THE STREETFIGHTER

A Star original

Now a major Columbia film
starring Charles Bronson

Novel based on the screenplay
written by
Walter Hill, Brian Gindoff &
Bruce Henstell

indoff &

THE STREETFIGHTER

Gordon Newman

A STAR BOOK
published by
W. H. ALLEN

A Star Book
Published in 1975
by W. H. Allen & Co. Ltd.
A division of Howard & Wyndham Ltd.
44, Hill Street, London W1X 8LB

Published by arrangement with Dell Publishing Inc.

Printed in Great Britain by
Richard Clay (The Chaucer Press), Ltd., Bungay, Suffolk

ISBN 0 352 39833 7

ONE

Times were hard. And didn't look like getting any easier.

Chaney was moving on.

Gray icy rain slanted into Chaney's face as his feet crunched the soot-blackened shale along the tracks. Ahead of him the wide open plains of Missouri stretched nowhere. Nowhere country. He stopped and thought about that, his face becoming a picture of seriousness. That's where Chaney was headed. That's where he had come from.

Things had a way of coming round.

Distantly behind him he heard the train pick up as it approached the gradient. He moved out of sight behind a paint peeling real estate hoarding. Farther up the track where the gradient grew steeper he saw other bums, broken, dismal figures, lost men waiting to scramble aboard the train, with no real place to go. That wasn't a good spot to climb on, Chaney figured. The train would be crawling at that point and the bull would be keeping a sharp watch. Their problem.

He pulled his cap low, adjusted his lumberjacket and hitched up the canvas duffle bag that was slung across his hard shoulder. When the locomotive reached the gradient he would make his move, jumping on as close to the caboose as he dared. That was always the safest spot he'd found. The bull would be watching for those bums getting on as far as possible from him. He stood for a second against the rain, chewing a matchstick, and judging the train's approach. Boxcars rattling, wheels clattering over worn joints.

The Missouri–Pacific's rolling stock was rotten. There was no money in railways anymore, and since the Wall Street crash no one was spending the money they were lucky enough to be left with.

Chaney had lost money then like everyone else. He had had something besides and had lost that too. In his years on the road since that time he figured he'd about regained it, and he wasn't ever giving up on himself again.

He was going to keep moving. Going to jump the train now

approaching because it looked to be going south, and that was a better place to go than Kansas City, Missouri. For a week he'd been in this mean city, with the cops looking to bust his head if he got out of line, and a broad looking to bust his balls. Now he was walking on apiece. Staying free. Chaney knew about commitment and it wasn't for him. In his past there had been army camps, jails, the wire-pens of depression. And there had been the dames. Just once he'd been a willing victim, got himself hooked. Just once he'd made himself so vulnerable he couldn't maneuver. Never again would he let himself crash like that. From now on he planned to stay loose. And anything that tried holding him, any broad, any shooter, even any feeling that proved too random he'd cut dead. Right now he was cutting out of Kansas and didn't figure to come back.

The train hit the gradient, its tender piled high with coal. The empty freight cars slid past Chaney. He let them go, they were for the bums up the line. Isolating the one he figured might be lucky for him, Chaney glanced past it to the end of the train. He saw the caboose, there was no sign of the bull. He edged forward from behind the peeling hoarding. The train was going faster than he figured. But he could make it.

Chaney sprinted to the train, his strong pace keeping him easily alongside. His boots slapped down on the wet shale, sometimes slipping but not failing to propel him forward.

It was then he became aware of someone else making for his car. The man must have come off the track farther up.

Wiping the man from his mind, he freed the hasp and held the latch for a second or two. With cold, numb fingers he worked open the latch and slid the heavy wooden door back. He tossed in his duffle bag, wrenched up and just hung there for a moment, his face showing a slight smile of defiance to the rain, the bull he had avoided, this town which he'd licked. Then in one neat movement he jack-knifed himself through the open boxcar. He was on his way.

He made to slide the car door shut, then he saw stumbling helplessly alongside a real bindle stiff. A dog got a better deal, even in those hard times. A dog had more spirit. He paused for a second at the door, waiting for the man to make his jump. Instead the man's gray face suddenly cracked and he wailed.

'Gimme a hand!'

Chaney shook his head. He didn't owe the man anything, not

even the door he was holding open. The man stumbled on, saw Chaney's unconcern, then suddenly made a leap. It was suicide. His legs went no place he wanted them to. Crazy. Chaney, seeing him heading under the wheels of the train, swung out of the car, grabbed his arm and hauled him aboard. He landed heavily on the floor.

Chaney didn't say anything. He turned to the door, paused a second and watched the afternoon slide by. Then slammed it shut. In the darkness he sat with his back resting against some empty packing cases. He listened irritably to the raucous breathing. After a moment the stiff had recovered sufficiently to speak.

'Jesus,' he said. 'Was I lucky to make that one.'

Chaney chewed on his match. The man echoed surprise at his silence.

'Hey, that was a close one, wasn't it?'

Chaney withdrew farther. Already he'd given this man a lot more than he was obliged to.

The continuing silence and the darkened car finally impressed itself on the man.

'Okay, okay,' he said, and crawled to the rear of the car. 'Gee, I sure was lucky to make that one.'

Just for a second Chaney let it go. 'You didn't make that one.' His voice was stoney.

Then there was silence again, broken by the clattering wheels as the train struggled up the gradient. Chaney heard the bull go across the roof. The bindle stiff heard it too. Chaney had a dollar on him. He'd buy a hundred miles off the guard if he looked into his car. The man would have to take his chance.

They weren't disturbed.

Chaney had no notion how far they traveled. He dozed a little, woke, ached, slept a little more. When he awoke again he saw the yellow light of morning through the ventilators in the roof of the car. He smiled, knowing it was a new day, and he was coming into another city.

'Where d'you figure we are then?'

Chaney glanced down at the bum. He shrugged.

'Ain't the place we got on,' he said.

He rose, the train slowing a little as it passed into the switching yard, the wheels jumping noisily over points badly in need of attention. He slung his duffle bag across his shoulder, and with one heave threw open the door. The sunlight hit him and he creased his face. He saw an old pickup truck stopped on a gravel road, the city skyline beyond. Two kids were in the rear of the truck, one of them, a ten-year-old boy, stood and watched the train. He saw Chaney. Their eyes held on to one another, like they knew one had been there and the other was going.

As the boy and truck disappeared from his view, Chaney swung out of the car and edged along to the ladder. He hung there looking beyond the switching yard. The city of Baton Rouge rose up before him.

There was a blast of steam as the train slowed further, cars slammed against their couplings. Chaney jumped from the ladder and landed standing in a gravel. The train moved on past him and Chaney turned away. Something collapsed behind him, and he turned back. The stiff had come off the car, straight out of the door, had lost his footing on impact and crumpled on the gravel. Chaney shook his head. Seemed like a setup to him, this guy always landing in the shit. It was the way the guy really wanted it. Maybe he figured people like Chaney would always give him a hand.

He looked at him, his face impassive.

The stiff suddenly got scared.

'I ain't got nothing you want,' he wailed.

Chaney held his look. The man certainly had nothing Chaney wanted. He had started weak then allowed his weakness to reduce him to nothing. Chaney had seen too many people like him. And guessed that if ever he let go, or gave into weakness, this is what he'd become. He would never let that happen. Never give in to weakness, never look to anyone else for something he wanted or needed. He'd make it alone.

The man couldn't work out what was going through Chaney's head. He tried a grimace, then turned it into a weak smile.

'Get your ass up outta there,' Chaney said.

The man seemed shocked, but suddenly came quickly to his feet. Chaney smiled in surprise, shook his head and turning, started away.

The smile was a mistake.

The stiff figured he could open on it, reach into Chaney.

'Hey,' he called after him, 'you got any money?'

Chaney stopped, but didn't turn round. I smiled, he thought, I gave up something of myself, and now I gotta buy it back, or give up some more to this jerk. He checked his lumberjacket pocket. All he had was five singles. The stiff came on again, wailing.

'How about a buck. I'm flat. Call it a loan.'

That did it. Chaney shoved the money back into his pocket and walked away. The guy wanted a loan, he wanted a relationship. Chaney was moving on.

The stiff called after him bitterly, 'Some goddamn day you'll need it, and you're gonna get the same.'

Chaney kept walking, his face set hard. When he had crashed, that one time he had needed it. He didn't get it. He hadn't even asked, he had got up by himself. But the stiff ain't strong, he told himself, and maybe next time nor will you be. Chaney went on walking, dropped a buck on the ground and kept on going.

The bindle stiff smiled like he hadn't in weeks when he saw the green flutter down.

Baton Rouge in the early morning was cool and peaceful and deceptive, but Chaney could still figure out the sort of city it was. Bill-boards, streets, store-fronts and parked motors gave it all to him. It had its industry, where those lucky enough got jobs, it had its rich gentlemen living in smart houses on smart streets where cops patrolled; its opportunists and racketeers licking the depression the only way they knew how, and it had its share of those who didn't know how. No way at all. Down-and-outs and wasted men, Chaney saw them littered all over the town. The streets, the market places, the warehouses empty since the firms went bust a few short years ago. It saddened him a bit, but he was resolved not to let it weaken him. Those in their fifties who a few years back had been all set up, they were hit the worst. He couldn't see his own future. Forget them, he told himself. He was only looking to the next bend in the road. At one time he had figured up the odds on a future and had laid out his claim which the world went and smashed, stole everything, and he still hurt. Hurt in a way that caused anger to continue within him, caused him to resist all inclination to ever do it again.

He would only look to the next bend, the next meal and the next place to sleep. That's all he wanted. Between times, and he was always between times; he was just moving through. He'd give this town maybe a week and he'd be pushing on. Maybe it wouldn't give him that long. Before then he needed some money from somewhere. Four singles wouldn't get him far. Chaney needed cash badly, but he was careful as to how much it cost him in getting it. He wanted it coming to him easily. No emotional strings or ties. It was just the money he wanted. He figured maybe a day when he had a good stash of money, when he was free enough, maybe he'd try to make a future for himself again. But other times he suspected he would never even try and shoot for it again. Somehow in stacking up enough greens to earn his freedom, he lost the spirit that set him free, found himself entangled in too many people's lives. He bought his way out, gave up everything he had had, and that had damn near cost him everything.

Things had come round again.

One thing which sure as hell kept coming round was this need for dough. There didn't seem much opportunity for any hustling on the streets he passed through. The gas stations didn't want pump attendants, they wanted skilled mechanics. But Chaney had no papers except the wrong ones, and figured anyway he was worth more than twenty cents an hour.

Chaney stayed on the streets all morning, that was a long hot morning in Baton Rouge; especially as he hadn't eaten or drunk anything apart from water. But he had got the geography of the place and its feel, and he had seen things which had interested him. The bar he eventually settled in was a low-ceilinged joint, the scarred counter running its length, with booths done out in a faded plush opposite. Chaney moved past a couple who could afford to drink professionally; a guy like himself; a busted-out hooker; couple of shooters discussing the local elections. He seated himself at the bar and called for a Jax. Scotch was usually his drink but not when he was only holding four singles. The beer slaked his thirst and he set his mind to figuring some angles.

Someone put a lazy number on the jukebox, and Chaney distractedly turned to watch a woman who began dancing by herself. She was cute. Too cute, Chaney decided. She'd want too goddamn much. Since his crash, Chaney had an inbuilt red warning system, fast as a brush fire, with broads like that. On each beat of the music she moved her ass provocatively from side to side, her hips thrusting out like she was screwing. But the chick dancing before him wasn't after hooking him. Chaney turned back to the bar; when he wanted some ass he chose it himself; he had it on his terms, or he had no ass at all.

He glanced down to where a tall, angular man sat watching the woman. But he wasn't interested in her ass at that moment. He was looking at her face, and Chaney saw his eyes say something to her. He got it in a flash then, the reason for the broad's ass display. He smiled thinly and waited. Soon he saw the angular man position himself alongside a little guy wearing a cheap business suit, who Chaney recognized as the pigeon.

The woman closed on the little guy, turning her back on the upbeat of the number, swinging her ass like it would bust out of her dress.

The pigeon was all eyes. He had never seen an ass like it, and he wanted it. And wasn't she offering it to him? He twisted a little in his seat with the excitement. His mouth parted as the slow boom-boom-boom of the number put her ass not six inches from him. Chaney saw it coming any moment now. The tall, angular man was oblivious to the pigeon, who didn't even notice him brush past and go on into the mens-room. On the brush he'd made a well-shaded leather hit, and had got clean away with it. It was something Chaney had seen often, and he had to admit it was pretty well set up. He had no sympathy for the pigeon, but saw a chance to make a little cash here himself.

He waited until the record ended and the woman walked away to finish her drink. He measured the pigeon with a look.

'Your wallet just walked into the john,' he said. 'You got hit while she was shaking it.'

The pigeon gaped in surprise. His hand reached into his empty pocket and he seemed suddenly in pain.

'Son of a bitch,' he muttered.

Incredulous. For he didn't want to believe he'd been taken, that that woman had suckered him. He stared over to her indecisively. She was already on her way to the door.

'Hey, you. God damn it!' He was the center of attention in the bar and embarrassed. The woman had gone. He stared at the door, wishing he was gone too.

Chaney leaned toward him. 'The one you want's in there,' he said.

The pigeon screwed his eyes, and looked nervously from

Chaney toward the mens-room. He was neither big nor brave and didn't reckon on getting into a situation he couldn't handle. He sat there stockstill.

'Want me to get it?'

The pigeon blinked, a tremor escaping down his face as he looked at Chaney.

'I don't need any trouble,' he said.

'No trouble,' Chaney said, and made to stand up.

The pigeon grabbed his arm. 'Listen, maybe we ought to forget it. I only had eight bucks.'

Chaney smiled. 'I'll take half,' he said.

The pigeon's face creased. 'You sure it's worth it?'

Chaney shrugged. 'Four bucks is four bucks.'

The pigeon paused a second, thinking over the proposition. He didn't want trouble rebounding at him. But the guy before him was big, six foot, maybe, powerfully built. That was what counted. He looked like a seaman, or perhaps a one-time lumberjack. He was a guy he wouldn't have liked to get in bad with. He had made up his mind.

'Okay by me,' he said.

Chaney nodded, and caught the bar tender's eye. He gestured toward his duffle bag on the bar.

'Keep an eye on that for me.'

The pigeon followed as he crossed casually to the mens-room. He got a little frightened just seeing the way Chaney handled the door when it jammed. Chaney hit it with his knee, bursting the door open. The controlled violence set the pigeon shaking. This guy, he thought, certainly knew how to use himself, but he felt he was getting into a situation.

Chaney stepped into the john. It was L-shaped, with brown graffiti-scarred walls and old yellow urine-encrusted porcelain right before him. Tucked round the corner the pickpocket stood before a spotted mirror combing his hair like it was an occupation. He turned too casually as Chaney approached, the pigeon behind him.

'You got my wallet!' the little man blustered.

The pickpocket made a gesture of surprise. 'What the hell is this?' He raised both hands as if inviting a search. 'You're crazy. I'm clean,' he said.

Reaching across to the waste receptacle Chaney knocked off the lid. The wallet was there on top of the garbage. He pulled it out and turned back to the pickpocket. He could see his way to the four bucks easily now.

'What's all this to you?' the pickpocket said resentfully.

'Business,' Chaney replied, the threat held in his calm tone. The pickpocket saw that this guy, whoever he was, wasn't going to let up, that he was looking for a piece. The whole number was blown, and he knew it. Expertly he snapped out a blade, held it quivering in the silence that immediately followed. Knives had an eloquence of their own.

Chaney steadied just a moment, sensed rather than saw the man's nervousness. He stared him in the eyes.

'I don't think you're that good,' he said.

'Come on over and see.'

The pickpocket beckoned with the blade. He knew no guy would walk right into a blade however tough he was. But Chaney started forward, wallet still in hand.

The pigeon was more scared than either the pickpocket or Chaney.

'Wait a minute,' he said, 'I don't want this kind of trouble. Jesus Christ. It's only eight bucks.'

Chaney figured he was afraid of getting hurt. He didn't look at him, but held the pickpocket's look, doubting the guy's spirit was as keen as the blade.

'Four bucks,' he said, 'Half's mine.'

He was moving forward before he'd finished speaking. He flipped the wallet straight at the pickpocket, hitting him slap in the face. Chaney's timing was good, he wouldn't get a second chance. He shot his right forward, and didn't miss. The blow lifted the man backwards into the mirror, fracturing it. He fell forward with the splinters, blindly thrusting with the knife as he did. Chaney dodged it, came back fast, hitting the man again with his right, this time in the side of the neck. As he went down lower Chaney suddenly one-handed the man's wrist, threw him outward and twisted up the arm until he could feel it wrenching against the socket. He knew what pain it caused.

'Don't break it! Please don't break it!' the pickpocket screamed.

Chaney added some pressure by raising his hand. He heard a faint crack, and then the knife fell to the floor.

'You got it! Don't break it! Don't . . .'

Chaney held his grip. He looked impassively over to the

pigeon, as though they were both in there taking a leak.

'Now you can come over here and get our money,' he said. 'The gentleman is perfectly willing to return it.'

The pigeon edged forward. This was a situation and the violence disturbed him. His hand shook as he reached out into the pickpocket's jacket. He pulled out some bills. His face broke with relief, he looked up and smiled.

'Eight bucks,' he said, then faltered, 'I mean, four. Four bucks are yours.'

Hesitating, undecided about breaking the man's arm, Chaney finally released his grip. The pickpocket fell to the floor, reaching round, trying to ease the pain in his arm as he watched them split the bills.

Chaney pocketed his four.

'Nice doing business with you guys,' he said.

He whipped his duffle bag from the bar and went on out to the street. He got himself a sleeping place in a downtown flophouse. The fat guy who ran the place talked round a cigar butt in his mouth and tried to take him for a dollar. Chaney argued in favor of fifty cents, with some hot water. He could have shaved cold.

Back on the streets of the state capital Chaney was looking again, and avoiding the cops. There were more interesting parties than him to bust.

The bustling deep-water port with it's confusion of docks, and sheds, and people who knew how to look after themselves, that's where the action would be if there was going to be any. He had heard of the action as he had moved about town. He felt at home in that kind of neighborhood.

As dusk began to fall the hunger he had felt all day reached its peak. He ate about this time. He didn't mind getting up mornings without food, but he didn't like going to bed hungry. Seeing a neon-lit diner he turned in to get himself something to eat.

The place was rundown, garishly lit and it didn't appear too concerned with achievements in hygiene. The waitress, a hard but good-hearted woman wearing a stained apron, looked like she would rather have been participating in a dance marathon, and the fry cook farther down the counter, glistened with perspiration, looked as though he'd just finished one.

Chaney sat at the counter, and dropped his duffle bag at his feet. He was beat and needed food. The waitress approached.

'What do you want, big boy,' she said wearily, without indicating any menu, or looking at him.

'Bowl of chilli. Cup of coffee.'

She looked at him now, leaning an elbow on the counter, and cupping her chin in her hand to do so.

'You got any money?' she asked. 'I've had my year's supply of dishwashers.'

That kind of response was something Chaney had learnt to live with. He reached into the pocket of his lumberjacket and pulled out a dollar. He held it up. The waitress smiled, and eased herself off the counter.

'One bowl of chilli,' she said. 'Flying right up!'

The chilli wasn't the best in the world, but then it was as good as Chaney had eaten. While he ate Chaney read a newspaper he'd picked up during the day. It contained a lot of stories of depression. People crying out about their problems, some of splashing into useless heaps. There were more results than causes; the results were more newsworthy, more spectacular. It disturbed Chaney because it put him in touch with his anger. If anyone at all had reason to cry out it was him. Yet he stayed in on top of it. The whelps and the weaklings crashed out. He guessed they had no options. He folded the newspaper and slid it onto the stool next to him as though disassociating himself with the society it reflected. He had his own problems; and he was angry. If I could use my anger to lick my problems, he thought, I guess I'd be a rich man, maybe a free man. No, he decided, anger never freed anyone; men were prisoners of their emotions, s'why they went splat on the sidewalk off the fifteenth.

Through the front glass of the diner Chaney could see a railroad siding with the huge warehouse sheds, the superstructures of cranes towering behind them. As he sat watching a Buick Marquette drove up. Three men climbed out and sauntered into the shed. They were followed by others on foot. This interested Chaney, for it was too late for any kind of warehouse work, and these guys had never worked in a warehouse anyway. He thought maybe he was onto something. He signaled the waitress to refill his empty coffee cup again, and turned back to the warehouse where some more men were now entering, a couple of them sparring with each other. That gave it to Chaney. He smiled. He had found some action.

'Mister,' the waitress said, hovering with the coffee pot, 'this ain't a rescue mission. Third refill costs you a nickel.'

Chaney suddenly stood up, no longer interested in that third cup. A couple more guys arrived across the road. He put a nickel on the counter. The waitress started to pour the coffee.

'Tip,' he said, and moved out of the diner.

TWO

The shed was lit only at the far end by a couple of naked lamps high in the roof. Shadows criss-crossed the ramps and stores below, but pale light flooded an open rectangle formed among packing cases. Here was gathered a group of men. Some were seated on packing cases; some of them just stood; some of them were shabby; some of them weren't; all of them wanted to make a few bucks; all of them were expectant. In the center of the gathering stood four men. Two of them were hitters, huge, hard-muscled, both going about two-twenty pounds. Neither looked particularly bright, both of them obviously having necks far stronger than their brains. They glared at each other angrily, because that was where they believed their power over their opponent was derived. Neither paid any attention to the actions of the other two men with them. All they were interested in was hitting and winning.

One of the other two men in the center of the rectangle was Spencer Weed. Everyone called him Speed. He preferred that. Speed was smart and quick and goddamn clever. At least that was the image he had of himself, and when Speed believed in something, he usually got enough energy together to convince others, or at least enough others to get him by, get him a living for the minimum effort. He was a big city boy who dressed in sharply tailored suits and used cologne, and these days spent just a little too long in the barber's salon having the grays touched in to match whatever else was left. Speed was past the first flush but denied it to himself and so was hanging on like hell to what traces of youth were left in him. He was tall and elegant and high-stepping when he walked, like a fine bred Tennessee walking horse. A lady friend had once said that to him and he had liked the analogy. Speed was a shooter, a high-roller, but a man who all too often tried filling inside straights. From city to city Speed rolled around the south, trying to be a bigshot, and rolling on again when things didn't quite work out. He'd had a couple of hits with the law, but they were good healthy gambling convictions, and Speed bore no grudges.

Proud at least to be acknowledged a gambler, rather than a tinhorn cardsharp.

He moved away from the men in the center toward the spectators. He had a well-oiled smile, that in any other profession would have been called winsome.

'Two-fifty on the scratch!' he shouted, holding up a roll of bills. 'Need somebody to nurse it. How about you, my friend? You look like an honest man.'

He offered the money to an oaf, figuring he was too dumb rather than too honest to run off with it. The oaf reached forward slowly. He grinned, revealing a big mouthful of gums.

'Atta boy,' Speed said, like he was addressing his dog, and handed over the money.

Don't tangle with big men, was a motto he kept before him like a hungry man reads a lunch menu. It was true right now he dealt with big men, lived on them, sometimes loved them, sometimes hated them; but he never physically tangled with them. Some of them were good for money, and those that weren't were morons. For Speed was all set as a pick-up fight manager. First he found himself a good hitter, matched him right, hustled the punters, and picked up the potbet when his hitter won. When his man lost and his reputation was through, Speed ran out on him. Speed was that smart; he didn't ass around with losers.

'Okay!' he said to the oaf. 'Don't run away now, friend.'

The oaf gave a sheepish grin, the words not registering.

'Just a little joke, friend!' Speed gave him a reassuring pat and turned to the gathering. He walked slowly along the edge of them, slightly stifflegged, beautifully polished shoes picking his way across the grease-stained floor.

'I'm good for another two-five-oh on the side!' he called. 'Anybody want some? Who can get it up against my hitter? He's a peg-leg, and's three parts blind. But don't let that influence you friends.'

He gave a big, all-teeth smile. Discussion issued from the crowd, a couple of shouts, and some insults, then the sweet voice of a taker.

'I want fifty!'

'Got it,' Speed said.

'Twenty-five,' came another call.

Speed beamed. 'Be my guest, friend, be my guest. Anyone else?'

The crowd talked quietly among themselves. A couple considered Speed's hitter, and laughed. Speed's beam had long since gone. No one ignored him like this. His fighter was good; he knew it but they didn't.

'Look, I got one-seven-five for anybody wants to take a sporting chance!' he called. 'I heard you boys had money to burn up here.'

The crowd weren't taking chances like that. Speed's face crumpled at the shortage of chancers. The trip out from New Orleans wasn't even going to break even. If he went back broke he'd probably get his balls busted from his ever lovin' Gayleen,

'Nobody betting. Jesus, maybe we'd better start selling tickets!'

From the center of the ring the other shooter who had been talking to his hitter moved toward Speed. He was called Caesare, a small, energetic, businesslike man. His manner of drumming up business on the other side of the fight contrasted highly with the flashy panache of Speed's manner.

'Three on the side?' Caesare called, holding up three fingers, each representing a hundred.

'Thirty,' a tall man replied immediately.

'And ten,' came another voice, happier about betting against Caesare's man. There were a number of small takers.

'Right,' Caesare said, 'now how about the biggies? Anybody?'

If any of the men had big money they didn't want to know. They remained silent as they were at Speed's proposition.

'Real big spenders,' Caesare chided. 'Real highrollers we got here. Why don't you assholes go and see a movie instead?'

He waited a second more, then glanced over to Speed, who waved his hand at him and moved over to his hitter.

'You had your chance!' Caesare called out to the crowd.

Speed took his hitter's face in his hands and slapped him affectionately a couple of times.

'Hear me now,' he said, raising his voice against the sudden increased stirrings of the crowd. 'You got to want it. All right!'

The hitter nodded slowly. Speed gave him a big smile, and turned to the center as the crowd edged in closer for the fight.

'Okay. Here we are,' he said.

'Let him go,' Caesare said.

Speed touched his gray hair nervously. It was a habit he justified by telling himself he was touching it for luck; it was as near goddamn silver and that was his lucky metal. In truth he was pretty anxious for he had little faith in this hitter of his. He had been a bitch of a fighter at one time, but that time wasn't now.

A hush fell on the crowd as the two fighters came through the weak pool of light and approached each other. Ritualistically both opened and raised their hands, and holding for a moment, their gestures reaffirming each was without palmers or rings. Then they dropped their arms and took their fighting positions. They were ready.

From the darkened area of the warehouse, Chaney moved forward from the position where he'd stood watching the preliminaries. He didn't gamble on anything as random as another man's talent, but had he, of the two he'd have put his money on Caesare's man; and on himself against either of them.

Immediately Caesare's man got off a good left jab to his opponent's face. It probably didn't hurt. It hurt Speed, who was already chewing his fingernails. Gayleen had only manicured them for him yesterday. Trying a kick, Speed's hitter gave too much warning and was knocked smartly backward for his trouble. Then Caesare's man closed in on him. They began grappling. There was no referee or rules, save that which said the man on his feet at the end was the winner. They started pulling each other's hair; they went down and rolled over.

Powerful men, Chaney thought as he watched, but without any kind of grace at all. He smiled as they began scrabbling around like a couple of punchdrunks, clawing, getting up, kicking, punching again, and stumbling round the dimly lit circle.

The crowd, who were making neither shooter rich, were entertained and shouted and called. Those of them who had laid out money on Speed's man were pissed off at the show he was putting up. Others only wanted their money back. Speed was screaming.

'Stupid! Stupid! Tear his head off, you dumb mother.'

The fighters continued to brawl. Chaney figured whoever came out on top would do so by chance. They had no finesse, no skill. Speed's man, in response to Speed's call, loomed forward and tried gouging out the other's eyes. It got him too close and left his body unprotected. Caesare's man saw his chance and took several blind but solid shots at the body. He was still swinging his arms when Speed's man went down on his back.

'Open your eyes, idiot!' Caesare shouted to his hitter.

Speed knew it wasn't going to be his night. He wasn't even going to waste energy telling his man to get up. Here I am, he thought, a smart Tennessee walking horse, stopping the traffic, and I have a hitter makes me look like a prick.

His hitter climbed up in a daze and turned to Speed. Caesare's man gave him one in the back of the neck, and he collapsed at Speed's feet.

'If I'd eaten,' Speed said when the man stirred again, 'I'd throw up on you.'

The crowd closed out the ring now. Caesare slapped the back of his hitter, and made his way to collect off the oaf with the potbet.

No one bothered with Speed's man.

No one bothered with Speed except Chaney. He watched him strut angrily toward the warehouse exit, bitching those who had his money. There was a man with a problem. The way he looked, Chaney figured he maybe even had an ulcer. Chaney decided he had the solution to the man's problems. He moved swiftly down through the warehouse after him.

Speed was unaware of anything other than his sick heart, his angry thoughts and hungry stomach. He was headed for his favorite spot in this stinking town. It was an oyster bar which looked a little exclusive, but with prices which didn't cut too deeply into the wallet. Speed's wallet was wafer thin after the fight.

The bar was the one thing that redeemed the state capital for him that night.

It had an eat-all-you-want counter for forty-five cents. Around the rest of the bar were the familiar night-time crowd. Guys in loud checks with too much liquor, making up to women who didn't give a damn anyway. There were other more discreet couples, some at the end of affairs, others maybe just getting going. Tonight Speed didn't want to know any of them. Tonight they weren't his people; tonight he was a loser.

He helped himself to a dozen on the half shell from the counter, and went and sat alone. He was pissed off. Didn't care too much about his hitter; hitters came and went, and even the duds could be matched right to make a little side money. What he cared about was going back to New Orleans broke and having to suffer Gayleen's shit about what a wonderful shooter he was.

Angry thoughts churned on and his oysters disappeared.

He got up from his table and with a shy smile to the couple of women in his path, he maneuvered himself back to the eat-all-you-want counter.

'Hey, friend,' he said expansively to the black behind the counter, 'I guess I could use about six more here, and another lemon.'

He turned back to his table, sighed wearily when he saw muscle-boy sitting across from his place. Then moved back over there anyway.

Chaney, sitting at his table, watched his approach. He acted like he hadn't a care in the world. A façade was as meaningless as his fine clothes, Chaney thought.

Speed took his seat and pulled a copy of the *Police Gazette* from his pocket. He started reading and eating without so much as a glance to Chaney.

Then, still concentrating on his newspaper, he said, 'You can start anytime, friend.'

Chaney introduced himself.

'Chaney.'

He considered that was about all the man needed to know about another man's past: the name he'd taken six years ago.

'That's your name,' Speed said disinterestedly. 'So what?' He was still reading the *Gazette*.

The number of dummies he got approaching him, he tended to click right off the second he saw a chest over thirty-six, unless it had a big pair of boucing tits on it.

'We can make some money,' Chaney said.

S'what they all say, Speed thought. It was such a familiar story he'd have made a fortune several times over had he set it to music.

'Right,' he said glancing up from the sheet. 'I'm all ears, friend.'

Patience was something Chaney had because he knew about control. He studied the man for a moment, knowing he wasn't being taken seriously. He didn't like that. He watched Speed pick up another oyster, then turn back to the paper. He let out a breath, his patience holding.

'That piece of business in the warehouse tonight,' he said. 'You set it up.' He leaned into the table.

'Happens all the time,' Speed said matter-of-factly.

Chaney took up an oyster from the plate. He wasn't hungry, but the gesture had the desired effect.

'Why not have one,' Speed said, looking at him now.

'Why don't you stop feeding your face?'

That brought Speed up sharply. He looked around the restaurant, then licked the gum off his fingers.

'I suppose you been down the long hard road.' His tone had changed noticeably now.

'Who hasn't?' Chaney shrugged.

'Jail?'

Chaney stared pensively at Speed. 'You a policeman?'

A smile of appreciation crossed Speed's face of misery. Then, 'I just like knowing where a man comes from.'

Chaney's eyes narrowed. 'Where I come from,' he said, 'nobody asks.'

There was a pause filled by the clatter of the restaurant.

Speed blinked, blank faced.

Chaney held his stare. He didn't speak easily of his past. Unless the odds were secure, he felt that giving out on his background was giving up something of himself. In a second Speed slapped down his newspaper.

'Well now, you got any objection in telling me where you're headed, friend?'

With a shrug, Chaney said, 'Maybe New Orleans.' That was as far south as he wanted to go, it was warm there and no harder to get along than in the next place. The Florida weather was more comfortable for someone on the road. But the cops there were something else. They'd shoot you with your hands cuffed behind your back.

'Well,' Speed said, 'my home from home. Small world, friend, ain't it.' He gave him a big come-on smile, but none of it meant anything to him.

Sensing the strength in the man opposite. Speed began to maneuver. 'Well you look a little past it, friend. Besides I already got a hitter.'

'I saw him. He could handle that, I guess,' tossing the oyster back on Speed's plate.

Speed made a reckless gesture with his elegant hand. 'So the son of a bitch fell on me tonight. But I match him right I can still make some nice change.'

'Small change,' Chaney said.

There was an intenseness about Chaney's tone which held Speed's; then he decided he was just a big boy hustling him.

'Look, friend,' he said, 'I get a lot of volunteers. Every town's got a bar, and every bar's got some bum in it who thinks he's as tough as a nickel steak. But that doesn't mean I should lay my money on him.'

Speed finished, the case was closed, the big boy could get up and leave now. But then Chaney reached in and took out his money.

'I got seven bucks, and nothing else. Bet it on me,' he said.

Grimacing thoughtfully, Speed guessed this guy must be either plain dumb or pretty good. Whichever, Speed was curious to know. Then he was a compulsive gambler.

'Go on,' Chaney said, and threw the bucks on the table.

Speed looked at the bills. They were folded neatly like they expected a lot more to join them. He'd never known a hitter before who would bet on himself. And he knew he couldn't go lower in the league than the hitter he recently parted company with. So maybe, he figured, I'll find out if this monkey's for real, or if he just escaped from a funny farm. Then he side-stepped from habit.

'Ain't a lot to lose,' he said with a laugh. 'Seven dollars even in these times.'

There were no doubts in Chaney's mind which way it was now. He could see it clearly. He stared straight back at him.

'It's all I got.'

Speed was almost touched. It was like a hooker telling him she could do nothing else. He said. 'So let's see what we can do. Walk me to my hotel, we'll talk.'

They left the oyster bar, into the close humid night. Two paces along the street set Speed's pores oozing sweat. He looked at Chaney. The heat didn't seem to bother him at all.

'S'gonna rain,' he said. 'It'll ease the heat.'

They walked in silence ignoring the propositions they were getting on the street. Occasionally Speed would smile politely at the hookers, tip his hat and tell them he was too young.

'You got a girl, Chaney?' he asked like a man who couldn't

keep quiet for too long. And when there was no reply, 'Screwing's about all anyone should do in this heat.'

His discourse moved from sex to life; to fighting. Chaney listened to the man with only a fraction of his attention. He was figuring nothing but the money he could make from fighting. Money which could give him a lot more freedom than he had now. Yet he distrusted it all. He distrusted money even when he had it, he distrusted its impermanence and everything it could buy. Once you'd been really down you didn't forget, and you didn't trust the system anymore. Yet perversely Chaney wanted that which supported the system, money, even though he could survive without it. When he had been down, had lost everything he had cared about, he had got up off his ass without it. But it had left him with a contemptuous distrust of the rich. He wanted money now as a safeguard, in case they tried forcing him down that low again.

'Understand,' Speed was saying, 'you got to understand about being a hitter. This is a trade for people who know how to handle themselves. You stand there all alone and there ain't no place to hide.'

Chaney smiled to himself. He'd learned how to handle himself the hard way. He reckoned there was no place he couldn't stand all alone and not stand up. Yet right there, he was hiding too. Hiding his heart, his loss; his past. He immediately cut that thought with the same ruthlessness with which his own roots had once been cut.

'There's one rule and one rule only,' Speed continued, 'don't hit the guy once he's down. Now if he don't want to get up, that's his business and we collect. How you knock him down, that's your business. Hit him, kick him, bite him, don't make no difference. But most of the real good ones deal with their hands.'

Speed turned to Chaney. He was walking, staring ahead abstractedly.

'Hey, you listening to this advice, friend? I could charge for this.'

Chaney nodded.

Speed frowned anxiously. Still he couldn't quite work the guy out. One fight, he figured, I'll fix him up with one shot, see how he shapes.

'Okay then,' he said. 'Now you reckon you can beat that

monkey who put my hitter down tonight?'

Chaney just looked at Speed, who immediately got the message.

'Okay, okay,' he said. 'Then I'll fix it. He's an oaf sure. But remember, handle him like you would a blind pig. And if you go down that's the end of our little love affair, okay friend?'

With three neat little jumps Speed was on the top of his hotel steps. He turned back to Chaney, who was looking at him like he was nowhere. Speed didn't care for that look.

'Christ, now what's the matter?' he said. 'What do you want of me?'

'I don't want nothing,' Chaney said. 'Just set it up for tomorrow night.'

'You pick me up here around eight tomorrow evening.'

Without another word or gesture Chaney turned away.

Speed shook his head, and went into his hotel.

Chaney headed on in the direction of the flophouse. He wanted a fight. He wanted money. He didn't want a relationship with a shooter or with anyone else. Whatever came out of the fight he was staying on his own. He was not going to be owned by anyone.

THREE

At 7 p.m. the following night, Speed slipped on his lucky vest and studied his face in the hotel mirror. It was lean and handsome. Some dame had once said pretty; she hadn't stayed the course. Tonight it was shining a little, shining with a winner's luck, he decided. Somebody up there was looking down on him. And about goddamn time too. After tonight this trip out from New Orleans was over and he was headed back home to sweet Gayleen.

Just how sweet she'd be depended on the greens he'd have in his pants pocket. Right now he was down. Way down. Even when he had put up his last one-fifty on his new hitter, and assuming he took the pot, he would still only break even, unless the side bets really rolled.

He patted loose gray strands of hair into place. In the pink-shaded hotel light there was nothing between the gray and the silver. He was going to be lucky tonight. Pull it all in, pay off the big dude his seven bucks, and take off for home. Maybe he'd rest up for awhile till his luck really hit.

He stepped back from the mirror, and pulled into his jacket. He looked pretty good, and that was always a sign when things were going to start hitting for him. He beamed at himself. Did he believe he was a winner tonight? You got to believe it, he told himself, show you believe it. His face crumpled. He wondered. He was already making plans to drop Chaney off immediately after the fight, win or lose. There was no future with a one-off small-shot. He wanted a real hitter. But believe in this boy, he told himself, just tonight show you believe in this boy.

He beamed again, willing belief. Smile, baby. He twirled his rabbit's foot around his finger, caught it on its seventh turn and thrust it decisively in his pants pocket. He collected up his plugged nickel and silver dollar off the wash stand; he had rituals for each of those. Games, he thought, goddamn games gamblers played. Then sweeping the bills and loose change off the stand with his hand, he thrust those into his pocket and strutted out momentarily believing in his success.

Chaney picked him up in the street as he emerged from the hotel. Chaney nodded in response to Speed's nervous greeting, but he said nothing. His workmanlike calm seemed to upset Speed a little as they rode a cab across town to the docks.

In the warehouse men, a lot of the faces who had shown last night, had gathered down the end. Most had something to say about something.

Letting Speed make all the running, Chaney casually followed on. He measured his opponent who was waiting to go, knowing he had the distinct advantage of having once seen him work out. He had other advantages anyway, mainly that he could hold tight on his anger; it was cool, contained and so powerful when he used it as he did, it required someone like Chaney himself to stop him, only someone better. Anger controlled like this was something that counted way above mere strength. And then there was Chaney's ace in the hole, which was Chaney himself. He never ever gave himself up.

His opponent looked across at him with contempt in his eyes, but Chaney could see no caution there. He had got his weakness, confirmed what he had seen yesterday. All the man had was his brute strength.

Caesare his manager believed that was enough. He measured Speed's new man by the performance of the hitter last night, and reckoned he was onto a good bet. And realized that the crowd thought the same way as he went about inviting bets in his usual energetic way.

'This man's a fool for punishment!' he joked, indicating Speed. 'Just wants to throw his money away. Any of you want to go down the same road?'

The crowd offered up no takers. Just a couple of laughs. Caesare played on it some more.

'Now there's got to be somebody out there who wants to bet his man. Where's your sense of American fair play, boys?'

'After last night?' A guy in a four-dollar shirt called out.

'Not anybody? Somebody ... Looks pretty good to me.' He paused. 'I'll give you two to one ... Three to one ... ? Those sort of odds don't come around every day. Shit.'

The men ignored Caesare. He gave a disgusted chuckle that suggested he had wasted his time coming.

There were a few more punters coming through the opening

of gray light, two or three others emerged from the shadows of the warehouse and joined the group in the lit area. But Caesare didn't think he had any takers there. He glanced across at Speed.

'Guess you boys aren't as dumb as he is,' he called, and stepped aside.

'Big shot,' Speed muttered, feeling embarrassed at this response to him and his hitter. Then, adopting the old façade, stepped right into the center, all teeth and business.

'One-fifty in the pot,' he called. 'I got the same for anybody that expects a repeat.' The words almost stuck in his craw.

The bets came in. The men flagging greens at the end of their arms. Speed flashed around in his smart suit, snapping up the bills irritably. These assholes, he thought, like a lot of mothering hyenas.

'Gimme fifty.'

'Twenty here.'

'I'll take forty.'

'I'll take it. All of it,' Speed yelled. 'You'll see.'

'A crazy man!' someone shouted.

Speed ignored it, he had to. He was gambling now. Chaney could've been a cripple and he'd have still taken the money against him. Besides his reputation with Gayleen was at stake. That broad! He hoped he wasn't crazy.

'Who's betting? I got fifteen left.'

'I'll do it,' a big man in a baseball cap reached out with his money.

'Amazing courage,' Speed joked.

He glanced over to Chaney. He liked to think it really did take courage to bet against such a man. What age was he? Hard to tell. Forty? God, he was an old man, too old for this game. He looked older than he did last night. Speed flashed him a smile. Chaney's face remained impassive. Then he remembered this man was betting on himself.

'Another seven. I just discovered. Who wants it?'

An old man waggled an old hand with money in it. 'I'll fade it,' he said.

'Got a bigtime gambling man there,' Speed let out. 'That's it now.'

He looked round for someone to hold the money. The oaf who had held it last night grinned at him.

'Atta boy,' Speed said, stepping across and laying the fold on him.

He came quickly back to Chaney, put a hand on his shoulder. 'I did my part, friend. He's all yours.'

Casting his eyes skywards, giving himself up to the gods now, he moved to the side with the crowd. The assholes suddenly sickened him. One of the bums leaned on his suit, like it belonged to a friend.

'You pissant,' he said bitchily, 'lean somewhere else.'

He turned back to the ring, worried the bum had dulled his winner's shine. Chaney and his opponent moved out. The derision of the crowd toward Chaney hurt Speed's ears. It was his judgement they were attacking; his personal esteem. It was worse than Gayleen's chiding. Chaney stood coolly looking at his opponent, which only invited more yells and jeers. Speed got off a tiny prayer. If you had the crowd with you you were halfway home, and here was his hitter forcing them right against him. He closed his eyes for a second, then opened them again. Chaney was still standing calmly before this side of beef. Suddenly Speed got a kind of strength seeing him like that. Something about him, he thought, maybe he's a stayer, a survivor. He's got balls. Maybe he ain't going down.

Still Speed stood there, his nervousness eating his stomach, fingers sliding through his silver hair.

'Hey, Pops, ain't you a little old for this?' Caesare's hitter grunted arrogantly and looked to the crowd for appreciation.

Chaney simply took off his cap and tossed it to the ground, followed by his coat.

The crowd fell quiet. This was it; always that same expectancy before a massacre. Speed could hear his heart thrashing, feel the acids eating his stomach. It was always the worst moment for him, especially when he'd never seen his hitter fight before. What a dumb bastard! Maybe Gayleen was right about him.

Chaney's eyes never left his opponent's. He raised his palms slowly and without threat. There was nothing half-hearted about Chaney, but nothing wasteful in his gestures either. All of his movements showed great economy, fine balance. He saw his opponent's hands shake as he lowered them. That didn't indicate fear, simply lack of control. He wouldn't be able to stand his ground, he would make the first move. Chaney mapped out his own moves, there wouldn't be many. He would wait for him, let him walk right into it.

First-time hitters always went out to their man. They were that keen to prove themselves. Here was Chaney unmoving, waiting to get mopped up. The features of Speed's face seemed to crowd anxiously around his nose as he saw Caesare's man move in. Chaney feinted a blow, drew the man's reaction, then let him have what he expected in the first place – a driving left straight between the man's eyes. Once was enough. The man juddered at the impact, and went out like a match.

The crowd weren't ready for it, some had blinked and missed it. The fight was all over; they were shocked, cheated.

Hardly believing his eyes, Speed shook his head. He had seen it, and now saw the answer to a gambling man's prayers.

Suddenly the crowd started up. They shouted at Caesare and protested, but no one could deny the result. The hitter they had made bets on was on the floor. Chaney was standing over him like he hadn't moved. He looked across to Speed.

Brimming with rediscovered confidence, Speed came forward. He splashed his sudden rejuvenated spirit all over the crowd like champagne.

'Didn't I warn you,' he shouted. 'Didn't I just warn you boys? I said you needed courage to bet against my hitter.'

He stepped through the dispersing crowd to the oaf and snapped his fingers. The oaf grinned and handed him the roll. Speed tossed it and turned back to Chaney.

'You got your money back,' he said. 'Come on, we'll make the split later.'

Slowly Chaney turned away and reached up his coat and cap. Something about his manner dampened Speed's spirits. He immediately feared the worst.

'Hey, you ain't running out on me, are you?' he said in a slightly stricken tone. 'Listen, the plans I've already made for you, they're something else. You don't get a second shot.

'Look you said you was heading down to New Orleans. Jesus Christ, we'll get on the Overnight Limited together. We'll move right on into the big time.'

Chaney suddenly smiled, not with pleasure, but amusement.

'I wanna go to New Orleans,' he said. 'But that's as far as I'm looking at the moment.'

Speed slapped his back. They were on their way. Speed with

all his old racy arrogance, Chaney with a lot of reservations.

The Overnight Limited to New Orleans left on time with Chaney and Speed on board, comfortably ensconced at the rear of the Pullman car. It was a long forgotten experience for Chaney to be traveling this way. It beat traveling the freights, yet he felt slightly uncomfortable another way. Something about those flatly respectable passengers reading and sleeping along the car made him feel edgy, made him think of the bindle stiff he'd so recently traveled with and the kind of treatment these people were likely to give him. His focus fell on the seat opposite and his black duffle bag laying there. When that was full of money, he decided, he'd split.

Alongside him Speed was counting out the winnings, some of which he'd already blown on a quick celebration drink at his hotel. He was feeling expansive and generous. When Speed's spirits were high there was nothing he couldn't do. It was always the same. And he could never quite believe those inevitable crashes when they came until that final kick in the groin. He was a typical gambler whether it was pickup fights, poker, craps or anything that ran.

'Just like anything else in the world,' Speed said with a knowing grin. 'Got to have money to make money. There's your fourteen and ten to have a little run on.'

He handed over the bills, giving Chaney a reassuring smile. He was one hitter he didn't want to let fade away.

'We got plenty of time to work out our official deal later,' he said. 'We're going to get plenty more of this stuff, don't worry about that. New Orleans, Old Crescent Street, here we come, my hitter and me got it made!'

Tucking the roll into his pocket, he pulled out a hip flask and offered his partner a shot. Chaney shook his head. Speed didn't get it. He was riding high, so everybody ought to be floating too. He gave Chaney a mean smile, but it didn't work and broadened it into a real flash of ivories.

'Yes, sir,' he said. 'Here we come. High, wide and handsome.'

Chaney hated to have to come down on a man as happy as Speed was right now. But by not doing so, he felt he'd be giving away his power and the freedom he had. A couple of bad moves and you sometimes found yourself enmeshed by a wall of obligations. Chaney was staying loose. The ends all untied, no obligations nowhere. And he was going to sever

Speed's choking tentacles clean before he really believed he had him.

Chaney spat out the match he'd been chewing, pulled down his cap and closed his eyes, listened to the rumble of the train making its way through the night.

He awoke with the first hint of squint of light. The rest of the passengers in the car still asleep. He lifted the shade a little and watched the countryside of cotton and corn roll by, its flatness relieved only by the occasional eighty-foot derricks of the oil rigs that were getting going and the smaller Samson posts pivoting the walking beams that continuously pumped the oil up from those that had come in. Black gold making men in far away offices rich, and worried about whether the price would hold at ten cents a barrel. Prisoners of the system.

The sun was well up as they approached the outskirts of New Orleans and most of the passengers were awake. Chaney watched the city grow on the horizon. It was sophisticated, yet unashamedly tawdry, with an air of constant fatigue but not regret for previous indulgence; a slight bleariness hovering above its paint peeling weather-boarded houses, while over the whole hung steamy skies which had rolled up from the sea. Chaney figured he might stick around for a while, already he could taste the old French flavor, sense the southern bigotries, the independence that left you unimpeded.

He was standing with his bag slung across his shoulder when the Overnight pulled into Union Station and glided to a halt, giving a final blast on the whistle.

With Speed, who only half awake was still riding high, Chaney moved through the main concourse. The station was pretty much deserted, save for a few blacks looning around with even fewer passengers' baggage. Speed had given his grip to a boy. Chaney carried his own bag. As they moved toward the exit on South Rampart Street Chaney caught sight of an old bum drinking from a bottle and shuffling around looking for pennies. Speed didn't even notice. But Chaney identified with him, and as he did, felt a nagging doubt, and mistrust, about his involvement even thus far with Speed.

Behind them from the revolving doors Chaney heard footsteps. A woman's urgent footsteps, crying out to be heard. Speed, who had been searching, turned round when Chaney did.

'Sugarplum!' Speed yelled.

Chaney studied the woman as she planted a light kiss on Speed's cheek. Her glance flitted across to him as she did so, measuring him curiously. She was dark and pretty and had a good figure and expensive tastes. She was attractive enough to turn heads even at that hour, and guys might have fallen for her immediate showiness. But for Chaney it signaled one thing: look out.

'How'd it go, Speedy?' she asked with too much interest and not enough concern.

'Rough start but a fast finish!'

Speed kissed her again. She cocked her head a little. She looked like she had been up all night rather than had got up to meet the Limited.

'How much?' she asked.

'Even,' Speed confessed.

'Wonderful,' she said sarcastically.

Chaney continued to watch, cool and detached. He could have matched those two a mile off. Speed was hanging in there; the woman was merely hanging on.

Speed tried reproving her. 'Always be pleasant around strangers, Gayleen. This is Mr Chaney. Chaney, Gayleen Schoonover, my permanent fiancée.'

Gayleen took up the introduction with a hard stare at Chaney. 'Pleased to meet you,' she said.

Chaney gave nothing to this woman at all. They began walking across the forecourt.

'So come on, where'd you park it?' Speed asked Gayleen, looking at the one or two motors that were around.

'Just right over behind that truck.'

Speed turned, all smiles again, to Chaney.

'I got a big old Buick and lots of room,' he said, 'I like driving a big car.'

Chaney took it in and gave a nod. 'I'll say goodbye here,' he said.

Speed's face dropped. He glanced from Gayleen to Chaney and a spark of anger flew into his eyes. 'Hey wait a minute, we got plans to make. Remember?'

The craggy, leather face creased accommodatingly. 'I just want to walk on a piece. Feel my way, get reacquainted.'

He stared hard at Speed. His stare said he owed him nothing.

He made his own way. Speed hadn't taken in what was happening.

'What about our partnership?' he said.

'I don't like to rush things,' Chaney replied.

Speed suddenly saw his luck reversing and screamed, 'Don't like to rush things? Look, you know what you're walking out on. What about our deal?'

Gayleen smiled at Speed's frustration. When a man was in that state she had the power over him and when she had the power over Speed she almost loved him. 'Always be pleasant around strangers, Speed,' she chided. Then turned to Chaney, and letting the silent tension hang a moment, asked, 'Are we going to see you again, Mr Chaney?'

'A question I'm dying to know the answer to,' Speed bawled.

Chaney made them both wait. He might have made it lighter on Speed, but Gayleen had really set it up; so he was going to kick right back in her face. He gave an indifferent shrug.

'I might turn up.'

Turned and walked away down South Rampart toward Canal Street. Out of their lives.

Everything in Speed fell flat. 'Son of a bitch,' he said dismayed. 'Hey! Royal Street. 17. Look me up, hear.'

Gayleen stared after Chaney. There was a challenge on the hoof. Someone in pants who said he didn't need her or anyone else had to be tried.

'Who was that guy?' she said, still watching him.

Speed shook his head. Wanted to cry. There went his dreams of the bigtime. Everything. He felt like a down-and-out.

'Money, walking bankroll,' he muttered. 'Let's get some breakfast.'

FOUR

Chaney hadn't felt so good in a long while. He had twenty-four bucks in his pocket, he was walking free. The morning heat was still very pleasant, the day hadn't got up and into gear yet, it didn't have the greasy, torpid feel to it which it started to get around noon when folks were about ready to drop in the bars and on the benches under the palm fronts in Audubon Park.

Almost instinctively Chaney headed down toward the water, passing quickly through the French Quarter. That time of morning was about the only time of day or night that the Quarter showed any sign of change, at that time it was kind of caught off guard, like a corpulent whore with her makeup and corset off, uncertain whether she was working or sleeping. It was at that time Chaney felt his greatest affinity for the place, being unimpressed by the hustling razzonatazz that went on through most of the day and night.

He walked down Rue Toulouse which brought him onto Decatur Street opposite the Jackson Brewery, the smell of beer hung in the air, mixed with the tarry smell that came up from the Mississippi just beyond the railroad tracks.

Climbing the ramp onto the levee, Chaney paused to watch the early morning movement of the river. There wasn't much activity yet, boats moored up and down the river were waiting to be worked. Stretching, as if throwing off the last remnants of stiffness from the train journey, Chaney realized how good he felt. Horizons here were as wide open as they had ever been since starting on the road. Here he didn't want to look back into his past. The homing instinct wasn't a worm he had inside him, not anymore. His home, his wife, his children, everything, it had all been destroyed.

Standing there on the levee, staring across the river to Algiers on the far bank, where he saw the Canal Street ferry start out, Chaney became aware of movement down to his left. He tensed expectantly, there was nothing that said he couldn't be jumped and robbed, or the attempt made. Chaney spun round ready for anyone but felt a little foolish when he saw a kid; a boy of about seven years old, who at once threw Chaney back into his past. He slammed a shutter down hard, but it was too late, he had identified this kid with one of his own. Questions resembling concern assaulted him, he wanted to know immediately where this kid had come from, what sort of deal he got and was going to get out of life. He had been sitting by an oil drum and was now standing. Maybe waiting for his old man's ship to get in, Chaney thought, or maybe he was just looking for someone to latch onto, buy him breakfast.

Look away kid, Chaney thought, getting his feelings on the right side of the shutter, you found yourself a non-runner. A kid looking at you, measuring you, made you measure yourself, and Chaney was none too sure how he really liked himself these days. What did the kid see? Another workless drifter with next to nothing to offer? Maybe. Or Chaney who had once been a father and a family man? Perhaps. He guessed some part of him would always be that man, despite his resistance. However, not a future part, he made no allowance there. Even recognizing this attraction for the kid whom he now passed along the levee, he knew he could never again take on all that he, and those like him, represented. It was all something Chaney had irretrievably lost and he was surviving without it.

He walked on, feeling the kid's hungry eyes following him, curious at the look he had given him. Shit, what had he seen there? Hope? Was he less in control than he believed he was? Chaney was about to stop, but dropped a buck on the ground instead, and kept on walking. Chaney didn't like getting involved, not with another person, much less with his own feelings.

Crossing the railroad tracks back over Decatur, Chaney intended moving down river beyond the French Quarter to the rundown docks area to get himself a room, but passing Jackson Square he stopped. The winos and the stumble bums who slept there were being rousted out by a couple of cops who were laying their nightsticks across the skinny shoulders of the sleeping men, bringing them awake with screams. Anger spread through him, he pressed his fist hard against the iron railing around the square. One of the cops, a fat guy with a clipped mustache, saw Chaney and paused to take stock. There was an arrogant challenge in his look, demanding to know what

Chaney had in mind. Then as if to say there ain't nothing you can do about it anyway, buster, the cop laid his stick across a drunk's skull, laying it open. There wasn't anything Chaney could do but move along; if he let anger carry him through those gates he'd never have made it. The cop would have drawn his gun and shot him before he was halfway.

The clapboard buildings down near the waterfront were the most rundown, and happily accommodated those who hadn't quite the guts to be dead, along with those who were but didn't know it. Behind the crumbling façades there were seedy, illegal gambling houses whose lights hadn't been off for days; there were sawdust joints selling fifteen-cent beer; smoky poolhalls and smokier brothels. Everywhere Chaney saw down-and-outs, panhandlers, broken people who were going to stay that way all their lives. He pushed them out of his mind and passed on to another area of the city.

Breakfast was easily afforded now and the newly baked croissant and fresh coffee were very tempting, but he passed. Breakfast wasn't a habit he wanted to acquire in his current flush. Recalling the lumps those guys back in Jackson Square were taking was enough to cut his appetite anyway.

A sign outside a house in a narrow decaying street off Burgundy Street said Rooms. Overspilling trash cans stood in the streets for rats and cats to pilfer from in competition, and blacks and whites alike without work or prospects lounged on stoops and porches.

Chaney climbed the three steps of the rooming house and pushed into the hallway, lit by a naked bulb in a dust laden wire basket. He rapped once, hard on the first door. Eventually an old man in a torn shirt and stained pants opened it a couple of inches.

'What you want?'

'A room.'

Water spilled from his eyes as the old man screwed them up to consider Chaney. He scratched at a sore showing through his thinning sand-colored hair and finally nodded. Leaving the door, he went back inside somewhere, then returned with a bunch of keys.

'Up the stairs,' he said, and began to climb up on a bad limp.

Chaney followed slowly. He said nothing. He wanted a room.

Nothing else. He waited on the top of the first landing as the man opened the door. The old man looked back at him. Again his eyes squinted like he was no longer sure about offering the room as a place for a human being to live in and was trying to make out whether or not Chaney fitted. Chaney didn't wait for an invitation. He walked down past the man and into the room.

He stood in the center of the bare floor with what seemed like a decade of dust and dirt engrained in it, along with stains of too many forgotten, anonymous occupants. With an unchanging expression Chaney's eyes spanned the gray, cracked and peeling walls. Along one wall was a small bed with a broken leg and a chock of wood under it, and a couple of blankets and a grease-stained pillow. By its side was a night table knocked together with scraps of wood. In the middle of the room were two chairs and another small table. The kitchen area was a hot plate, icebox and sink next to each other on the wall. He took in the rest of the room with a glance. There was nothing else.

Chaney remained immobile. Behind him in the doorway the old man began shuffling. Maybe he figured Chaney would turn it down. When he didn't and he saw the prospect of actually letting the room, he came closer to reality. He started in on his sales-pitch.

'You get a lot of sun through the window,' he said, coming into the room flapping his cuff, making a feeble gesture to sweep off the dust from the table; if he'd run a diner he'd probably have done the same with a plate. 'Fix the place up, could be real nice.' He stopped, looked at Chaney's impassive face, and wondered. 'Real nice,' he muttered nervously.

Chaney was hearing the old man, but wasn't listening. Music was coming in from outside somewhere. That interested him more. Perhaps the old man really believed the place could be done up, real nice, or believed it mattered.

'It's fine,' he said.

He tossed his duffle bag to the bed, looking at it lying there. Like no other thing, it was with him everywhere.

The old man couldn't believe it. 'You'll take it?' he said. 'Well I got some furniture down in the basement you could use.'

'I like it the way it is.'

The old man squinted as Chaney moved across to the grimy shaded window. He stood there looking down to the street.

Across from this building outside what appeared to be a bar, a spasm band looned around in a wild kind of shuffle dance. A passerby tossed them a coin and a Negro boy pursued him down the sidewalk on his hands. Chaney liked it a lot, liked the life he saw down there despite the shit they were getting. Over the curiously harmonious bumping rhythm of tin cans, pan tops and washboard the old man suddenly spoke up again, unaware of the competition.

'Six bucks a week,' he said optimistically.

'I wanna rent it not buy it.'

He freed two singles from his fold and held them up. The old man laughed in nervous anticipation and plucked the two dollars away from Chaney.

'Sure you don't want that furniture?'

Chaney wanted the man to go now. He turned back to the window, watching the dancer with the band, and rocked his head from side to side. The old man waited, as if believing there should be something more to this transaction. He put the two singles in his pocket and nodded his head, not really understanding the way some people lived. He placed a key on the table, gave a last glance to Chaney's back, hoped he hadn't bought himself trouble and limped out, closing the door behind him.

Chaney turned into his bare room. He gave a smile, some of it for real, some of it cynical and a little sad. Sure he liked the room the way it was. Impermanent, barren, impossible for him to spread roots. That's the way life was now, without roots. Roots meant he couldn't easily move on, which was the one sure thing he would always do. The time before when he set them down and thought them strong enough to withstand whatever wind of change he had been proved wrong and they were torn from under him. He wouldn't let it happen again.

All he was looking for now was what he had got, a broken-down room which he owed nothing, and expected nothing from. Home was his black canvas bag and its meager contents, a blanket, shaving tackle, spare socks, spare pants.

He took off his cap and dropped it on the table. He was tired and wanted to sleep. The bed creaked and rocked and shuddered when he laid on it like it was about to collapse. But it held. He could still hear the street band, and from above him in the rooming house heard a radio playing. It reminded him that in joints like this other people made their homes, and he thought then who it might be playing the radio. He figured it was a girl, for occasionally he caught the sound of a shuffling step as though she was dancing a little. Chaney tried denying it, but just then he felt the need for a little female comfort. If I wasn't so damn tired, he thought; maybe later. He put back his head. On the ceiling above him was a blade fan. Chaney smiled, reached up and flipped the switch over the bed. There was no action. He prised himself off the mattress and hit the blade with his hand. It began turning, faster, till it was running to speed. He laid back, smiling. All it needed was a little help. Watching the blade lazily churn the air pleased Chaney. He always liked things going round and round.

It was night-time when Chaney awoke. He woke as he always did, suddenly, eyes open wide and instantly alert. The fan blade was still turning overhead. He was conscious of two needs. Food and a female. I get up, he thought, I go and get them. I survive. He took up his cap, the key from the table and went on out.

The city was more comfortable for the darkness disguised the garbage and decay. The centers of light provided just enough distraction.

In an eating house without a band and the floor covered in peanut shells and sawdust, Chaney got himself a huge plate of chicken, red beans and rice for twenty cents. When he'd finished eating he stayed on a while watching the activity around him, envying some of it, yet at the same time wanting no part of it, not the couples who were enjoying each other so much. He considered the two hookers outside on the street, each had the opposite side of the street. Neither were for him. His need wasn't that frail.

Soon he moved on, walked with hands deep in the pockets of his lumberjacket, along poorly lit streets from one area of light to another. He got hustled in poolhalls, and hustled in bars. But didn't see what he was looking for.

When he walked into the Pearl Cafeteria it was late and there were few customers around. It was an end-of-the-road type of place, checkered oilcloth covering the tables, and dead light bulbs left in their sockets. The counterman in a white t-shirt under a stained apron, had given up for the night, and sat down one end of the divider, idly smoking a cigarette while reading a paperback western.

Chaney hit the counter top with the tips of his fingers, causing the man to jump.

'Coffee. Black.'

'That's all?'

'That's it.'

The counterman turned to fix it. Chaney looked round the place. It was anonymous enough for him to feel at home. The customers were people he'd seen all over; you looked at them and you forgot them; mostly their lives were wasted. But Chaney didn't like to think this way when he knew so much of his own goddamn time was spent in the same places.

'Black coffee.'

The counterman set the cup down. Chaney didn't take any notice. He was looking across at one of the tables. There a lone girl was sitting, just sitting, nothing else, not putting out at all. Chaney decided she was the one he'd chosen. Without taking his eyes off her he put a nickel on the counter, picked up his coffee and walked over to her.

'Mind if I sit down?' he said.

She lifted her head and her eyes met his. They were querulous, doubting and mistrusting. She had troubles and Chaney didn't want them loaded onto him, not even for as long as it took to drink his coffee. He turned away.

'Sorry,' he said dismissively.

She called him back. 'I'm just having a cup of coffee. I don't own the chair.'

Chaney smiled, turned round again. He hesitated, but justified the move as being on his terms. Sitting, he looked at her straight. She avoided his look. She was no blue-eyed darling, but there was something of the original about her. Attractive in an odd sort of way, with a curiously animated face. He guessed that every thought that passed through her head registered here first. Her eyes were enormous, like a horse's, and despite time probably being down on her, they still had some sparkle. Chaney reckoned she'd been through the mill, knew the score, and probably had life enough to take another shot. When she did look at him he could see the ghost of her youth in those large green eyes. They seemed to ask for a lot, but were too distrusting to ever accept anything. Her face said she didn't want trouble; not anymore in her life. Which was all okay by

Chaney. He wasn't offering much. What he did want he could go after straight and level.

'You want to talk, or just want to sit?' he said.

Her look hardened as though she resented the way he just took her over; yet because she felt a need that he could answer as well as anyone she couldn't tell him to get lost. So maybe what she really resented was that need which made her so weak. Chaney saw it already, saw the essential difference between them, and how he was going to score.

'Maybe I'm waiting for somebody,' she said, 'you think of that?'

'Maybe you are.'

'I am.'

Chaney didn't believe her but let it go, figuring she just wanted softening up a little.

'Got a name?' he said.

'Lucy.'

'Hello, Lucy,' He gave her a smile.

For a second or two she tried refusing it, then cracked, smiled openly, and about gave herself up to him. Chaney had made his point.

'Who you waiting for, Lucy?' he said.

She took in a breath, paused looking upwards, then came down, smiling and saying, 'I'm waiting for someone to buy me another coffee.'

Chaney smiled and told her his name.

She tilted her head thoughtfully, considering the name. 'Chaney.' She made a face indicating the name was okay. It fitted him.

Turning, Chaney gestured to the waitress, who was yawning, waiting for shut-up time. He pointed down to Lucy's coffee cup. Lucy was waiting for him, waiting for him to fulfill her need other than for coffee. And he decided he'd let her have it at once.

'Live round here?' he said.

Her tired eyes closed a little. The old mistrust and doubt filled her face. She'd forgotten how many times people had tried to pick her up.

'Didn't take you very long to get around to that one.'

'I thought maybe I might walk you home.'

She stared at him blankly. Usually they weren't this quick or this straight. There was something about the guy, about his honesty, which she liked. Yet she was frightened too, frightened of giving herself over, of trusting, making herself vulnerable.

'Not likely,' she said, letting her attention go to the waitress who approached.

Chaney shrugged. 'Just asking.'

They both watched the coffee cup being refilled. The waitress departed, left them staring at the steaming black liquid. Both looked up at the same time and stared with nothing to say. Chaney wasn't going to start in on small talk. There was something he wanted. He had made his gambit and would wait, figuring she would come around. She needed too much.

For a moment she appeared even more lost, and chewed on the pulpy flesh inside her lips during the silence. She wished to Christ he'd say something, anything to get the ball rolling. When he continued to stare, in that easy, pleasant way, his rugged face not too hard, she thought she'd make a move.

'Still, not moving,' she said. 'It's been the same all day.'

Chaney questioned her with a look.

'The weather. I reckon it'll break soon though.'

'You do.' It wasn't a question and gave her no natural opening. He didn't know shit about the weather, only that most people complained about it. He wasn't about to.

'Come on,' Chaney said and rose, picking up her purse. That panicked her. She stood and he simply handed it to her.

She looked at him, suddenly smiled.

'Oh, you're good!' She paused, then said, 'You want to walk me home.'

'That's what I figured I'd do.'

'Okay,' she said, and got out from the table. 'I'll let you walk me home.'

They came onto the sidewalk and moved in the direction she indicated, Chaney with his hands in his lumberjacket pocket, Lucy by his side, swinging her purse. Neither making contact of any kind as they walked. Chaney stared ahead up the dimly lit street, waiting for Lucy to move her ground. Eventually she put a hand under his arm and walked in step. Chaney smiled.

'Well, you want to talk, or just walk?' she said, a bit uneasy at his silence.

'You want to talk? Talk.'

'I wish I goddamn well knew what you wanted.'

Chaney looked askance at her. She seemed pretty vulnerable to him with her uncertain expression beneath her pageboy bobbed hair. Her light summer frock added to the impression. It wasn't that she didn't have anything much in the world, he just felt she just didn't have any strength. He doubted she would survive alone very long.

With a cynical laugh Lucy flagged her hand toward one of the houses.

'Home was a bit like this, you know. A girl had two chances in my home town, stay and be bored or move out and take your chances.'

From one of the porches came an uproar of laughter and a raucous whistle. Lucy was unaffected by it.

'I've seen worse,' Chaney said considering the street. 'Nothing happening can be a lot better than something you don't figure on.'

Not being a gambler he had no high hopes now, and wasn't looking for any.

Lucy shrugged. 'Depends what you're looking for,' she said. 'How about you?'

They stopped outside one of the three-story dwellings.

'I don't look past the next bend in the road. Never could see any farther than that.'

He was offering nothing, Lucy realized, no future; just the moment. Could be a good moment, she thought, but could also be trouble because she needed love too much, she needed to be loved. That was part of her need. She pushed her finger abstractedly against her forehead, and tried a smile at him. Then moved on up the porch.

Either side of the porch were two doors. She fumbled in her purse for a key and shoved it into the lock of one of them. She'd just about got the door open, when the door opposite pulled back a few inches.

Lucy sighed wearily and turned to the elderly woman who was there.

'Good night, Miretta!'

When the woman saw Lucy she quickly shut the door.

Her own door open behind her now, Lucy felt vulnerable. She turned to Chaney, but didn't meet his eyes.

'You want me to come in?' he asked.

'No, I don't.'

Chaney considered her wan face. She wanted him in there, she needed him, and he knew it. 'You sure?' he asked.

'Listen, Chaney, I thank you for the walk, but I've got a husband in jail; no job, no prospects and I don't need any trouble in my life right now. And letting you into my place means trouble.'

Chaney raised an open hand. 'I wasn't planning on bothering you.'

'What was your plan?'

'I guess it's just fallen through.' He stepped down from the porch. 'Maybe I'll see you sometime.'

Lucy bit her bottom lip. Much as she might like the guy, she figured she had played it right with him now anyway.

'Maybe,' she said, and turned in, shutting the door.

Pausing, waiting for the light to disappear from behind the door, Chaney smiled to himself. He'd see her again.

FIVE

By noon Speed still wasn't fully awake and only half-up. But up or down, the way his luck was running these days it didn't make too much difference. He was propped on his elbow in his Murphy bed, and on his third cup of coffee which he had had to make. With a thick pencil he was circling potential winners in the scratch sheet from the back of the Pic-Times.

Gayleen rolled over and jolted his elbow, making him bite off the end of the pencil. He spat it out irritably, and considered her still asleep. She was an amazing piece of ass, but she wasn't bringing him any luck just now. Something about her had upset Chaney at the station. Just for that she ought to have been bounced. But he guessed he'd rather sleep with her than Chaney.

There was a guy who was lucky, Speed thought. A guy with no goddamn needs at all. He tried to dismiss the thoughts of Chaney, still being pissed off at the way it had come and gone like that. A dream, he wondered if that's what Chaney had been. A hitter old enough to sucker the punters but good enough to cream the opposition.

He went back to the daily racing form, looking for a sign.

All three-legged no hopers from what Speed could see. Come on lady, where are you. I'm looking for you. Maybe there was something running named silver. There wasn't. Only Golden Thorn in the third. Then he saw it, My Man in the sixth. The horse's name leapt up off the page as if in mockery. That was it, Speed knew it. He didn't even have to circle it.

The knock on the door when it came was sharp, like someone was out collecting. He wasn't running any markers right now, but there was all the usual stuff without too much pressure which someone usually finally got around to calling for.

'All right!' he yelled, when the door was banged again.

Reluctantly he got out of bed and stretched; then moved to the door and cautiously opened it. His face suddenly beamed like pure gold. Chaney was standing outside the door as large as life and twice as beautiful.

'Well hallelujah! Jesus Christ,' he said. 'Good to see you, pal.'

He threw open the door and expansively beckoned Chaney inside.

'I'm mighty glad you found time to drop in, friend.'

Chaney stepped in and casually looked over the place. He wasn't impressed with the bargain Speed had with the world if this was all he was getting in return for the price he was paying out. Speed saw the look on his face but wasn't going to let it worry him. Chaney's walking through the door like this was the piece of luck he'd spent yesterday praying for. And whatever the apartment lacked in comfort, Speed made up in smiles.

'Come on into the kitchen and we'll get the morning started right!'

As Chaney followed him toward the kitchen, Gayleen stuck her head out from under the covers and he glanced at her. Disinterestedly she rolled back into her pit. He looked at Speed, wondering what made her worth it to him.

'Don't mind sleeping beauty,' Speed said, maneuvering Chaney into the kitchen, as if Gayleen, out of sight, was a problem out of his life. 'She's not one to rush into a day's work.'

Turning back from the kitchen, he regarded her sleeping form. 'Are you goddamn *it*?' he yelled. Times like this when his luck suddenly turned good and he knew he had to grab it fast, he realized she was a millstone. Jesus, if only he could do without her as a cushion for the hard times. 'How about some breakfast around here,' he said not looking for a fight. 'We got an important guest.'

Gayleen went on ignoring him and giving out little signs as if asleep.

'Christ on a crutch,' Speed muttered.

Watching him give up with a shake of his head and a shrug, Chaney couldn't help liking Speed this morning with his façade stripped away, couldn't help feel something for him seeing him surrounded with all his weakness. Like so many of his contemporaries, Chaney figured, Speed simply liked to crucify himself now and again by loading himself up with problems. There was a masochistic pleasure dragging a crucifix up a hill, and sometimes it was easier than standing alone. But it was one weight Chaney didn't need, and one he didn't plan to have put on him, regardless of his involvement with Speed now. Chaney was staying light except for the greenbacks he was going to pick up.

Turning around and facing him, Speed switched off that air of desperation he got at Gayleen's hands, and his face lit up, hope and bravado jostling for prominence. Chaney just smiled. Speed looked a little ridiculous in his baggy gray undershirt, and shorts from which stick skinny legs sprouted. He sashayed to the icebox with the swagger of a successful fairly who had just seen his make. In a suit and two-tones he might have worked. Whatever impression Speed was creating he wasn't letting it worry him. Chance had brought Chaney to his door this morning, and that meant his luck was running good again, and that inevitably meant money. He glanced back at him, all smiles.

'How about a beer? It'll take the dust off,' he said like it was some excuse.

Chaney gave a nod, and sat down at the kitchen table. Speed excitedly took a couple of bottles of Jax from the icebox, cracked them, and came and sat opposite Chaney.

'Well, I assume you want to talk a deal, my friend,' he said. 'We go fifty fifty on scratch bets and expenses.'

Chaney waited, sensing he had finished. Speed still had to learn if he believed he'd just take whatever was handed down to him. Disinterestedly he took a pull on the cold beer.

'Side bets I keep seventy-five per cent,' Speed went on. 'That's how it works.'

That's how it don't work, Chaney thought. That's why hitters always end flat, busted out before they even reached his present age, on the floor of a bar-room somewhere. His glance turned from the mess in the kitchen and flicked across to Speed when he spoke.

'Sixty-forty, in my favor on scratch. Side bets down the middle,' he said casually.

There was no kind of proposition in his voice, a big flat nothing. Speed's pan contorted.

'I'm telling you the going rate,' he said. 'What's normal. Ask anybody.'

'We'll do things different.'

'Why should we?'

Chaney looked at him. 'Right now you got a percentage of nothing.'

Speed didn't need it rubbed in this morning.

'That makes me about even with you,' he said.

Chaney pushed his bottle aside and stood up from the table. He gave a look at Speed dismissively. They weren't even and never would be, Speed had too many needs. He turned and started out of the kitchen. Speed jumped up. He couldn't let him go.

'I'm just supposed to trust in you. Not me, pal,' he said.

The words had no effect. He saw Chaney continue out. He'd really thought they were even. Seems they weren't. Maybe Chaney did have something that he didn't. Jesus, he wouldn't like to barter with this guy for anything.

'All right,' he yelled as Chaney reached the apartment door. 'We'll do it your way.'

That second Speed felt himself grow a little older, a little weaker.

Turning Chaney gave him a level stare. At moments like this he sometimes didn't like himself. But he would have liked himself a lot less accepting another man's terms. Anyway, he wondered right now if Speed had ever really expected anything else. Speed, he figured, lived his life waiting for luck to touch him, and rarely went out to make either his own luck or his own life. On a different level he was like the bums and the bindle stiff, he waited for life to shove him around.

'Look,' Speed sighed. 'I'll level with you. Things are slow. I can't even pick a horse lately.'

That caused Chaney's face to crack wide open. It was pointless telling Speed that he had never really chosen anything.

'Could you ever?' Chaney said.

Speed shrugged, not wanting to think about it. All he was concerned about was getting Chaney and he had done that. But he had lived on his nerves there for a while. Gayleen's can sticking up under the blanket annoyed him and he let some of his anger and frustration at her.

'Can a man get some breakfast around here?' he screamed. Gayleen was unmoved and completely ignored him. Speed hadn't really expected anything else. She couldn't even toast a muffin.

Back at the kitchen table he paused for a second in pale sunlight which shone through the dirty window. Sunshine was usually something to be avoided, if possible, for it made him feel old, made him feel he was missing out on so much that was going on around town. He lightly touched his hair, it probably looked good in the sunlight, like real silver. He gave himself a collusive smile, feeling a little like he did when shooting crap. You threw and threw and you lost everything. Then you gave up, felt easy and lightheaded, but decided on one more shot; then that careless throw won you everything. You lost it later but that didn't matter, not at the time. And Chaney, he figured, was that careless last throw, and a winner he was sure. He raised the Jax and tipped some beer down his throat.

'You know, I got a great feeling about this. We can make some real money. Next week I'll get you something set up. We'll go in light. Three, four hundred.'

It wasn't what Chaney wanted. Chaney wanted all or he wanted nothing. By going in light he'd be rolling around south forever. He wanted a big deal or he was going to look to make it for himself.

'Maybe you ought to think a little more positive,' he said.

Speed looked askance at him. As a comment on his life as a gambler it was an understatement. But that look Chaney continued to give him impressed Speed a lot. Speed decided then and there this time he was going for the top. With Chaney he reckoned he had a chance. He smiled. It was his best smile. It was for real. No nervousness, no kidding himself.

'Yes, sir, I got a real feeling about this one,' he said. 'A real feeling. We'll go for the top. Chick Gandil. He's the big shot. This could turn into something special. You and me. I feel it.'

'Keep one thing straight,' Chaney said, his tone bringing Speed down just a little. 'I came here to make some money. Just fill in some in betweens.'

That was all Chaney wanted, nothing long term.

'In betweens. Hell that's no kind of living,' Speed said, his thoughts still fixed firmly on running a top going concern.

'It suits me. When I get enough change in my pocket, I'm gone.'

Speed shook his head in dismay. Chaney had a lot going for him, he thought, but like so many hard-hitting boys he was just a little naïve. How many times had Speed himself figured on going into a poker game and quitting when he had enough change. It never worked out that way, any dummy should have known that. You got to like things in the game too much, and you wanted to stay on. You could only ever leave the game by leaving a little piece of yourself on the table. And no one who gambled liked doing that.

'Pal,' he said wisely. 'Things usually have a way of being more complicated than that.'

Finishing his beer, he dropped the bottle in the trash can.

'Let's get started anyway,' he said. 'Gimme a minute to make myself shine, and we'll go see the man down here.'

Fifteen minutes was how long Speed took to spruce up and shine, he'd have liked half an hour. His suit gave him the look of a successful man, and with the luck he figured on Chaney bringing him, it changed the whole of the interior too. As they stepped down the street to his Buick, he had all his old flash charm about him.

So much so he drove like crazy across town to the river. He parked near an old wooden landing stage, where a tugboat was moored alongside a barge.

'Now on,' he said, 'there's not a thing can go wrong for us!'

Chaney said nothing, simply followed Speed over the shale road leading to the river landing.

There was a big crowd around, but different from the scum who watched the warehouse fighting up in Baton Rouge. Chaney could almost smell the money. Some were standing on the stage looking down, while others leant against a tugboat. But down on the flatbed of the barge was where the majority stood in a tightly compressed crowd.

Speed and Chaney moved down onto the barge among the spectators where most of the action was. Shouts and bets buffetted off the sides of the barge, money quickly changing hands.

Seeing Chaney in comparison to the hitters here, one of whom was reputedly the best there was, Speed began to let tiny doubts creep in.

'We'll put this trip down to research, part of your education,' he said conspiratorily. Wondering if it wouldn't be part of his too.

Chaney didn't reply, his cold, assessing stare was taking in the fighters, the crowd, the whole set up, measuring, calculating. Finally it settled on one man he saw seated on a high chair near to the center of the crowd like he was the main attraction. Chaney guessed he was, the fighters were incidental to this man's presence. He was New Orleans gentry, a young, arrogant well-dressed man in a neat white linen suit; there was a touch of the light about him. Chaney immediately identified him with corrupt city and state officials and crooked cops bought in to protect his vested interests. He probably owned one of those villas out on Orleans Avenue. His ancestors were planters, and probably slave owners too. He was the man born with a big stick which he kept waving at Chaney wherever he went.

'Who's the one up on the chair?' he asked Speed, the name being immaterial.

'Chick Gandil. That son-of-a-bitch has broke me three times. He's the one we're going to shake. That's his hitter below. Jim Henry.'

Chaney's look fell on the hitter Speed had indicated. He was smiling and very confident, but Chaney didn't figure it meant much. His opponent was a swarthy bare-chested man with a lot of muscle and not much idea what to do with it. Good for changing tyres if he was told how but wouldn't have made it on his own initiative. The man's shooter was making his pitch around the crowd.

'Last call! Bets!'

'I'm laying two to one,' Gandil said in his soft lazy southern drawl, but enunciating every word.

'He's giving two to one on Jim Henry,' the shill echoed. 'Let's hear it now. Can't get any better than that, boys.'

Glancing at Chaney, Speed gave him a wink that suggested they were getting there.

'I'm going to cast some bread upon the waters,' he said, and snapped his fingers at Gandil's shill. Here it went, his last careless throw. He was already setting Chaney up for the big fight. He tossed it out loud and clear.

'A hundred against curly on a marker.'

'No markers,' the shill told him.

Speed became indignant. He was really on the skids today if he couldn't get a marker. 'Since when?' he said. 'Chick, boy. You know me!'

A lazy smile passed over Gandil's lips. Speed was a sucker, if ever he saw one; he'd like to meet a hundred of his kind a day. There weren't many who'd go against his man.

'Take it,' he said.

'Two hundred to a hundred on a marker,' the man called. 'Who else? Anyone? Last call!'

A couple in the crowd who had been hesitating finally decided to come in, figuring that by the law of averages Big Jim Henry had to fall; no one could last for ever, not even him.

'Fifty!'

'Twenty, here.'

'Got them. Last call. Anymore? All right.' He glanced at Gandil for approval, and got it. Let's get down to it!'

The ring was immediately cleared on the flatbed of all but the two hitters, Jim Henry was still smiling.

'Hey,' he jeered at his opponent, 'don't get nervous kid. It ain't gonna take but a minute.'

The crowd laughed. He had a good reputation and they were looking to see it shatter. There was silence as the fighters stepped out, raising their palms. They got started. Jim Henry suddenly closed in, slammed the swarthy man back against one of the bulkheads. Before he knew what had really happened Jim Henry followed through, giving him no opportunity to block those solid punches he hit him with. The man was briefly lifted off his feet, then collapsed. There was obviously no contest but the man on the deck hadn't believed it until that point. He'd come here believing he could prove himself, and that got him to his feet again. But only for a second. Jim Henry slammed him down again, and this time he stayed down.

The result was a foregone conclusion which had been anticipated by the crowd, and despite their secret wish for Gandil's man to crash they laughed and jeered at the beaten man, slapping Jim Henry's back.

'And that's why he's the best,' Speed said.

Unimpressed by what he'd seen, Chaney replied, 'Is he?'

Although the man hadn't stayed long enough for Jim Henry to give any sort of performance, Chaney had seen enough.

'Nobody's beat him,' Speed said. 'Not many want to try nowadays.' He turned to Chaney, gave him his biggest smile of the day. ''Cept us,' he said. 'Few fights first and we'll set it up.'

'So long as it's worth it.'

They climbed up from the flatbed and down the landing stage toward the Buick.

'Oh, it'll be worth it,' Speed said at length, still trying to finally convince himself. 'You don't think I just gave a hundred away, do you?' Speed shook his head. 'No sir. Chick Gandil's one of the biggest money belts in town, and I'm going to set that son-of-a-bitch up for as much as I can shake out of him.' He held open the Buick door.

With that kind of talk Chaney figured he could really get to like Speed. He liked a man who tried.

It was night-time when Speed finally let Chaney off. Chaney having refused an invitation to eat with Speed and Gayleen.

Instead he bought some groceries in the store on the corner of the street and headed back to his rooming house carrying them in a brown bag. He heard the spasm band playing before he turned into his street and saw them. They gave him a lift. These people seemed to have a good time and it must, as sure as hell, beat working. As he passed he flipped them a dime, and one of the boys immediately put a tin on his head flicked over and spun himself like a top. Chaney grinned with fleeting pleasure before moving on.

Crossing the mouth of a narrow garbage-filled alley between two dwellings, a noise attracted his attention. He peered into the darkness, figuring he'd see another bum laid out. But he didn't, he saw a cat. It had just pushed over a pail of garbage, and now sat poised about to forage through it, but first checking Chaney was no real threat. Its eyes stayed on him, waiting for him to pass. Hard times, Chaney thought, about to move on. Then he felt a kind of sadness for the cat and stood there a moment longer, wanting to give to it, and feeling no fear over what the cat might put on him. With a cat he reckoned he could find the right balance of friendship that suited him. And when he was through he could give the cat back to the garbage bin.

The cat still didn't move. Nor did Chaney. When he took a step toward it, the cat glanced about, preparing to quit the contents of the garbage bin which meant so much to it. But it hung on there, and hung on just a second too long. For Chaney suddenly moved forward scooping it up under its belly. The cat tried and Chaney pulled back, he'd been here before. After a while the cat quietened, and once under Chaney's arm seemed surprisingly resigned to it's fate.

At the top of the stairs in his rooming house, Chaney sat the cat in the top of his grocery bag, while with his free hand he unlocked the door. An obese woman shuffled down behind him, but Chaney didn't even give her a look.

In his room Chaney found a bowl by the sink and put a

little bread and milk in it. Placing the bowl on the floor, he shoved the cat toward it and grinned, watching the skinny animal lap up the food. He emptied the contents of his grocery sack into the icebox. He hadn't bought a lot, just enough to fulfill his needs; canned soup, coffee, sugar, a loaf of bread, a quart of milk, fifty cents worth of steak, half a dozen apples. Nothing else. Tomorrow he'd get some fish for the cat.

He wasn't in this town to set a fashion in dinner parties, he was here to make money. From every fight he intended to pile his money up a little higher, and before every fight he would bet half of it on himself. He wouldn't ask another man to do what he wouldn't do.

Taking three cubes of sugar from the bag, he crushed them and placed the grains on a sheet of newspaper. He put the newspaper on the window sill, then opened the window. He turned back to the table as the cat, through eating, jumped up on it and began preening itself. Chaney looked at it, and reached out and touched it. Immediately the cat began to trust him and nuzzled its neck against his strong finger. That was a start. Chaney then shoved it onto the floor.

Several flies had dropped onto the sugared newspaper when Chaney checked. He shut the window and carried the paper to the table. Reaching into his pocket he took out some money. Fourteen singles, the same seven he originally bet on himself, plus the seven he'd won. He put half back in his pocket, those he'd bet on his first fight, and counted those remaining. He put the seven down on the table, these he was going to bet on himself and his next fight and all he won. He'd given himself seven fights, that would be enough.

He watched the flies flitting about over the sugar, settling, rising and settling again. He considered for a moment how much people were like these flies. Their need for the sugar was as great and they put themselves at the same risk, waiting to be caught. He shook his head dismissively, waited a second longer, then his big hand flicked out. He held it closed before his face. Slowly he opened his palm. He almost smiled.

He had won his first fight.

SIX

Having set Chaney's first fight the impetus of it all had got some good feelings running in Speed about this whole operation. But right now, the morning before the fight, he was as nervous as hell. If everything suddenly fell flat, if lady luck suddenly skittered away like those ducks on Lake Pontchartrain when a plane managed to get up off Shushan airport, he'd be a ruined man. And a lonely one. Gayleen would leave him. Sure she needed him right now, needed him to supply her needs and he enjoyed that. But if he failed to come up past scratch this time she'd beat it. Miami, that's where the little lady had her sights set. Three years ago Speed and Gayleen had a little dream about getting enough dough together to take them to Miami in style. Somehow it hadn't worked out, somehow they seemed to prevent each other getting there. Frequently she threatened to leave and take off by herself. Sometimes Speed wondered if he shouldn't let her go. At times it seemed he would make his own way down there a whole lot easier anyway. He needed around ten big ones to set up a serious gambling operation down there, and hadn't really come near to it in three years. Whenever he started in with the makings it was always swallowed up by something Gayleen needed right then, some kind of rip-roaring diversion that lasted for days and left the Quarter or the Fairground, or wherever, reeling, knowing that Speed had been. But with Chaney he figured he had got the wind in his sails that would take him all the way to Florida in style. Yet he was nervous. He'd had Gayleen press his suit and had spent a dime getting his two-tones one shine. Even his old lady had to admit he looked a goddamn successful son-of-a-bitch today. He knew it too, but still he needed something extra to give him that final filip of confidence. He needed to see Chaney win again.

Behind the wheel of his Buick all his nervous energy raced through his foot on the gas pedal. But as the big car slid across town he began to feel the pressure ease. In fact he felt almost good by the time he reached the intersection where he'd arranged to meet Chaney. He saw him standing near a stop sign while still some distance off, and decided he looked a stayer. Speed wheeled up and braked hard, grinning out through the open window.

'You ready?'

Chaney didn't reply, figuring the man was a knot of nerves to ask such a dumb question. He climbed calmly into the car and Speed powered away like a drunken hot-rod driver.

The venue was in a field down river. Warehouses bunched like impassive spectators. The whole place had the smell of bilge-rot. Adjoining the field was a demolition operation; lumps of metal hung from the cast iron frame of a dry dock shed. But not much work was in progress. The labour was out for the fight.

'That's it,' Speed said.

Chaney's glance swept the venue and settled on the stagnant puddles from recent rain. Speed misread the look on Chaney's face.

'I'm going to get my goddamn two-tones ruined,' he said as if that was his contribution. 'Come on.'

A crowd of some fifty or so men had gathered near a brick pile. The sight of them, most of whom seemed friends of the muscle-boy who was fighting Chaney, brought back all Speed's nervousness. Muscle-boy looked a toughie, he thought fleetingly, as he made his way to the muscle-boy's man to get things started.

Waiting quietly and calmly Chaney gave no indication to the crowd of what he might be capable of or what was going through his mind. In fact not that much was. It was a fight, a piece of business, and when they were ready he would get it done and leave. Yet now as he stood there regarding the crowd, he recognized just how much of an integral part of the set-up he was, and wished he could be away. Free. These people were waiting for him and he hated the involvement, even for five minutes, however long it took him to earn his money.

When the betting was finished, the insults and shouting all over, Speed came back across the clearing. He laid a thin, delicate hand nervously on Chaney's shoulder, and glanced back toward the big muscle-boy and his shooter.

'Okay,' he said trying to reassure himself more than Chaney, 'that's him. Now listen. He puts his pants on the same way you do. When he farts he smells just the same as you do – well, perhaps a little worse. Nothing to worry about. Nothing except money, being able to eat and have a place to sleep at night.'

Coolly Chaney's look met those before him as he removed his coat and cap. Speed had so much to lose; his dreams; his woman; his money. Chaney had nothing to lose, which was why he was going to win. He passed his cap and coat to Speed.

'He's just ugly,' Speed said, neatly folding the lumberjacket, 'that's all. What's important. Keep your head down, stay calm and want it! Okay?'

'Anytime.'

Unable to really believe or cope with Chaney's calmness, Speed guessed he was by comparison straight off the farm when it came to positive thinking. He looked back to the muscle-boy and his handler and yelled at them hoping to boost up his confidence.

'Anytime! God damn it, anytime you think you're ready.'

The muscle-boy flexed his shoulders in a little mocking dance, which spooked Speed a little and he screamed at him. 'What we waiting for? Make your play pencil-neck!'

The muscle-boy's shooter turned to Speed, 'Hey, you. Shove it!'

Speed jerked up his fingers. The muscle-boy moved forward. Speed retreated as Chaney went out to meet him.

They stopped center of the clearing. A light breeze coming across the open field carried with it a stronger smell of bilge-rot, but also for Chaney it carried with it the smell of freedom. He thought he'd like to be as free as that, as light as that. But here he was in a commitment with muscle-boy, if only to earn the cash to enable him to be free. He stared into the man's eyes and slowly raised his hands showing the palms. He was out in the open and would stand, take anything that came to him, and throw it back. Unlike his shooter, if he didn't believe he could take it he would never have stood up in the first place.

Not letting muscle-boy take him in a rush, Chaney went out to meet him. Muscle-boy tried a left hook, which would have hurt Chaney had he not swung away. Believing he could crowd the old man, muscle-boy went for a big one, but missed. Chaney walked around it, and a couple of right crosses he saw coming. He could see the man getting mad at being made a fool of. He was getting mad and getting desperate to prove himself; so Chaney let the man beat himself for him, and played him, his hands and arms held loosely, his palms slightly open. He knew he had the guy beaten already. This guy was too concerned with the impression he made on other people, that was how he measured himself. How many he could knock down was too important for him ever to measure himself as a person on the ground, at rock bottom. Unlike Chaney who didn't need to hit the guy to know he was a man.

The muscle-boy accepted the invitation Chaney gave him, and tried another big one. Chaney danced away from it, and while the man was still collecting himself, let him have it twice hard in the face. The muscle-boy took it with more than a little surprise, and just looked at him for a second, trying to measure the old man. Anger burst through him and he suddenly tried a kick, but Chaney caught his foot fast, and threw him backwards. He went over, into a puddle.

A whisper of a smile crossed Speed's face. The guy's around him were all howling for the muscle-boy. They weren't guys Speed would care to tangle with and he felt uneasy among them. But he felt good about his hitter putting muscle-boy down like that, and momentarily forgot about the assholes around him.

Muscle-boy waited a moment on the ground. When he figured he had Chaney's tactics worked out, he got up and went straight down again as Chaney slid in with a solid right from nowhere muscle-boy saw. Retrieving himself, mad and reckless now, he got up and fell flat down yet again, as Chaney proved his total control. It was almost effortless.

Never before had Speed felt so much affection for a hitter. It was like Chaney was his alter ego. It was Speed out there proving himself a real man, he didn't need a sharp suit or two-tones, just his muscle – no, just his strength.

Chaney stood his ground as the muscle-boy began to rise yet again. He figured the man had nothing left in him but a wail. He was right. The guy stumbled to his feet and tried a headlong rush. Chaney didn't move, the blow that he stopped him with caused muscle-boy to hang in the air almost frozen. Chaney hit him with a couple of short jabs then moved out so the man couldn't hug him. He crumbled forward, his face hitting the wet ground. It was all over.

Chaney walked over to Speed, ignoring the murmurs of surprise, of disgust, of indignation from men who had lost their bets. He remained calm and in control as he took his cap and coat from Speed. The fight might not even have involved him.

'Holy Christ,' Speed said, still dazed at his success. 'Very pretty. Very nice.' His doubts were no more.

Chaney pulled on his coat allowing himself a brief smile. Deny it or not, it was nice to be appreciated, and Speed certainly let you know it. Then Chaney looked up.

'Let's get the money,' he said, almost as if for a second they had forgotten about it.

'Nobody ever has to tell me about that, my friend. No sir.'

Speed strutted across to the gathering around floored muscle-boy, a Tennessee walking horse once more. On the proceeds of this little number he could have himself a couple of the sharpest suits in town. Maybe a fine linen one like Chick Gandil's.

'All right, gentlemen,' he said expansively. 'Now you've seen how it's done. I believe this is mine.'

From one of the onlookers, he snatched away the pot, then looked over to muscle-boy's shooter who was busily tending the beaten champion.

'You got anything else you want to say?' he invited.

'Yeah. Get hosed!' the man called back.

'Don't think I haven't tried, friend,' Speed retorted with a grin, drawing a laugh from the men close by.

Finding Speed, Chaney took the cash out and peeled off five singles from the wad. He started across to muscle-boy. Speed was staggered and came after him. Chaney stopped before muscle-boy, whose head was just clearing, but not enough to understand the five notes Chaney dropped into his lap.

'Are you crazy?' Speed demanded, pursuing Chaney as he turned away.

'We won some. We can give a little back,' Chaney said.

'So give me back the bundle before you go into the mission business,' and he plucked the rest of the money from Chaney. 'We'll make the split when we get back. Right?'

Chaney drew in his step as they made their way toward the Buick.

'Well, Jesus,' Speed said. 'We can afford to celebrate together!' He considered Chaney's uncertain face. 'You know what a celebration is?'

Chaney gave a shrug. 'So we'll celebrate,' he said.

Speed bounced into the driving seat, full of secret smiles. Then cocked his head to one side and confessed winsomely, 'Gayleen and I give each other a hard time when we go out together. With you there we'll really shake up the joint!'

As the car headed out across the field Chaney was still and silent. He didn't want to celebrate, and even less if it meant bailing Speed and Gayleen out of the stranglehold they'd put around themselves.

But the three of them went to a crowded bar in the Quarter. It was too crowded for Chaney's liking. There was a party of tourists singing along with the popular tunes the black jazz-band was playing to accommodate them. They'd move on to eat or have their photograph taken holding a monkey, and another crowd would take their place.

Chaney, Speed and Gayleen sat in a back booth. Chaney drinking whiskey from a short glass, while Speed took beer from a pitcher. Since the evening began Gayleen had been angling at Chaney by putting Speed down, but he had let it ride, wanting none of her and no part of their domestic quarrel. He remained as distant as he could without being openly hostile. The lady had shown a dandy streak, but not until Speed took out the prize money and started counting it into separate piles did she flash a smile that really showed her spirit.

'Eighty, ninety and two hundred,' Speed counted, with a satisfied smile. 'Victory does have its rewards, friend.'

He pushed the piles toward Chaney, who took them up and pocketed them. The day's business was complete. Soon he'd be on his way out of this joint. Speed put his own money away. Business concluded, he was then ready to really start celebrating.

'Things go right we're going to be just like a state fair,' he said. 'Bigger and better all the time.'

'Great hopes and high expectations,' Gayleen said cynically, with a knowing look to Chaney as she raised her glass.

He didn't return the toast and ignored her proposition. She had great hopes of Speed getting higher each night, and when he didn't she looked around. But Chaney wasn't looking to be anyone's substitute. When Gayleen saw she wasn't making any kind of hit with Chaney, she turned irritably to Speed.

'My glass is empty, Speed,' she said.

'Always demanding, Sugarplum ... aren't you?'

'But don't you just love it,' she came back at him.

Speed gave her a shrewd look, which he didn't very often. 'Sometimes I wonder,' he said.

Only since meeting Chaney, since he had seen how far he could go, had he wondered just what the cost was of attempting to fulfill Gayleen's needs. Maybe, he figured, it's because I don't ever really fulfill them that I go on trying. Shit! She was a piece of ass, and like most ass the more you hit it, the more they wanted. You could never win.

In so many ways they were ideally suited, Chaney thought, they deserve each other. They hung together like a couple of punchy fighters, believing they needed each other, not knowing what way to turn if they let go. They grew to depend on the pain and the anguish they managed to inflict upon one another. As he sat there isolated, alone, the couple by his side bitching unnoticed in the raucous din that filled the bar, Chaney's thoughts irresistibly turned to his wife and family. He had enjoyed the relationship he had had with her, and when she'd gone, along with the kids, he hadn't been able to move, not forwards nor backwards only downwards. And as a result had considered all such relationships in the light of what he'd felt like without his. He couldn't understand why no one else felt similarly, and simply figured they didn't hurt as much as he had, hadn't loved as much as he had. So many people played life, played at living like it was a game, and that's what he distrusted most of all. People playing like Gayleen. They were the ones you had to cut.

'Here!' Speed caught the arm of a passing waitress. 'Another pitcher of beer. Another glass of wine, and one more for my friend.'

'What's your label?' she asked Chaney.

'Wild Turkey.'

He watched her slip off to fill the order.

'Now, let's get down to it,' Speed said in a businesslike way. 'How'd the bones hold up today, Chaney?'

'No problem.' Chaney opened out his hands. One was just a little puffed along the knuckles. 'Just the head spot,' he said.

'Take care of them, that's important.'

Chaney was amused. He guessed Speed was playing out his part. He knew how to take care of himself. But he let up a little as the waitress approached again and set down their drinks.

'Maybe,' he said, 'I should just keep my hands in my pockets all day.'

'Not a bad idea, friend,' he beamed. Good as Chaney was, he'd seen too many big boys get careless with themselves. 'Things stay right, we're going right to the top. I got it all worked out on the way to take Gandil and his baby. I'm going to set it up just as soon as I can. We got a chance at some serious money.'

Gayleen came in right on cue. 'In other words a meal ticket,' she said. Three years was a long time to be with Speed, and in that time she'd heard enough talk about serious money. Gayleen knew Speed was a gambler and had him figured for a loser and guessed he was always going to be that way. She'd hung on waiting for the break, believing in it at first. Now she was getting impatient, and when she got sufficiently impatient she even got over her laziness. She decided she'd give Speed one more chance; with Chaney she figured he was making a half decent throw. If he didn't score she'd look around for someone else with more than car fare down to Miami. Someone like Chaney maybe. There was a guy who had it all, if only he chose to give it out. He had it and she wanted it. She needed so much, always needed someone to fill her needs. Jesus Christ she was even horny for herself. She turned a flashy smile to Chaney.

Speed apologized. 'You'll have to forgive Gayleen's direct way of talking. It's part of her charm.'

'I noticed.'

She was irritated that Chaney didn't even look at her. So if I ain't bait, she thought, maybe someone else is.

'If you need some company,' she said, 'I know a girl for you.'

Chaney smiled to her. 'I like it better when I find my own.'

Speed tried to iron over the tension brewing. 'Man's got to have a natural release,' he said. 'Can't let the skirts get to you though. Perfume tonight, smelling salts tomorrow!' He filled his glass from the pitcher, and raised it to Chaney. 'Happy days and to what should be a hell of a team.' He turned the glass up and drained down in one.

'And to lively times ahead,' Gayleen said, lifting her drink.

Chaney lifted his glass. 'Here's how we lost the farm,' he said vacuously, and swallowed the shot. 'I'll be seeing you.'

Without another word he rose and walked on out. Even the

close night air outside was a relief. He was glad to be free of the bar and tourists and Speed and Gayleen. They couldn't work it out, and he thought they both resented their need for each other, which made it one hell of a relationship. Yet it was a relationship and one they lived with, he reminded himself. He had little more going for him in that area right now than the bums down in Jackson Square. But even with that realization he knew he couldn't pay the price. Maybe a relationship with a woman who would accept the moment. A woman who didn't want strings or ties. Lucy drifted through his thoughts and he wondered about stopping by her place. He decided he'd leave it awhile. He didn't need it that much anyway.

If he got lonely through the night, well, there was always the cat to whistle to, and his money to count.

SEVEN

Lady Luck was back with Speed. He could smell her perfume in the air all around him, and like a beautiful lady he wanted to stay with he was treating her with respect. Today and right on through, he wanted that lady by his side, for today he was going to throw the hook to Gandil. It would be a gamble at the best of time, but now more especially for Speed because he had a little case of the shorts, and would first have to borrow the bait. So if Gandil didn't snap just the way he wanted him to, Speed would find himself running a big marker to a man who would make him more dead if he didn't pay up.

When one lady was with a man naturally she didn't like any other being around, and Gayleen hanging on his balls and bitching was just something he didn't need. She was already ploughing through his share of the proceeds of Chaney's fight, and insisted on being motored around town to collect a few of the little luxuries she claimed Speed had kept her starved of. The trouble was she had given him a good time last night, one of the best and he hadn't the heart to deny her.

All this, and Speed had so much to do today. He stood at the door of his apartment, waiting on her like she was Dietrich combing her hair.

'For Christsakes get it done, and let's go. I don't even spend this long on mine!'

'Not this morning you didn't,' she said. 'How do I look?'

'Terrific, Sugarplum. Absolutely.'

He held the door and she paddled through. He paused a moment looking over the apartment before leaving. He figured to say good-bye to this joint just as soon as he'd clinched the biggie. Already he could see himself maneuvering on the scene down in Miami. Sharp white suit, the right degree of tan; every hair perfectly matched silver. Jesus, what a sight, he'd stop the traffic.

'Come on, Speedy!'

'Lady be kind,' he muttered, and quickly shut the door.

'Kind?' Gayleen said.

'Wasn't talking to you, baby.'

Speed with another little smile to Lady Luck, headed out for the Buick. Gayleen curled in alongside him.

'My business first. Then yours,' he said.

'Big-shot,' she replied as he started the car, jamming his foot to the gas pedal. 'When the hell we getting rid of this goddamn Buick, anyway?'

'That depends how this morning goes,' Speed said, gunning away into the thin traffic down Royal, swinging out and around a man sauntering across the road, and shouting at him.

The Absinthe House bar on the corner of Bourbon and Rue Bienville was a nice place to drink if you were a tourist or a rich lush; it only closed for three hours in twenty-four, 3 a.m. to 6 a.m. Marcel Le Beau was neither, but that was where he hung out a lot – they couldn't help the type of customer that got mixed up with the nice people. The bar was open, but looked closed; it was that time of morning, and Le Beau was there doing business with whoever had the need and could meet his requirements.

When Le Beau was eight years old he had a little chip on his shoulder because he thought his parents loved his elder brother more than they loved him. He was right, they did, so he killed his elder brother with one of his mother's kitchen knives. Not much had changed in Le Beau's thirty-odd years since; the chip had got bigger, and the death toll had gone up. He started his loan sharking in reform school, first extorting nickels and dimes then loaning it out, taking a quarter on the dollar. After someone he was collecting off put a blade through his throat, he found it profitable to invest a certain percentage of his capital in hiring thugs to look up those whom he couldn't get to personally.

People like Speed used Le Beau all the time, and always short term; they couldn't afford it any other way. But some people used the loan shark long term and Speed didn't envy them one bit, no sir, especially not on those days the interest fell due.

Leaving Gayleen in the Buick, he crossed the narrow sidewalk and pushed against the old doors, rattling them a little nervously as though they were locked. He saw Le Beau sitting at one of the marble-topped tables at the back of the room, protected the whole time by two lieutenants, one of whom

Speed knew as Doty, the other was just muscle. They were a pretty mean bunch and he got no pleasure from having to deal with them. There were four other customers in the bar and a black clearing empty beer kegs near the door, which crashed into them announcing Speed's presence. As much notice was taken of him as of the black shuffling around. The three pairs of eyes from the back flicked up at him, as he made a beeline for them.

Jesus, the price of taking Gandil was almost too high, Speed thought, as he moved forward, giving a nervous clap of his hands as if to announce himself further. No one took any notice. Plunge in, he figured, a big smile guaranteed success. They'd see he was a winner. Not that that would impress Le Beau, who always won regardless. He started across the tiled floor, his shoes squeaking like a rusty bicycle wheel.

'Gentlemen,' Speed was being his most winsome.

But the silence that followed was as heavy as clay. Then Le Beau's flunky, Doty, a squat toughie built like a steer, finally gave Speed some attention.

'So?' Doty said.

Speed levelled. 'I need a short termer, a thousand.'

Doty looked at the tough between Le Beau and the aisle. Something seemed to amuse him. Maybe the prospect of the tough taking out Speed's teeth.

'That's a heavy taste. How short?' he asked.

'Hour. Maybe two,' Speed replied.

'Price is fifty. By the hour.'

Eagerly Speed stepped forward, wanting the deal, believing it was done. Doty didn't move, but just looked at Le Beau who went on with his paper. Speed waited. When Le Beau spoke not a muscle in his face or neck moved.

'I've done business with you before,' he announced, slowly folding the paper – now he was onto Dixie Dugan.

'About a year ago,' Speed said with a regular-guy smile. 'I got it back to you, every cent.'

Le Beau turned to him, not impressed at all.

'Yeah. You paid back my three bills. But you ran another marker from Auber to do it. That one you didn't cover so well,' he said.

Speed gave a shrug, knowing not a detail had been missed by the shark. 'Three weeks over,' he said. 'Big deal.'

'Closer to three months.' Le Beau's rasping voice strained from his lungs; it wasn't difficult to understand why he allowed Doty to do the talking.

'Look, I'm clean,' Speed said, a reed of desperation rising thinly through him. 'It's straight now, Mr Le Beau. What's the difference?'

'There's a big difference between me and Auber,' Le Beau croaked. Speed knew the difference, here it was that difference not simply between living and dying, but dying painfully and slowly.

Le Beau gave his lieutenant a nod and went back to Dixie Dugan.

'Okay, Speed,' Doty said grudgingly, 'that's nine-fifty you get.' The loan came at fifty bucks a day up front, and fifty a day thereafter. It wasn't negotiable.

Doty's dexterous fingers quickly counted off the nine and a half bills from his wallet. He paused a second before handing them over, liking this bit of the job.

'Don't be late,' he said, having no need to underline the threat.

Speed gave a thin smile, he knew just how implicit the threat was. His long fingers plucked the money, and turned on his heel. He needed a drink, but not there. Oh Lady treat me better than this, he pleaded.

The one in the Buick wasn't treating him nice. Driving up Rue Bienville to North Rampart Street, Gayleen started in on him again, wanting him to take her shopping. He pulled up outside the Athletic Club and cut the ignition.

'How long you going to be?' she wanted to know.

'Just wait here, Sugarplum,' Speed replied.

'I don't feel like sitting out here all day,' she bawled.

'You don't have to worry about it. Just a couple of minutes. Don't start complaining.'

'I don't want you getting caught up in any game in there, Speed.'

'It's business.'

He took a deep breath. Taking the Lady's heady perfume down into his lungs he stepped out of the car like he owned the Athletic Club.

'Here goes nothin',' he murmured as the black liveried flunky held the door open at the top of the wide perron, bedecked with palms.

There were one or two lean men cutting their way through the pool like they had the next Olympics in mind. They didn't disturb the fat men by the pool who were undecided whether to take a dip before or after lunch, and were only considering it at all because their masseur had told them it would do them good.

Five towel-draped men sat at a cast-iron table on the far side of the pool playing drawpoker. Chick Gandil in a towel robe and silk ascot was one of them. There was a lot of money on the table.

Jim Henry, Gandil's hitter looked less menacing fully clothed. He looked uncomfortable sat to one side as he was. He'd have liked to have been in swimming or working out on the weights. He saw Speed's approach around the pool first and glanced at Gandil, who bumped the table for three cards.

Gandil wasn't a snob when it came to business. He wouldn't have had Speed in his house as a guest, but would have had no objection at all to his coming there to play cards, always assuming he could raise the ante. He assumed it was business that had fetched the small-time shooter here now.

'Hello, Speed,' Gandil said, as the man arrived at the table, sweating. He was always pleasant in business when things were going his way.

'Hello, Chick boy,' Speed said wearing an expansive front.

'How's my personal pigeon,' he asked, endeavouring to take the sass out of him.

'Just stopped by to pay off my marker.' He produced the two bills and dropped them on the table in front of Gandil, who registered it, then flicked one of them into the pot on his call.

On seeing the size of the pot some of Speed's expansiveness shrunk.

'Raise one,' the man alongside Gandil said, showing the color of his money.

Gandil nodded, then turned back to Speed, seeing his expression. 'I'd asked you to sit in but it's a big game.'

Speed laughed. He was planning a bigger one for Gandil. 'Couldn't anyway,' he said like he was in the running. 'I'm keeping a lady waiting.' He made no move away from the table.

Gandil turned back to the game as the betting came round.

'Raise two,' he said indifferently.

Speed felt deflated. The world along with Spencer 'Speed' Weed was going to bust with trying, these five sat with large money on the table like they weren't aware of either.

'Guess you heard I got a new hitter,' he said to Gandil.

'I'll see it,' a man with a large cigar and even larger belly said.

'Word gets around. A maverick isn't he?'

Speed gave a laugh. Chaney was certainly an animal, and sure enough no one yet had branded him with a mark of ownership. That's how Gandil thought of his hitters.

'He's a real hitter,' Speed said. 'Might even work him up to peanut brain over there.'

He made a face at Jim Henry, who bristled, half-rising off his seat. He turned back to Gandil who threw in another three to the pot.

'I'll ride,' he drawled, and turned to Speed. 'No mystery about it. Just takes a thousand dollars on the front line. Then you get a chance at my hitter.'

Speed played him along a little more. He felt the Lady pulling for him now.

'I can get the money,' he said.

Gandil turned to the game. The judge with the fat cigar had just folded. He studied the pot. Covered the bet and raised, and turned back.

'You making an offer?' he asked Speed.

Speed strung it out now. 'Not me, pal. My hitter's an old man. Starting late. A man would have to be crazy, or get long odds,. to mix with skinhead over there.'

He pulled up shortly, noticing Jim Henry getting a little restless at the abuse. He gave him a smile, which only added to Jim Henry's irritation.

'That's three,' a player said.

Speed laughed it off, but could see how much he'd riled Jim Henry. Wouldn't ever like to meet him without his boss to keep him in check.

'What kind of odds you looking for?' Gandil suddenly invited.

'Five to one.' Speed had been rehearsing his pitch.

'I'm a Christian gentleman, Speed. I don't even keep slaves anymore.' He got a laugh. 'Three to one.'

'Deal!' Speed said, apparently losing his nerve and throwing the fold from Le Beau on the table.

'Looks like you got hustled there, Chick boy,' one of the players said amused.

Gandil looked at him sternly, then at the greenbacks. Something was going on and he didn't like it.

'Somebody die and leave it to you?' he said curling his lip contemptuously at Speed.

'Three to one. Money's on the table, Chick boy.'

This display of enthusiasm was too much, Gandil thought, even for someone as short on style as Speed. He'd known him stay cooler than this. Something wasn't on the level, something he hadn't figured yet.

Just as Speed calculated the big gambling man rejected the deal in the only way he could – he felt like kissing the Lady, he knew was hovering over him.

'You think I'm going to fall for that sucker play?' Gandil demanded, 'I don't like being hustled by a hope and prayer artist. You want three to one, fine. But you're not getting it that cheap. The pot bet goes up to three thousand. Come back when you get that rich.'

The words Speed was hearing were sweeter than he imagined. Three to one with three Gs down in the pot. Chaney was going to bring nine thousand home all in one hit. With the Lady smiling on him and positive thinking, he'd be powering the old Buick down to Miami in no time.

'I'll be back,' he said, reaching to pick up the grand from the table. 'Nice meeting you, gentlemen.'

He started away but paused as Gandil made another bet against the last remaining player.

'Plus one and call.'

The player opposite produced a flush, and Gandil threw in a deadman's hand. Gandil was on a bad streak.

'That's the way it goes, Chick boy,' Speed said beaming.

A hope and prayer artist! He'd show him. He started out, a lot of bounce in his walk, and a big, high smile across his handsome face. Everything was rolling for him now.

Except Gayleen. When he got back to the car she was steaming.

'I told you not to keep me waiting, Speed. I got things to do.'

Speed wasn't listening to her, he was thinking about the run he was on now. He didn't intend stopping until he scooped that pot from Gandil. This was one time in his life when he was in control. Nothing was going to stop him winning this time. Certainly not Gayleen.

'For the kind of money I have been talking about you can wait till Christmas, Sugarplum,' he said, and then he allowed himself another huge amassed smile. 'It worked. I pushed Gandil up two thousand on the going rate, and got three to one for my trouble. Three to one.' He whooped causing heads on North Rampart Street to turn. 'Wait till Chaney hears.'

'When do we collect?'

Speed rolled his eyes up as if about to draw off and punch her. Always demanding the goddamn money. What kind of sucker was he to keep on even trying to fill her needs?

'Listen,' he said, 'right now we got to get this thousand dollars back to the owner before I get both my legs broken.'

He hit the starter and swung the car back down through the Quarter.

'We're going to move fast,' he said. 'Two fights or so, then we'll take Gandil. Shit or get off the pot, that's the way Chaney would like it. We'll go out of town to make some money first. I don't want his reputation gettin' out of hand.'

'With me Chaney don't cut no way,' Gayleen said petulantly.

'So see it stays that way!' Speed snapped suddenly jealous. Gayleen might have some plans herself for Chaney. Crazy, he thought, all this time I can't get her off my back, then as soon as she threatens something else, I need her there like a cripple needs a crutch.

'The big boy's got no interest in broads anyway,' he said.

'Maybe he should see someone about it. You too. A doctor or something.'

'Just what I'm going to get him fixed up with,' Speed said. 'Just to make sure things go smooth on our way to the top. He might need some professional fixing up.'

Gayleen looked at him as the car arrived outside the Absinthe bar. She groaned, knowing what Speed had in mind.

'Oh, Christ, not that jerk.'

Speed slammed the door on her. She sat there boiling. Something good had to break for her soon or she was going to get really mean.

EIGHT

Speed was out to pick up some professional help in his bid for the big time. Having fixed up another fight for Chaney, he wanted the help right along with him just in case of trouble. That's if they could find the man. They were detouring on their way to the fight venue.

As the days went by and the showdown with Gandil's hitter got closer, Speed seemed to get so highly strung he was now little more than a jumble of stretched nerves covered with some fancy clothes. The way he was driving the Buick today, had it been a hearse, he would have frightened the stiff right back into life. But not Chaney. He sat alongside not saying anything. Speed couldn't work out his mood.

'What's eating you?' he asked, looking at him as he did almost running off the road.

They had driven across Huey P. Long Bridge and were headed out on highway 90 toward Houston.

'Nothing,' Chaney said. 'I'm ready for business.'

There was nothing bothering him, nothing but the evening itself and the memories it brought. There was a soft red sky which the sun didn't want to leave, and bunches of cumulus cloud no bigger than powder puffs; the landscape that reeled away from him begged to be ploughed and planted but wasn't, the road that rolled away under him was like his own past, gone behind him but not forgotten. It all made him a little sad, conspired to bring afresh his memories of the life he had had with Alma and his two kids. Even the small town they shortly entered off the highway threw him back into the past. It had that familiar, unhurried atmosphere of most small towns that grew up around the highways. The town was nearly deserted where people were in to their evening meals. That was how Chaney best remembered Bluffton Georgia where he once lived. Even the first house which Speed stopped at reminded him of his past; it had that same look of impermanence, like someone had knocked it together not intending to stay. And the pentecostal church, to which they were directed. It was no different to the baptist church where he had buried Alma. It had the same tiny bell-less steeple over the front porch, and the same paint flaking weatherboards.

'I'll see if our saviour's in here sniffing a little joy,' Speed said. He entered the church just like he would a beer joint or whorehouse.

Chaney was grateful to be left alone. After a little while he climbed from the car, he stretched and sucked in lungfuls of the dry warm air, before walking into the peaceful churchyard. The low sun stretched shadows the length of the narrow paths. and little phosphorescent discs danced on the gravestones. Chaney stopped in the center of the path. He didn't want to go on. He didn't like going back, digging through that great secret trunk of memories. Yet he could never forget it; and the two small graves of children he saw before him brought it all back whether he liked it or not. He hated himself and got angry when he hurt like that, yet still he couldn't forget it. That was the one thing he couldn't cut out of himself.

Alma, Jackie and Mary, they were his family. Before the really bad times hit they'd lived together in hope, not much hope, but always enough to believe that things were going to get better. Chaney had worked a piece of land that he and the bank had owned, along with the house he had. Life had been tough, but there had been some satisfaction in the belief that it was your own, and that those you loved around you loved you back. They had all loved too damn much and trusted too much. They had trusted him.

But when the really bad times started to roll, it was the poor who got hit first. The banks had to protect their investors and their profits. Loans were recalled and when they weren't met, the banks foreclosed on the property held in mortgage. Hopes and dreams were hard to sustain with empty bellies through cold nights. His children hadn't understood and had cried; Alma didn't complain, but Chaney saw what was happening to her. He hit out. But banks were the most important institutions in those troubled times, he was told. If they weren't solvent the whole country would go to the wall. Chaney hit out at the men who ran the banking institutions; they also ran the police.

He didn't see his wife after his trial, not alive.

Turning back toward the little church, he wanted Speed to

return, wanted to move again. Strange how right now he wanted Speed. Chaney needed to set up one pattern of life in order to escape from the agonies of that previously destroyed pattern. He brushed a fly from his head and spat out the match he'd been chewing. It wasn't really the way, one pattern led to another, then another and always there was hurt. The way was to cancel out the need for any pattern was to keep moving. Time to walk on a piece. Time for Speed to come back out of the church.

In the church Speed found a small congregation all with their goddamn heads bowed like gamblers shot dead over a table, and he couldn't figure out who was who. Up in the pulpit a woman with a mouth like a chicken's ass spouted a few words, making a noise like the other end of the chicken. But Speed riding with luck, wasn't concerned.

'When Jesus comes to claim us
And says it is enough
The diamonds will be shining
No longer in the rough...'

Speed wanted the diamonds shining sooner than that. Eyes searching, he moved along the aisle. He spotted a crumpled little man in a crumpled white linen suit huddled up alone in one of the pews. A smile stretched across his face and beckoned him. The man didn't move. Speed became irritated. Although the man was a believer, he had probably come here to score some dope.

'Pssst! Poe,' he said too loudly. The man looked up. 'Come on Poe. It's important.'

Raising his eyes with a frown, Poe took a weary breath and stood. Speed walked out, and Poe started after him.

Outside the church, even in the pale evening sunlight Poe recoiled like a night anemone. Poe was a small, fleshy man with white hair. He had a putty-like complexion which suggested no kind of outdoor pursuits and a faceful of nervous tics. His white suit was badly stained, especially around the fly.

'What the hell you doing in there?' Speed said.

'I've always been a student of comparative religion,' Poe replied in whining, yet what the uneducated might assume to be, educated tone. 'If you went to the trouble, you would find that the Pentecostals present a number of points of interest.'

'Forget that crap,' Speed said as he started for the Buick. 'This is important. We're back in business. Now how much doping you doin'?'

Poe gave a sigh. 'Unfortunately, my means this month are not such that I am able to continue my explorations into the stratosphere of imagination.'

'I mean to tell you I'm not talking about spare change.'

'Let's not bother with negotiations,' Poe smiled. Poe needed money and here was his old friend Speed pointing the way. 'Given my present condition I am a willing participant in any medical blasphemy,' he said.

It didn't matter to Poe what he was going to have to do. He called himself a quack, and had once been very well intentioned.

They approached Chaney who was resting against the rear fender of the Buick. Poe stopped before him. For all his bizarre affectations he was an intelligent man, and he immediately recognized a kind of affinity with Chaney, a kindred spirit. It was the sort of instinctive thing which two men have who are opposites in style yet headed for the same end. Chaney was the strong man who didn't cry, while Poe sometimes cried in order to stay strong. In Chaney he saw the man he ought to be, never would be. In himself, he suspected Chaney saw the man he might be, weaknesses all to the wall, and never would be. As much as he cared for his friend Spencer Weed, Poe could never feel quite that way about him.

'Chaney, this is Poe,' Speed said. 'Like I told you, he's good. Cut eyes, broken noses, takes care of all hurts and pains.'

'Save those of a spiritual nature.'

'Cut that crap, Poe.'

Without standing up off the fender Chaney studied him.

'I have little enough to recommend me, two years of medical school,' Poe said it like in Chaney he saw a man who might one day be badly in need of treatment, which he wouldn't be able to give.

'Two years doesn't make a doctor,' Chaney replied.

Poe frowned. 'While in the third year of my studies a small black cloud appeared on campus. I left under it.'

'He always talks that way,' Speed interrupted. 'What he's

saying is, he was a hop head, dyed in the wool user.'

'I have a weakness for opium,' Poe said mildly.

Chaney stared at him a second. For some reason an image of Alma rushed into his head. He quickly let the shutter down, yet he couldn't dislike Poe after that. He saw that somewhere behind him life had given him a hard time. He was still living with hard times, and so maybe, Chaney thought, he understands hurts and pains and understands about life.

Anyway Chaney liked the way the man tried to hold on to something. Even if it was hopped up bullshit. The man was down but he wasn't letting himself get beaten. He wasn't fighting like Chaney; maybe he didn't have the anger in him. Yet he was there taking it, not taking it seriously, but making the whole of it, life, the good times and the bad times, just a goddamn joke. That took another sort of strength.

'Some habits are hard to break,' he finally said with a smile.

'You speak as though you have been there.'

Chaney didn't reply, he was thinking of something else.

'A victim of circumstance,' Poe went on. 'Some are born to fail, others have it thrust upon them.'

Chaney couldn't go along with that. Habits, like his own anger, were hard to break. But all habits could be broken, and all circumstances could be changed. Only Poe's acceptance of himself as victim kept him there. That's one thing Chaney would never accept.

'Your hands please,' Poe said, reaching out and taking them. 'No protruding knuckles, good. No calcium deposits, good. Large hands, good. More area to absorb the concussion of a blow without breaking. A simple matter of engineering stress.'

Poe dropped Chaney's hands.

There was something about taking care of someone which gave him a kick aside from the fact that this one was taking him to the top. Speed cocked his head and smiled. He would look after Chaney. Chaney would pay him back.

'No bony ridges on the face,' Poe said, examining it, pressing and pulling with his fingers. 'Very promising. Your skin looks reasonably thick. I would say that there's a good chance that you're not what Speed, with an unfortunate turn of phrase, refers to as a bleeder.'

'Like I told you, he's good,' Speed said. 'Knows his stuff.'

Chaney looked at him. Again he felt this resistance about being taken care of, though recognized that Poe might once in a while be useful. If someone took care of you they usually wanted too much back. With Chaney it was only business, and he'd let them know that was all he was offering.

'How much?' he wanted to know.

'Expenses and ten per cent of what we win. It's the standard,' Speed replied.

Ten percent. Chaney considered it the same way he might consider dropping the odd buck on the ground for the bums. He nodded.

'So let's get to it then, partners!' Speed said, strutting energetically around the car.

The dash and panache Speed had mustered at the moment of agreement about Poe, vanished as they got to the iron foundry where the venue was, and his nerves had returned. This he had no doubts about Chaney being able to handle; it was that step nearer to the biggie that was making him jittery. He started to repeat his advice about the hitter to hand.

'I said it before, I'll say it again. Watch his feet, he's a kicker. He goes straight to the balls.'

'I'll remember,' he said wearily.

Screwing up his face, Chaney pushed the last cobwebs of Alma from his conscious thoughts as he stared across at the expectant crowd. Those earlier thoughts had left him feeling fairly exposed. He didn't feel too much like fighting this evening, but his surface anger had left him now.

'You got one thing more to remember,' Speed repeated. 'He's got a lot of friends here. They're used to seeing him win.'

'You told me that before.'

'I did? Well, I like to make a point. Let's get to it.'

Speed sprung out of the car like he had St Vitus's dance. Poe walked calmly alongside him. Chaney followed on, but waited off by himself, while Speed did his shill on the pigeons.

Inside the foundry where the cherry red furnaces were blasting, the noise hardly slackened, even though nightworkers began gathering for the fight.

From the crowd of men who swiftly gathered Chaney got a feeling which he didn't like, they were all too close, too knit together; they probably hated outsiders, anyone not in line with the pattern of their own lives. Chaney felt how they tried dismissing him even before he'd taken off his cap and coat. He began to feel the anger he had earlier, it rose up in him again; their wisecracks suddenly penetrated that shell which he'd believed impervious. They called him old man, he was compared to their boy. He decided he'd finish this one before it got started, he'd show these guys he didn't need them. They had nothing he wanted.

The knowing wink and slap on the shoulder Speed gave him as he moved out into the clearing meant he'd made a good deal. Someone in the crowd asked if he needed a walking-stick. There were roars of delight when his opponent feinted a couple of rights, then suddenly tried to kick him in the balls. Chaney stepped around it, to disappointed noises from the spectators. The opponent came in again, feinting a kick before going for the real one. But as his leg left the ground, Chaney shot out his own right leg. The blow from his boot smacked the man in the gut; his stomach caved in, and he started to vomit. But Chaney wasn't done, as the man collapsed forward, Chaney hit him with a right and spun him round as he went down.

Surprise made the men silent. They stood shaking their heads at their hitter in dismay. Poe gave Chaney a thin smile of admiration, but not approval.

Collecting from the man who was holding the cash, Speed said sagely, 'Don't be a gambling man. Didn't your mammy never give that advice?'

As Chaney went for his coat and cap, a man full of anger and booze stepped out into the clearing. Chaney stopped and stared at him, he was dressed in greasy pig-burned overalls, and in one of his huge hands he held a length of heavy chain. He took a run at Chaney, and suddenly lashed out. The chain caught him across the forearm, cutting him. Chaney's reflexes were instantaneous, with the same arm he caught the chain and snapped against it. In his astonishment the man hadn't the savvy to let go. Chaney didn't exactly pull the man toward himself, but gave him such impetus that the punch he followed through with almost took the man's head off. He drew the chain in, figuring no one else would rush to pick it up. They didn't.

Speed's smile was magnificent.

Gravely Poe gave his considered opinion, 'In a week, I

would say. He might regain consciousness.'

The crowd shuffled around, some of them embarrassed. All of them avoided Chaney's look, as he passed through them with Speed and Poe.

Speed was full of their future plans during the return drive. Poe listened politely, occasionally adding his professional comments, throwing in the odd stanza of poetry. Chaney didn't say a word. Having had the cut on his arm tended, he was grateful to Poe. But he was still hurting, and he was angry. He was angry because he'd left too much of himself back there, made himself vulnerable. He'd vowed he'd never do it again. He had felt then that same surge of anger as he had when he had gone after those bankers who made a mockery of his life for living it by their rules.

He stared pensively ahead at the lights of New Orleans coming up on the skyline. Night-time and another fight behind them. He guessed Speed would go celebrate, and maybe Poe would buy himself a tubeful. The whole damn day had thrown him back into the past to the person he once was. Even now, after taking that lash from the chain, he couldn't kill the memory. Maybe he should take Speed or Poe's way out.

But he didn't. When they reached New Orleans Chaney dropped himself out. 'See you in a few days,' he said, and slammed the door.

He walked in the direction of his place. As he walked the city reached into him with its sounds and its smells and its people; it threw up that familiar eternal invitation, that promise in return for delay, that allure of dalliance. For once in a very long while Chaney responded. Tonight he wanted it too. He didn't want to be hurt or angry. He felt tonight he wanted to lose himself a little.

NINE

It wasn't a conscious decision. He could have gone back to the rooming house. He could have laid around with a bottle of Wild Turkey and whistled to the cat. He even wondered for a moment if he shouldn't get back and feed the cat. But once there, he didn't think it would be enough tonight. He needed to feed himself, needed to feed on some comfort and lose himself a little.

After stopping off in a bar for a couple, the next thing he knew he was wandering down that fading street where Lucy lived. Just wandering, with no real plans when he sprang the steps of the stoop and hit the bellpush. Didn't even know if she'd be in and he didn't think it meant too much to him anyway. He waited, his back to the door, looking out on the street at the people who were looking out on the street at him.

Hearing the door open, he left it a moment before turning. When he did he smiled.

'Chaney.' She was surprised. 'Thought it was a salesman or something.'

'No pitch. Nothing to sell,' he said.

She hesitated, and then smiled. 'So what are you giving away?'

Chaney shook his head in silence.

'That was hardly worth coming down the stairs for,' she said as if her life was full of such futile actions.

He said, 'I'm hungry. How about something to eat?'

She laughed. 'There's a real slump around my kitchen.'

'I'm not looking from you. We'll go eat some place. You free?'

She sighed, like it was an awfully big decision to make.

'So who you waiting for, Lucy?' Chaney wanted to know.

'I didn't think I was waiting for you,' she said.

Chaney shrugged. 'Looks like you were. So let's go.'

'Will you give me five minutes?' She hesitated again. 'Come on in if you want.'

'I'll wait here.'

She watched him turn away, lean over the stoop wall and stare out. She might have known he wouldn't come inside, not unless she really invited him. She promised herself she would never let him in unless he asked. Then she would just see where it went from there.

While Chaney waited he felt his arm throbbing, but the events of the day were slipping farther and farther behind him now, into his subconscious. He was about ready to break out a little; he felt like enjoying himself.

With Lucy he walked up the block to catch the trolley-car to Canal Street. Traffic was held up while a Negro funeral procession moved across town, headed up by a Dixieland band, the musicians all brightly dressed; behind the open coffin mourners followed, wailing and dancing.

Lucy studied the man's rocklike immobile expression as he watched them. There was dignity in his expression rather than pleasure.

'I bet you feel for them, don't you?' Lucy said.

'You don't, Lucy?'

The woman shrugged. The gesture was easy, relaxed, and Chaney liked the look of her slim shoulders. She appeared less vulnerable now.

'You know,' Chaney said, as they hopped on the street-car and he gave the operator ten cents, 'those poor dumb sons-of-bitches pay on the nail every week of their lives to ensure that they get sent off like this, right.'

'You don't think it's worth it?'

He knew it wasn't worth it, but didn't reply.

Lucy craned her neck in the seat next to him and regarded him trying to figure a way of getting into those thoughts. She didn't really think she had a chance.

'How do you want to go, Chaney?' she asked seriously.

'How do you?'

'Oh, a bit like that, I suppose, someone finally taking notice.'

'People in the street being entertained,' he said a little disgustedly, knowing Lucy and the people like those poor blacks back there had been entertaining the people all their lives. 'It's going to cost you, Lucy. Too much.' He didn't mean dollars and cents.

'But, Chaney,' she said like she thought he was a bit dumb. 'There's no other way of getting it!'

'Do without. How you die's all that matters,' he said with an air of finality.

They went to Kolb's, the German restaurant on St Charles Street, the main dining room of which was done out like a German tavern. Lucy thought it was beautiful. She hadn't been there before; nor had Chaney; he figured it was a night for new experience. The place was crowded, but they got a table without too much problem, a bit too near the Tyrolean orchestra. Customers sang along with the musicians.

It was the sort of thing Chaney liked more if he could keep a little distance from it.

'So what are you having?' Chaney said, taking up the menu.

The choice of food was rich. Images of bums starving on the road jumped into his mind but he resisted them. Chilli or fried chicken usually sustained him, but he had no real idea about fancy food. But tonight, he thought, he was out on a limb. The waiter recommended German steamed goose with dumplings and potato pancakes.

They said they'd think about it and ordered a pitcher of beer.

There was wide-eyed enjoyment in the woman's expression, like a kid at its first funfair. Funny, he thought, how she waits around for something like this and never gets up and gets it herself.

'Chaney,' she said excitedly, suddenly looking up from the menu. 'Listen to this. Listen, you can have hot lump crab-meat crowned with anchovy, how's that?'

'I'll take the goose stew.'

'Oysters in a spinach, herbs and absinthe dressing. Wow! Then for desert, listen, you can have Louisiana strawberries on sliced pound cake, covered with meringue shell filled with brandy and brought flaming to your table.' She paused. 'Jesus,' she said, 'who would have thought of it.'

The woman's obvious enjoyment pleased Chaney. It was a long time since he'd been with anyone who was so openly pleased. She went on reading at random from the menu, and he listened, not to the words, but the inflections and the high notes of her happiness, just letting them ring in his ears as he turned and watched the orchestra. Like it or not Lucy was giving him a lot tonight.

'So what are you having?' she said, suddenly bringing him

back to the table.

'The man's recommending the stew.'

'Oh.' She seemed a little deflated.

The waiter brought their beer and poured some. Chaney ordered the dumpling stew for both of them. Lucy sipped her beer and put it down, but didn't speak when the waiter departed.

'So what's the matter?' Chaney said.

She raised her shoulders vacuously. 'You get what they tell you's the best, or good for you, or available, ain't that always the way.'

'You could have picked anything you wanted. Why didn't you?'

'I don't know. Scared I guess.'

She was looking at him with a serious expression, figuring he was trying to say something serious too.

'You got the choice,' Chaney said, 'you have to make it before someone makes it for you.'

She was silent awhile longer, looking at him straight. Then she nodded. 'Yes, maybe I do.' Suddenly she smiled. 'I'm sure the stew's the best thing they have.'

Through the meal Lucy did most of the talking. He watched her animated face as she chatted away telling him of her problems and some of the good things too. He guessed she wasn't much different from a thousand other girls, but right now he was attracted to her, because in her circumstances, being broke with a husband in the pen for fraud, he figured she was prepared to accept just the moment without wanting to stretch it into a whole future. Chaney figured the isolated moments made for the best times. The danger was in letting them work as a softening-up process so in the end you tried dragging them out to an eternity, where you found the last moment was nothing like the first, and you weren't the same person either. And the price for that discovery was your independence and your freedom. Chaney had to stay a pioneer.

When Lucy wasn't talking they let the music engulf them, sometimes she would join with other customers and sing along with the orchestra. Chaney didn't. Their eyes caught each others' often, too often, and Lucy's look would escape back to the band. She was still mistrustful. In spite of the circumstances she'd recently been caught up in, it was her nature to ask for future safeguards, a means of hitting bottom and bouncing rather than hurting.

Around midnight, after Lucy had finished speculating on the sort of job she was looking for, finished telling of her hard years, she suddenly looked at Chaney and realized that she'd done most of the talking and that she'd been sitting alongside a stranger all night. He was Chaney, that was all, and she knew nothing else about him.

'You still haven't gotten around to telling me what you do,' she said.

Chaney looked at her, not attempting to answer.

'Well, it's something that people generally ask,' she went on.

Although that was true, the way Chaney stared at her made her wonder how important it was to know anyway. Maybe in her life she had worried too much about such things.

'Afraid I can't pay the check?' he said, and suddenly smiled.

'No. I'm worried because you never answer any questions.' She figured a guy had to answer a question sometime. It wasn't fair if he didn't; the relationship was one way. He wasn't giving anything. 'Tell me how you get your money? To pay Kolb's check and carfare.'

'I knock people down.'

That was how he operated. If she got too close, he'd be forced to cancel her out.

'You mean like a boxer?'

'Different from that. Pick-up fights. It's just something I'm doing for awhile.'

'You mean temporary?'

'That's right.'

Lucy paused and gave a frown. 'Funny way to make a living.'

'Beats changing tires at the gas station for thirty cents an hour.'

Lucy smiled. 'Somehow I doubt that was one of the choices.'

She considered him again, but she still didn't think she knew anything about him.

'So what's it feel like to knock somebody down?' she asked.

'Makes me feel a lot better than it does him,' he replied with a shrug.

Lucy didn't believe it. Didn't believe that's all there was to

Chaney. There was a lot there but she knew she wasn't getting it, not tonight and maybe never. She should forget him.

'That's a reason,' she said 'for the fighting?'

'There's no reason about it. Just money.'

'You got something in mind when your tin can's full?'

'Maybe I'll quit.'

They sat there in a long silence trying to get the measure of each other without revealing anything of themselves. The way Chaney fought was the way he played his relationships. He didn't particularly like himself when he was doing it. But if you didn't do it in a fight your opponent came in too close and you got hurt, and maybe in a relationship, too. So he knocked them down first.

Lucy shook her head and sighed. 'I choose to leave,' she said.

Chaney paused and then shrugged. He regretted it. He'd have been content to sit there another hour.

'You're learning anyway,' he said as he stood with her, and started out of the restaurant.

On the stoop of the house where she lived she turned to him, a troubled look on her face. It was trouble Chaney didn't want. He stepped back down to the sidewalk. He wasn't like Poe, he didn't have anything to give to heal pain.

'Got to get back,' he said. 'Got a cat needs feeding.'

Trouble vanished from her face, and was replaced by disappointment. Then she looked at him a little surprised.

'That's a reason,' she said.

Chaney stared at her, a little cruelly; she'd got too close. He walked away and Lucy turned in. She didn't know where she was over Chaney.

TEN

Something of a nervous disposition was what Speed had been inclined to even before he began shooting for the biggie, but now he'd about reached the stage where he was a complete nervous wreck. He planned one more fight for Chaney, before going after Gandil, and the tension was eating him up. He couldn't stand it a lot longer. Fortunately he wasn't much short of meeting Gandil's minimum price, and figured to do this the next fight.

Lady Luck was still blessing his every action. But he needed to be triply sure, and so drove up to the top of Canal Street where a better class of Negro lived. There in one of the houses screened by palms was a Voodoo drugstore. Charlie Two-Fingers, a Creole stud poker player had put him onto it. Charlie Two-Fingers had great faith in the lucky potions and oils on sale there. And notwithstanding the fact that Charlie was fished from the Mississippi having been stabbed to death. Speed had faith also. From the gray-haired proprietor of the illicit store he bought two vials of oil, one being fifty cents worth of luck around business, the other came at a dollar fifty was Goddess of Luck.

With Gayleen things were running down. She had no faith in the power of luck, believing it simply took you high and left you dry, or wet like Charlie Two-Fingers.

'Not this time, baby,' Speed reassured her, as he smoothed the oils into his hands, across his face and neck and onto his hair. 'Charlie just got unlucky.'

But he couldn't convince her. Sometimes he thought she wanted him to end broke, in spite of her continual howling for money and almost certainly because of it. Maybe she liked howling. Maybe she really liked to see him busted out. Maybe the prospect of Speed all-successful frightened her. The thought amused Speed.

Of course it never once occurred to Speed that somewhere in those craggy good looks and his finely touched hair, and the infrequency with which he screwed Gayleen, there was in his makeup something of the fag. If there was one thing that did make Speed scream like a fag it was Gayleen calling him one; and when that happened it was as sure a sign as any that a man wasn't facing himself.

Gayleen didn't mind his gambling activities in themselves, just that they meant too much competition, and his gambling successes weren't sufficient compensation.

'Gambling,' she said mockingly, 'is sexual compensation.' And reached for the book she'd read it in, knowing she'd get an argument.

'Nuts,' Speed said, pausing in front of the mirror.

'I have it on authority.'

Speed laughed. 'Whose authority,' he wanted to know, 'Peter Rabbit's?'

'Freud's,' Gayleen said. 'Listen. "The fluttering movements of a card dealer's hands," ' she read, ' "the thrust of a croupier's rake and the shaking of dice are subliminated forms of copulation and masturbation." '

Speed stared at her, suddenly angry. 'Don't give me that crap from some frustrated fag writer.'

Gayleen smiled, seeing that she was getting him worked up. 'Even Dostoevsky had an orgasm one night when he lost at a roulette table. What do you figure happens to you, Speedy when one of your big hitters puts someone down? D'you get it up?'

'Shut your mouth!' Speed screamed, mad that anyone should need to question his masculinity. 'It ain't me that happens to. I seen the way you were giving Chaney those big eyes.'

Gayleen gave him a real bitchy smile. 'Well, I've been missing out a bit lately, Speed.'

Speed exploded. 'Then go find yourself a pool cue, baby!'

Snatching up his jacket, he flew out of the apartment, knowing he had lost a couple of rounds that time.

Reluctant as he was to admit it, all too often after gambling he was emotionally exhausted. There were nights when he couldn't get it up and didn't try, this was why Gayleen was putting on him. But in a little while, he figured, after the biggie, he'd lay off and get into her. He sort of understood how she felt. Fortune was a goddess, and Luck a Lady, and Gayleen felt she'd been thrown over for this other woman.

Speed sensed it. Well, it was true, and she was going to have to bear with it for a while longer. He was staying faithful, at least until he got to Gandil.

In order to avoid Chaney's reputation reaching Gandil, Speed was planning to fix up another out of town fight. He figured the rednecks in the bayous wouldn't present any real problems, and were all keen gambling men. The man up that way who ran things could always be relied upon to come up with a worthwhile scratch bet. All he'd need was a call on the telephone.

Poe was already waiting at the bar when Speed arrived and looking more like the Poe of old. He hadn't quite run to a new white linen suit, but he had had the one he was wearing cleaned and pressed. He no longer looked like he spent his nights in the drunk tank. But Speed hadn't time to waste on compliments. Getting himself a beer, he went straight to the telephone and called up Pettibon, leaving Poe shooting the pintable. Poe, a pin-ball maniac, would happily spend most of the day sliding his ten-percent into the machine; but he was good on those tables, and even with half his attention on Speed at the phone behind him he could still run up to fifteen thousand with one dud fin.

'. . . I'm feeling quite fine, Mr Pettibon, quite fine,' Speed was saying, making expansive gestures with the Jax bottle in his hand. Then he paused, listening. 'What? Oh, I heard about him. Where d'you find this gorilla?' He paused again. 'Shook a few trees, I see.' It was a game, both knew. Each were giving the other the old flim-flam, but both observed the rules. 'Well now, friend, we got a prospect here. Think I could make you an interesting contest.' He paused again, listening to Pettibon's shill. 'Well, I do admire confidence,' he continued. 'I'm not sure our hitter's up to all this but he's real game. He's starting out late. A bit old, but real game. The kind that does a gambling man's heart good to see.'

Poe turned and looked over at Speed, who flagged a circle with his thumb and forefinger. Poe frowned thoughtfully, figuring that ten-percent coming in from the bayous would get him a taste. He shoved a nickel in the pintable slot and got another set of balls. He didn't know how long the whole thing would last of course. Speed's winning streaks had a way of not lasting. Chaney's would run down too unless he got out. But Poe doubted he'd do that in time. A man of vision, whether doping or not, Poe could already foresee the sorry end.

He believed in the inevitability of patterns, cycles and sequences of life, which were all but a preliminary to a more important afterlife. True, he believed there was a sort of recurring order in this life which taken at the right turn would lead one on to overwhelming fortune, enduring for one's stay here. But he didn't reckon that such a turn had yet come around for Speed. His winning streak would suddenly vanish overnight, only Speed wouldn't believe that Lady had left him, not until he found himself suddenly down and without a dime; with Gayleen vanished in pursuit of the shrillest whistle. Despite the strength he'd seen in the man, Chaney, like all hitters, would run out of luck and find himself slumping in the sawdust on the floor of some waterfront bar.

Speed didn't let up on the telephone.

'Last time I came up your way it cost me a ton,' he said and listened to Pettibon's counter. 'Now, don't talk that way. Nobody hustles you bayou people. Not a backwards child like me. Just name the time and place, we'll be there.' He did. 'You got it, Mr Pettibon. Good talking to you.'

Poe started a good run on the table. He was just reaching the point-score when Speed whooped with delight and slapped him on the back causing Poe to tilt the table.

'I told you a fat one,' Speed said.

Poe turned and smiled tolerantly. He sniffed curiously. 'What's that peculiar odor, Speed?'

'What? I don't smell nothing.'

'You got some kind of pomade on your hair?'

'Hell now . . .' He suddenly remembered the Voodoo oil. From the deal he'd just made it was obviously working. 'I got Pettibon up to fifteen hundred George Washingtons, that's what I got. That's going to pay some bills.'

'The dun at the door and the wolf at the gate shall be held in abeyance,' Poe said whimsically.

'More than that.' Speed beamed. 'This is going to take us right to that son of a bitch Gandil.'

Poe paused, took out a large white handkerchief, and wiped his nose thoughtfully.

'You're sure about Chaney?' he said.

Speed looked at him, disappointed that his friend should doubt him. 'Does a goose go barefoot?' he said. 'He's a natural! Let's pick him up and Gayleen, and let's move, we've a long way to go.'

By midday the Buick was blazing along a dirt road headed for a place called Baldwin which was way out on highway 90 beyond Franklin. Chaney sat alongside Speed in the front passenger seat, he was silent, and ready for business. In the back Poe sat next to Gayleen. Speed's neurotic excitement was winding him up again the closer they got and he let it out in a constant stream of chatter, which affected them all except Chaney, and near drove them crazy.

'Now, I never saw this guy work but they're all lintheads out here. Lean and mean.' It was the fourth time Speed had said it. 'Just apply the sweet science and get it finished, friend. Nothing more dangerous than wounded white trash. You'll go through 'em like butter.'

Poe piped up. 'Wounded lean and mean white trash butter is always dangerous.'

'This is not the time for your humour, drug store,' Speed shouted, glancing up at him through the mirror, and hitting a wide rut in the dirt road as he did so.

The car jolted and Gayleen and Poe were thrown together in the back.

'Speed,' she said, 'people generally slow down for holes in the road, for Christsakes.'

Speed flashed her an angry look through the mirror. When someone criticized his driving they were going straight for his balls.

'Do me a favor, just don't criticize the goddamn driving,' he said. 'Just do me a favor. You haven't even got a goddamn license.'

'Some of us agree with her,' Poe offered mildly.

Speed nearly screamed. 'Everybody's so worried about the goddamn driving, and nobody but me is worried about the fifteen hundred we got riding.'

'It is indeed a heavy burden you're carrying,' Poe said pedantically. 'A fortunate thing you have such broad shoulders.'

It was another slur against his manhood. That one did it for Speed. 'You want the car slowed down. I'll slow the goddamn car down and kick your ass right out the door. Then you can make your goddamn wisecracks to the trees and fence posts. You'd like that, huh, Mr Hophead?'

Poe bowed his head like a penitent. 'I apologize,' he said.

Watching Speed give the quack another look through the mirror, it seemed to Chaney that he was almost disappointed to have him apologize and end the scrap so soon. They were always bitching and they loved and hated every minute of it. But he was plain sick of it. He just wanted to make the fight and collect his money without having all these emotional scenes shoved onto him. It was as much as he could do to stop himself being dragged into them. His face creased with irritation as Speed started up again, settling into his victory over Poe, stamping his asserted manhood all over him.

'Damn right, you apologize,' he said.

But then Gayleen, never liking her man to establish too much ground, spoke up. 'Will you quit being such a shit, Speed?'

The counter-attack surprised him, so much so he missed seeing another rut and the Buick jarred into it, then out again.

'And slow down!' Gayleen shouted.

'You know I could kick your ass out too,' he yelled back.

'You don't want me in this car I'll be happy to get out.'

Chaney leant back his head. Speed wouldn't kick her out. He wanted her there. Howling and going for his balls.

'You think I live and die or care about your fifteen hundred?' Gayleen put in like she meant it.

'Damn right you care. What do you think you live on?'

Leaning forward, Chaney snapped on the radio. A loud shrill from a toothpaste sponsor suddenly cut their squabbling to complete silence. Then Gayleen spoke up.

'Well, excuse us for living, Mr Lord God Almighty.'

Chaney said nothing. If that was living, he'd sooner take a raincheck. They drove most of the rest of the way to the bayou town in silence.

The town's main street was deserted like it was church-time on a Sunday morning, only it wasn't Sunday. Most of the folks were gathered for the fight in a field out back of the town alongside the nearby bayou.

This was Cajun County and the locals had turned the

occasion of the fight into something of a fair. Alongside a barn that served as a boathouse at the bottom end of the field was a fish-fry and a band playing off key. Mules were being auctioned, along with wildfowl; they even had a bear in a cage.

'I thought you said it was a Cajun I had to fight,' Chaney said, his first display of humor surprising the others.

Eventually Speed came back with, 'You got it wrong, the winner fights that.'

The outsider's car was spotted immediately it entered the field and by the time it got down to where the action was a reception party had formed up from the main crowd. The six men who approached the Buick weren't hospitable, despite the fact that they were riding high, believing no one could lick their man.

Speed, edgy as hell again, pushed open his door and climbed out. Poe and Gayleen followed him. Chaney didn't move.

One of the six men was Pettibon. He was a man who had never said no to a rich dessert or that one last offer of a drink; a man who indulged himself. He was corpulent, very fleshy and perspired a lot.

'Good to see you, Mr Pettibon,' Speed said.

'Hello, Mr Weed,' he said, amused at the name. 'We been looking forward to your arrival to add to our little entertainment. Look what we laid on for you.'

'Mighty fine. Well, here we are. This is my fiancée Gayleen Schoonover and you know Mr Poe.'

'Sure I remember . . . Nice to see you again.'

Pettibon was impatient at these pleasantries, he was more interested in taking a look at Chaney, who was sitting in the front of the Buick, staring ahead.

'That's Chaney,' Speed said almost incidentally. 'He don't say much.'

Pettibon gave a derisory laugh. 'Things go to plan, boy, he won't be saying much later either.'

Speed was quick to come back at him. 'That's your plan not ours.'

Pettibon turned to Speed, drawing his hand soothingly around his neck that overhung his collar. 'You said he was green,' he said challengingly.

'Three-times out.' Speed played to him. 'He's real new to the game.'

Pettibon gave Chaney another measured look. Chaney turned and stared at him in a way that Pettibon didn't like.

'He don't look on the unpicked side to me.'

'Well, he got started real late in life.'

Pettibon turned toward the barn. 'Guess I'll let my man be the judge of that. That's him right over there,' he said proudly.

Casually Speed looked over at the man seated calmly by himself, thinking what a shame it was that such a good-looking boy was going to have his face messed up. He turned back to Pettibon.

'He looks up to the mark,' Poe said professionally.

'He'd better be. Course I could go in another direction. Let you folks take on a real fast.'

'What d'you have in mind?' Speed wanted to know, and grinned tolerantly when Pettibon indicated the bear. 'That's an interesting idea you got there, Mr Pettibon.'

'I thought it might catch your fancy.'

They let the idea amuse them for a few moments as Chaney slid out of the car and moved across to the cage. The bear hurled itself against the bars, trying to get free. Chaney didn't move. He wondered why the bear was there, where it was destined for. Certainly it would never again know the freedom of the woods.

'All things considered,' Poe said, believing Speed might even shoot for such a match if the odds were right, 'I think we'd better stick with the match we've got. When do you figure on getting started?'

'How about right now?' Pettibon said, and turned toward the barn followed by the other men.

'What about it?' Speed called to Chaney, who was watching the bear still. 'Let's do it.'

Chaney did it, too quickly, too easily, too professionally. The Catjun crowd was not pleased with the result and it had little to do with the fact that they had lost their money, this was to do with identity, survival, pride, all that had been riding on their fallen hitter. But most unhappy of all was Pettibon.

Speed fetched Chaney his coat and cap where he stood in the center of the hard earth packed ring towering above the fallen rawboned local hitter.

'Very pretty,' Poe said, not having tuned in to the hostility of the crowd. 'Very precise.'

Chaney smiled. Those sort of words weren't important, but they had more meaning when Poe said them. The good feeling he had was short lived when he picked up the mood of the crowd. This result obviously didn't fit in with their carnival plans.

'Better get the money,' Chaney said evenly.

'Nobody ever has to tell me that,' Speed said. And strutted across to where Pettibon was.

Pettibon waited like a man who *wasn't* waiting to pay out money.

'That's how it's done, Pettibon. I guess this just wasn't your day.'

Pettibon was angry. 'Damn small question about that boy.'

Speed gave a dismissive shrug and reached for the fold of money the man held in his hand. Pettibon wasn't about to give it up.

'What the hell you doing?'

'This is a big reverse for us,' Pettibon said. 'I didn't think anybody could go through our man that way.'

His cold, dull eyes fell on Chaney. He resented the way that man hadn't got a mark on him.

'You saw it,' Speed said. 'Obviously an error of judgement on your part.'

There was no such thing as far as Pettibon was concerned.

'Yeah, I saw it,' he said. 'It was too damned easy, like shooting birds off a telephone wire. Now Mr Weed, you said your man was just startin' out. And that plum was a lie.'

'That money's ours. There isn't any rules about this other than who wins.'

Speed was getting angry and he felt he was getting out of his depth. He pulled into his coat and then looked back at Pettibon. A number of Cajuns moved in behind, just waiting for the word from him.

'Something wrong?' Chaney said as he and Poe joined Speed.

'We got a slight problem,' Pettibon said. 'You're a ringer, Mr Chaney. That is my considered opinion.'

Backed by Chaney, Speed was getting very mad. He was almost forgetting his rule of life about not tangling with big men. He roared threateningly close to Pettibon. 'We want our goddamn money.'

'You want the money, take it,' Pettibon said like he was playing with a pigeon.

As if on signal one of the men from behind Pettibon stepped forward and stood with his folded arms, clearly displaying the revolver in his waistband.

Chaney saw it. If there was one thing which got him angry it was guns, especially when there was no good reason for them. He figured he could move fast enough to break the cowboy's jaw before he could draw it from his waistband. But that would start something with this crowd which the three of them wouldn't be able to finish.

'Somebody always shows up with a gun,' Poe said philosophically.

Speed screamed and stabbed wildly at Pettibon with his fingers. 'You goddamn sack of country shit.'

Poe was concerned that the situation was getting out of hand. 'Steady on Speed,' he said. Then more deliberately, 'These gentlemen are not refined.'

Pettibon indulged himself in a huge smile. The set-back wasn't working out too badly after all. His large nose twitched as he identified a smell that wasn't coming from the fish-fry. 'What is that peculiar smell, Mr Weed? Do you have some pomade on?'

Losing his money was one thing, but taking that kind of shit was another. 'You've had your nose up that bear's ass.'

Bristling at the insult, Pettibon said, 'I think you folks ought to get into your car and drive on back home. You've a long ways to go.'

Chaney nodded slowly. This guy was going to give him so much pleasure he almost liked him. 'Sounds like good advice,' he said.

'There's a man that's got some sense,' Pettibon's smile returned.

'What about the scratch money? We get that back?' Speed asked.

'Forfeit,' Pettibon replied. 'Now get on out.'

'Now wait on Pettibon, that's just what I call plain stealing.'

Chaney stopped him with a shrug. 'The man doesn't want to pay,' he said calmly.

Speed couldn't believe that he was hearing this from Chaney. 'Just okay, never mind, huh? That's what we're going to do? Nothing?' Furious at Chaney backing down like that, he swung round to Pettibon as if to hit him. 'Next time I come to this coon-ass country *I'll* bring the goddamn gun!'

Pettibon smiled. 'Well, you do that. Better make it a big one. Now you just move on out, 'fore we forget we're nice folks.'

Speed turned and started out through the crowd catching Gayleen's arm forcefully. Chaney followed. Poe shook his head ponderously like he was worried for the future of mankind.

Speed let out all his anger on the Buick, he punched the starter and slammed the car into gear. Gayleen slumped in the back seat along with Poe. Chaney sat looking ahead, quiet in a solid sort of way which gave little indication of the anger about to explode. Speed jammed his foot on the gas pedal and took off.

'A sorry spectacle,' Poe said. 'A very poor example of southern sportsmanship.'

'All this driving for nothing,' Gayleen whined. 'My God, breaks your heart.'

'Breaks my butt is what it breaks,' Speed bleated, unable either to keep quiet or still.

Then Chaney said, 'Let's take things easy. Drive around the backroads. See the sights, it's nice countryside.'

'What the hell are you talking about?' Speed snapped.

'Business,' he said. He looked across at Speed and smiled.

The lean man in the sharp suit grinned knowingly.

The expression faded when Chaney said, 'Speed, what the hell is that smell?'

Embarrassment stung Speed's cheeks. He wasn't about to say, especially not now that the damn Voodoo oils hadn't done him any good.

ELEVEN

They drove out beyond the bayou town until nightfall. When they came back it took them no time at all to find out which of the two bars Pettibon used; he owned one of them. They checked out both the front and rear of the bar. Chaney told them what to do. He was going to bust Pettibon good.

Keeping the lid down so tightly on his anger, Chaney became almost frozen inside. It wasn't simply the fact that he had been cheated that made him so angry, but the way it was done and the fact that it forced him into this sudden involvement which he hadn't bargained for.

Gayleen, driving the Buick, let them off about a hundred yards or so from the roadhouse which Pettibon owned.

Chaney said, 'Give me about two minutes, and then let go.'

He moved along the alley at the side of the bar, disappearing into the darkness of the shadows.

That Chaney, Speed thought as he stood feeling a little out of place with the wrench in his hand, he sure was something else. He glanced at Poe by his side, drawing no comfort from his presence.

At the top of the alley and along the back of the bar crates of empty bottles were stacked along with empty beer kegs. There was a lean-to men's room tacked onto the back of the bar. The door was ajar and there was a man inside taking a leak. Chaney waited wondering how long he'd be. If he was too long he wouldn't be able to make his move and Speed's effort would be pointless. The redneck had a big bladder and seemed to take forever. When the man eventually kicked open the door and returned to the bar Chaney followed, catching the door to the bar before it fully closed. Through the crack he could see into the bar.

Pettibon was watching the pool game in progress, one hand resting on the thick thigh of a large blonde woman next to him. Standing at the top end of the bar together with some others was the man with the gun in his waistband. Others sat around at the tables, drinking, arguing, listening to the jukebox.

There was an easy, unconcerned atmosphere which followed the good times that had started that afternoon.

Waiting a little tensely, Chaney saw what he hoped wouldn't happen. A man stood his beer down then started up toward Chaney to go to the men's room. He didn't get that far. His attention like everyone else's in the bar was immediately taken by the wrench that came crashing through the plate glass window, causing those down that end of the bar to cower back as splinters flew in.

Chaney slid in through the back door, moving fast and silently. He went straight for the dude with the pistol, hoping there weren't any other cowboys in the bar. He crucified him against the counter with a kidney punch, a good one, then wrenched him about, pulling the gun from his belt before the rest of the bar had time to register what had happened. When they did, there was Chaney as cool as Christmas, back to the bar, gun in hand.

The first one who tried him was the bartender. Sensing the movement behind him, Chaney swung round and hit him with the pistol, laying the flesh across his left cheek open to the bone.

'Well, look who we got here,' Pettibon said with a slight quake.

As if the bartender wasn't a sharp enough lesson, one of the pool players had to try him. The player suddenly swung out with his cue. Without losing his balance Chaney twisted away and the cue shattered across the bar. Chaney looked at the pool player. He'd just made one of the biggest mistakes of his life.

'Dumb,' he said, jamming the pistol in his pocket.

The pool player couldn't believe his good luck until Chaney hammered him with three punches which caused blood to fountain from the man's nose. He dropped like a lead weight.

Chaney looked around, almost willing someone to try him.

A vein of excitement raced through Speed, who now stood with Poe by the front entrance of the bar. He had never seen Chaney quite like this before, and didn't know what it was that had got him so riled up, but it was more than the money, he was sure.

Chaney's glance swept on, seeking out the man who thought he had a chance. Eyes avoided his now in case contact was mistaken for a challenge. He was going to take them all on, everyone who thought they could hurt him, and if he had to he'd kill them. His stare settled on the Cajun hitter whose face was swollen from earlier on in the afternoon.

'You want to try again?' he said.

The man wisely shook his young head.

'Anybody else?'

He waited a second, but there were no takers. He seemed disappointed. Right now he wanted to destroy the world. He turned to Pettibon, taking out the pistol as he approached him. He stopped just before him.

'Guess I got the gun now,' he said.

Pettibon screwed up his dull, hostile eyes and measured Chaney. 'Guess you do at that, boy,' he said. 'But I'm not sure you want to use it.'

Chaney stared at the man whose arrogance was inviting his own death.

'There's different ways,' he said casually. Without warning he swung the pistol in a tight circle and popped Pettibon in the side of the neck. He slumped to the floor.

'That's one of them,' Chaney said.

Leveling the gun at the man on the floor, Chaney's hand shook briefly in rage. He didn't know if he could stop himself now. It had happened before, and he hadn't stopped himself then. His hand tensed on the butt.

'You want to see another way?' he said.

The arrogance displayed earlier had all left Pettibon now.

'You owe me money.'

Pettibon reached a nervous hand to his pocket, and pulled out his wallet. He tossed it up to Chaney, who caught it left-handed. Paused, wallet in one hand, gun in other. He had the money. You got what you came for, he told himself, now bring in the gun. His grip didn't slacken on the butt as he opened the wallet, removed the money, then tossed the empty wallet aside. He glanced down at the gun still in his hand, then once more at Pettibon. As he walked slowly backwards to Speed and Poe at the entrance, the people in the room seemed to sigh as one. He turned back, considering the gun in his hand, then Pettibon. Everything in him screamed at him to destroy the man. He stood there a second, anger and hate trying to burst the barrier within him to the point of rage. But control held. He suddenly swung round and blasted the bar-mirror; his next bullet shattered the wallphone; then an overhead light. He blasted the jukebox, causing the music to jump then stop with a screech. The pintable was next to get it. The shattering explosions ripping around the place sent every one in the roadhouse diving to the floor. Chaney offered a cynical smile in the silence that followed; he was paying back a little bit in kind for his own hurt. He paused and looked down at Pettibon; leveled the gun and slowly locked it, watching the sweat break out over his face. He would live with that fear he was at that moment experiencing, the arrogant, over-indulged man would remember it all his life. Chaney turned, was about to throw the gun on the bar when he caught sight of himself in a portion of the shattered mirror. It wasn't as if it was him; he was seeing instead the man he had once been before his family all died, that man who had loved and trusted, and had wanted to give. Yesterday's man before the Chaney who now hated so much and mistrusted so much made his appearance. The reason the anger and the hurt continued was because he could no longer trust any person or thing other than himself, his own strength, and because of it there was at the core of him a nagging fear. He hated himself just then, and in a violent, futile gesture, he blasted the image of himself he saw before him. He watched them fall, knowing that dismantling the barriers and the person he had set himself up to be, would not be as easy. He doubted if he even could now anyway.

He threw the gun across the counter and turned out, passing Speed the money as he went.

The Buick came tearing down the road as they appeared outside the roadhouse and braked hard, overshooting them. They ran fast to the car and piled in. Gayleen gunned the engine, slammed the gear-shift forward into first and accelerated away. She may not have held a license, but she handled the car pretty good.

Speed was still very keyed up by the scene. 'Better drive faster, Gayleen,' he said. 'They got some mean mothering sheriffs up this way.'

'What was all that shooting?' she asked, treading on the gas and causing the car to suddenly surge.

As if the whole cause for the scene had been forgotten

Speed suddenly looked down to his lap and saw all the money. It took him a second to work it into perspective. Then he began laughing.

'Jesus,' he said, 'Jesus Christ.'

'A-men,' Gayleen said, uncertain why.

'Jesus H. Christ, Chaney.' He glanced round at the man in the back.

Relief broke out of Poe in the form of a song. 'As I walk along the Bois Boolong,' he sang slightly off key and with an odd pitch, 'with an independent air you can hear the girls declare, "He must be a millionaire". You can hear them sigh and wish to die; you can hear them wink the other eye at the man who broke the bank at Monte Carlo.'

No one ever really expected Chaney to comment. Nor did he. Nothing shared, but some parts of his body were still shaking. All in all he wasn't sure what was happening to him just now. He sat there staring out past Speed and Gayleen, ahead into the orange pools from the Buick's headlamps. Trying not to think, he was only vaguely aware of Poe's song and the noises the others were making.

It was dawn as they approached New Orleans. Speed and Gayleen having long since switched places, the latter was now asleep against his shoulder. Poe was asleep also. Chaney was awake, still avoiding thinking as he watched the light sneak up behind the iron superstructure of Huey P. Long Bridge, seeing then the silhouettes of boats tied up downriver.

Both Poe and Gayleen woke when Chaney had Speed drop him off outside Lucy's. It was a whim rather than a promise that took him there.

'Right just here's fine,' Chaney directed.

The houses were shut up, the stoops deserted now. The only activity in sight was that of the black trash collectors tipping the pails up on the back of their cart.

'Right here,' Chaney said, outside Lucy's house.

The Buick rubbered to a halt, in front of the horse drawn trash cart. Gayleen stepped out yawning and let Chaney out from the back.

'That where you live, Chaney?' she said like she'd at last got something on him.

Chaney ignored her, and stooped to Speed.

'Talk to you in a few days,' he said.

'You know who's next,' Speed said.

'My, my,' Gayleen said as she climbed back in. 'If it's not where you live then who's the lucky lady?'

Chaney continued to take no notice. Having got on top of his feelings again, needling like that didn't touch him anymore. He turned and started up the porch.

'You have a real big time now,' Gayleen called out.

He glanced back from the top of the steps as Speed stuck his thumb into the air. Chaney waited for the Buick to rumble away before turning back to the door. Ringing the bell he waited a little apprehensively. He needed Lucy just at that moment, wanted her; he felt hurt and exposed and could use a little comfort. His roots that had been so violently torn up six years ago were still aching, like the amputee's stumps in the cold weather, yearning a little for what was. Today he was no longer the same person, but just occasionally when time telescoped and he remembered who he was and what he had lost, then wanted comfort. He was just a little afraid now that he wouldn't get it.

He rang again on the bell, turned and stared pensively at the trash cart along the street watching the activity around it; one of the blacks hit the horse's rump and it pulled against the shafts, stopping automatically at the next pick-up point. He had worked his land with a donkey that was that smart. Hearing the latch on the door snap free, he turned back. It opened a fraction, the night chain still in place.

'Who is it?' he heard Lucy's voice say.

'Chaney.'

The door shut to release the chain then opened wider. Surprise chasing sleep from her large eyes as though believing an emergency might have brought him here.

'What do you want?' she said.

A reply wasn't easy for Chaney. His eyes searched her, looking for a more oblique approach now. There was none.

'Thought maybe you'd like to come out,' he said.

She pulled her robe closer about herself and looked at him, understanding but not trying to admit it. 'Are you treating me to a champagne breakfast?'

'Whatever you feel like.'

The look stayed in his eyes. She couldn't deny it then. She saw just what he was really asking. Finally he was asking her.

Either she could accept or she could shut the door in his face; she could only avoid it briefly.

'You know it's five a.m.?'

He didn't reply. He had no more words. He'd asked her and he wanted an answer. Just stood there watching her face, her odd expression of hesitation, uncertainty, disguising what she really wanted. And he wanted her.

'Christ,' she said, the moment of decision weighing down on her. 'I barely know you.'

'Yeah, but would you like to?'

Almost without her participation her head tipped in an affirmative. She wanted to know him, but she still didn't think she ever could allow herself to unless he chose first to open himself up.

'Why me?' she said.

'Because we're the same. You don't want any trouble.'

She chewed her bottom lip a second, sensing he would allow her no longer than that.

'I guess I can make you some coffee,' she said.

She pulled the door back and let him in. She led the way up to her apartment, through into the kitchen, feeling reluctant to give up all the ground at once.

'You want it black?'

'Black.'

The kitchen, like the rest of the apartment which he passed through, was small. There was an oilcloth covered table and a couple of badly chipped painted chairs, a battered Norge icebox, a gas stove, sink, few cupboards. The place had the look of a rented apartment. The pale light of dawn was insignificant compared to the unshaded brilliance in the ceiling by courtesy of the Louisiana Power and Light Company.

Chaney sat at the table, folded his hands on the top.

He watched Lucy fill the coffee percolator and set it on the stove with a light under it. Her movements were jerky, indicating her nervousness,

'Where were you?' she asked. 'You get thrown out your place?'

'No.'

She sat opposite him.

'I'm going to share my coffee with you,' she said. 'You don't share nothing with me.'

He was unmoving, unyielding. She stared at him, and he stared back at her. She didn't have any more choice she didn't think, but she had to look away. They'd want some cups, she realized and jumped up to fetch them. As she set them down the knuckles on her hands showed tense and white where she gripped the cups.

Was he not going to give anything else, she questioned.

'Knocked anyone down recently?' she suddenly asked.

He nodded slowly. The problem she had wasn't difficult for him to understand. But he didn't see that talk was going to resolve it at all. She had made her decision. For him it was the right one to relieve the pain he had inside, the fear. Now he wanted just to lose himself and maybe forget himself in brief physical passion. He didn't want anything else along with it.

'Gonna knock me down?' she said.

He shrugged. 'That what you want, Lucy?' He knew it wasn't, but he sure as hell wasn't about to promise her a rose bed.

She paused thoughtfully.

'Chaney,' she began, but didn't say anthing more. She turned the heat out under the coffee and stood with her back to him.

There was only one direction now. She took it. Chaney watched her as she moved into the bedroom-cum-sitting-room and stood by the Murphy bed that was down out of the wall. Following her, Chaney removed his cap and coat and threw them on the chair. There were dried sweat stains under the arms of his blue utility shirt, and he figured he could use a bath. Chaney closed the gap between them. His kind of strength bred gentleness, and that was how he was when he touched his hand to the side of her face.

'You're not the kind that's going to give up anything, are you?' she said quietly.

'I gave up something when I asked.'

She lifted her eyes to him, gave him a pale smile. 'And you're just looking to rent but not to buy?' she said.

'Something like that.'

She didn't know if it was what she wanted, she suspected it was, but knew she had to try. Times were hard and she'd got nothing else. She leant into him, placing her arms tightly around him.

'Just treat me nice, Chaney,' she whispered. 'Please.'

He ran his hand through her hair, and smiled in a way he hadn't smiled at a woman in a long while. He bent slightly and kissed her once on the mouth. The tension he felt in her shoulders slackened completely. Her robe was fastened by a belt which he untied. Beneath the robe she had on a slip. She was more skillful than he at removing that and did so. Then stood naked and vulnerable before him. He kissed her, and lifted her onto the bed. She eased the sheet up over herself.

She lay impassively, with one knee slightly raised, her eyes fixed on the plaster cracks in the ceiling while he undressed. He came to her hesitantly, slid in beneath the sheet alongside her. Their bodies touched and tensed instinctively. Then suddenly she turned into him and he held her. It had been so long coming between them. Their passion was as volatile as dry kindling, it needed only a spark. A sigh was enough. Her soft caresses quickly became random, grew wild, and her passion touched off his in return. He enjoyed her urgent pleasure, the soft words of entreaty she mixed with her kisses. He entered her, giving her everything physically he had to offer. He felt her clasp him, the sigh that parted her lips said she knew the contact was only flesh. But still her breathing quickened into excited gasps. His body trembled as he thrust into her, as if so long frozen, the thaw which now followed fractured him like brittle ice. Then her pelvis rose up to meet his and he felt a surge of pain through his whole body. He came quickly in her, like a man a long time on the road, his body pounding her. His abstinence now found her at the same precipice. Her body arched off the bed and she clung to him violently through her own orgasm. Afterward she lay still like she was beaten and had nothing left to give. With his eyes shut against the sharp-cornered world outside, Chaney lay in the woman's warmth. His body relaxed utterly, all the surface anger having vanished. Still he hurt deep within, but it was momentarily softened, not to a point of forgetfulness, never that, but to a pitch where it could easily be tolerated.

The cause was always there. He wished it wasn't, times like these he wished he could wipe the slate clean, forget the past and get involved with someone new. He wished he could allow someone new close enough to touch him. He couldn't do it.

Even Lucy now, with her tired used body, that had just given so much to him, wasn't really touching him. And for him to try and reach into her was only to aggravate his hurt.

The sight of Lucy's naked body, her breasts gently rising and falling in untroubled sleep, brought images of Alma to him, in those early days. Then an image of her lying dead popped into his head. The best and the worst juxtaposed as if they were one. Six years was a long time but it might have been only yesterday.

They hadn't informed him in the pen about Alma falling sick. They had made the mistake of telling him how poorly his children had been the year before; they had to confine him in irons after he tried busting out. His children's fever had developed into pneumonia and they hadn't survived the winter. The following spring Alma had taken up with someone else just to stay alive. She was just 'filling in' till Chaney got back. She didn't tell them the man she had taken up with got his money from dope. The state had buried her, albeit reluctantly, in a two dollar pine box.

The pusher whom he had hunted down after busting out of the pen had told him all that between the blows he was systematically raining on him. Just before he had beaten the pusher to death with his fists, someone else had shown up, someone with a gun. Chaney had been very angry. He had taken the gun off the man, and had shot him in the process. Afterwards he regretted the deaths of those two men, even though they deserved to die. As far as the upheaval in his life was concerned, their deaths made no difference. He had already killed a guard while busting out of the pen – he had had greater difficulty persuading himself that that man deserved to die. After he had killed the pusher, and how he had done it, he had made himself two promises. He would never let go on his anger again. And he would never get involved or let anyone get close again. With Alma and his kids gone, his life set on an irreversible course, he had cracked completely, had hit bottom and had come back up again. His way, the in-betweens, wasn't living, but it was life.

In the years since he'd held himself in and tried patching himself together. He was still working on it, but knew he would never be completely successful, for that he'd need to put down some more roots, and if he did that there was too much of a chance that men would show up with guns and haul his ass off to jail. Or just open up on him and whoever was around him.

Now as he lay peacefully with Lucy asleep on his arm that was as close as he would get and as close as he could let her get. He couldn't accept the whole range of emotions and obligations she wanted to give him. He would have liked maybe to reach in and touch her and maybe have her touch him a little deeper. Right now he wanted to just say, 'Thank you, Lucy, sorry it was only an inbetween.' He wanted to wake her and say it, but couldn't. Instead he just fell asleep awhile.

Later he would wake and he would move on.

TWELVE

Speed was showing all the symptoms of a gambler running up to a pay-off. He wasn't eating, nor was he sleeping, which wasn't surprising. He was holding three thousand in his pants which he was going to put up to Gandil. The minute he had it together in a roll he took off in the Buick to confront him.

He left Gayleen in the apartment, another night alone without him or what she wanted. This would be the last chance Speed got. If he didn't bring off the biggie soon she would quit him for sure. Then he would be left alone with his other inconsistent, unpredictable lady, the Lady of fortune. She had favored him enough to bring him this close, he felt he couldn't ignore her now. He just had to hope Gayleen would stick around a while longer.

At the fine mansion where Gandil lived just off Orleans Avenue Speed presented himself, full of expectations. He wasn't quite expecting dinner, but he did expect to get past the uppity Nigra in a monkey suit. The man informed him at the door that Mr Gandil wasn't in, that he was dining with friends in town. Getting the whereabouts of that dinner party from the uppity Nigra wasn't easy.

The dinner party Gandil was at was being held in one of the private dining rooms at the Roosevelt Hotel. Speed didn't know why he couldn't eat in the public dining rooms like plain folks. The reason was clear enough when he gained admittance along with Poe. Gandil was in the middle of dinner with another equally impeccably dressed man and two women who were neither their wives nor their sisters, but Jesus they were something. Even Poe noticed.

The atmosphere over the dinner table was light, sparkling, expectant, that was until Speed showed up shaking like a crap-shooter, with Poe behind him. Then it suddenly became tense, embarrassed, even a little confounded.

'Hello, Chick,' he greeted expansively, 'good to see you. How's tricks?'

It was like a sudden cloud burst at a garden fete, but

Speed was riding too high to notice a thing. Gandil was very irritated when he spoke. He was only a breath away from snapping his fingers and having this tin-horn shooter thrown out.

'This is a private gathering,' he said. 'I don't believe either of you gentlemen were invited.'

Poe noted the point immediately, but Speed laughed and waved his manicured hand dismissively at the company, as if the fact that he could now make Gandil's price made them social equals.

'You remember Poe here?'

'Mr Poe,' Gandil said courteously, absolving him of blame for the intrusion.

'Mr Gandil...' Poe smiled with difficulty at the company.

'Only keep you a minute,' Speed said, knowing like never before in his life he was riding the big one. 'Last time I saw you, you set a special number for that three to one. Now I'm calling the bet.'

'First you've got to get three thousand,' Gandil said contemptuously, but not without interest. 'Real, whole dollars, marker man. Otherwise the question is merely academic.'

Speed flashed his roll with such stumbling panache that the whole table couldn't be off seeing it.

'Want to count it?' he said.

Surprise passed briefly across Gandil's bland face and he considered the proposition for a moment. It was three thousand, money enough for serious thought, and who was it but a pigeon betting against him. Speed was always snapping at him for a big action, so now he was going to give it to him.

He gave a nod. 'You're a sucker, Speed,' he said. 'You want it, then it's tomorrow, tomorrow night. You know where.'

With the sort of deprecating gesture that only the wealthy ever muster, he waved the large starched napkin irritably signalling Speed out, now that he had what he came for. Speed, palms up like a hitter, gave a mock bow, as the waiter in tails and wing collar stepped forward.

'We'll do it,' he said.

Speed was there, he could taste it. But until it was over he'd be living on a high wire.

Whether out of perversity or a rich man's desire to bring a little light to a poor man's life, Gandil's favorite fight venue was Depression Colony. This was the Batture dweller's ramshackle shanty town located between Carrollton Avenue and the protection levee at the Jefferson Parish Line. It consisted of dozens and dozens of shacks made out of salvage materials, corrugated iron, driftwood, palm fronds and house boats propped level. All were situated on the raised butture between the main channel of the Mississippi and the three hundred foot wide burrow pit which was dug when banking the levee. At flood-time most of them floated away or were submerged and even those built on stilts weren't without their problems. But with the river low the butture was high out of the water and very dry and baked hard. It was as good as any for the fight and not one the cops were likely to show up at – that wasn't something that happened at Gandil's venues, and not just because the cops rarely went to Depression Colony.

The night was close in the city but out on the butture it was kept very cool by the light breeze that came across the river. There was a big crowd out for the fight. The Louisiana Power and Light Company didn't supply the colony so the venue was lit by pitch fires in tin oil drums. These gave off a dense smoke, which only Speed seemed to mind when it blew back on the crowd. He was convinced it had a personal grudge against him. The smoke never seemed to go near Gandil where he sat in the rattan chair that had been fetched over for him. As he moved about the crowd taking side bets from all those pigeons who expected to see big Jim Henry live up to his reputation, tension caused Speed to strut like a clockwork duck. Chaney by contrast couldn't have been more cooler. He sat on one of the benches that were fetched down, cap and coat on, arms folded, maintaining a Samurai's reserve. He watched a man without legs who was sat in a box-cart playing a Jew's harp for pennies. The melodic whine from the instrument held against his teeth found a level above the noise of the crowd and hung there as if to epitomize the plight of the local habitués.

The detached, cool-headed manner in which Chaney waited was easy for him. Unlike the guys around him, he had nothing to lose, not money or reputation. Chaney wasn't a gambler, but was instead a practitioner, he made things just the way he wanted them, and he was going to make the result of this fight the same way. That left no room for chance. Across the way he was aware of Jim Henry, flexing his shoulders at his own confidence where he stood alongside Gandil, occasionally leaning down to his boss with words presumably to bolster his confidence. He saw Speed break off his shill to the crowd and cut a line directly across the hard-packed earth to where Gandil was. He'd lived for this night and was savoring each minute of it. His performance had never been better, Chaney thought, never flashier. For the occasion he had bought himself a brand new twenty dollar suit, the only problem with it was that it made him look like one of those guys who sold patent medicines off the back of a truck to the dirt farmers of the Mid-West.

The build-up to the fight got to Poe a bit and he fussed around Chaney, casting himself in the role of boxer's second. He didn't worry Chaney any.

'Been a few unfortunate pilgrims busted their knuckles on that hard head of his ... old marble top. But he'll try to end things fast,' he advised. 'He'll crowd you, moves straight ahead like he's on rails.'

Speed, his face alight with nervous expectancy, suddenly loomed up in front of them.

'Lord God, I just saw it,' he exclaimed. 'Nine thousand dollars right there in the man's hand. Takes your breath away.'

Chaney gave him a look, then a smile. Speed responded, and came full face to him, he was so proud of Chaney just now he wanted to hug him. And he knew he was going to be even prouder by the end of the night. Chaney was his man, his big hitter, and he thought, his friend. He had brought him all this way into the big time, and he loved the guy. Sure he had his quirky moods, but when you were that good it didn't matter. He was a real professional, he could always be relied upon. After this night was through Speed had a feeling Chaney would never let him down.

'Now, look, what Poe's telling you is simple,' he instructed. 'He fights like a goddamn street car. Stay away from him until he gets tired.'

Speed patted his face a couple of times, enjoying the touch, then gave the mother of all his smiles. Chaney returned it with a fist placed against his chin. It seemed like they'd come a long way together since the night he first approached him in Baton Rouge. Strange, Chaney thought, how even without noticing it happening and despite not wanting it, time together attaches you someway. He stood up, dropping his coat and cap, as Speed turned toward the center of the clearing.

'Time!' Gandil's shill called. 'Bets in. All bets in now.'

Chaney met Jim Henry's stare from the opposite side of the ring, and held it evenly, seeing the man's anger grow at not being able to stare him down. Till now no one challenged Jim Henry this way and won. Speed noticed this silent first round of the fight going on and he enjoyed it.

Jim Henry was the first to crack. 'Hey, why ain't you at home taking care of your grandchildren, Mr Chaney?' he mocked.

Nothing stirred in Chaney. He knew what the insult meant.

'Talk it up over there, Jim,' Speed shouted, 'while you still got some teeth in that dumb head of yours.'

'I get done with your monkey I might come after you,' Jim Henry threatened.

'Only thing you'll be coming after is a doctor,' Speed retorted.

The crowd was becoming restive. The preliminaries and the insult period had gone on too long. They wanted to see some action.

'Let 'em work,' someone called.

'Start it! C'mon. Get 'em going.'

'We're ready over here,' Speed said.

All eyes turned toward Chick Gandil, waiting for him to give the word. What he did instead was make them wait on him a bit longer while he whispered some last-minute advice to Jim Henry.

Speed reckless with tension, stole his thunder. 'I hope that's a good prayer you're telling him, Chick,' he shouted.

The spectators laughed. Gandil gave Speed a look that indicated his displeasure. Then he gestured Jim Henry out to meet his opponent.

Chaney took two steps forward and raised up his palms, waiting for the man to repeat the ritual. But as his hands came up Jim Henry suddenly lunged at Chaney, who, anticipating the move, side stepped and jabbed him with a close right hook. He was irritated with the man, but having made a move like that and failed, he'd set himself up for the first beating and Chaney took advantage of it. As the man spun away from that first jab, Chaney got him with a left hook in the liver. The blows didn't have much immediate effect on Jim Henry, who threw himself back into things like he hadn't been touched. Chaney realized just how accurate Poe's information was about the man being knuckle-busting marble. Chaney got off a series of four jabs, each connecting with Jim Henry's face, driving him back toward the crowd like driving a nail into soft wood, but the big man merely blinked at each blow like he was blinking dust out of his eyes. Swinging a wild right which Chaney read clearly, Jim Henry slid a sly left hook in under his guard. Chaney felt it lay against his ribs like a sledgehammer. He knew then what he had only suspected before, the man carried a punch that he couldn't afford to be hit with too often, unless he wanted to take a lot of punishment. Encouraged by the blow he had just landed, the man thought Chaney would stand for it again; but when that left slid in this time Chaney wasn't there, which left Jim slightly off balance. Two straight jabs sent the big man spinning into the crowd, which immediately folded back, letting him fall to the ground.

The crowd loved it and roared enthusiastically even though most of them at that point looked like losing their money with Gandil.

Bellowing like an enraged bull, Jim Henry came headlong at Chaney and had he got hold of him would have torn him apart. In deference to his knuckles Chaney didn't try to stop him with a straight head punch, but side stepped and got off two short jabs. The blows were getting to Jim Henry now, but Chaney wasn't deluded, there was still a lot of danger in the man.

Watching the man career around the dirt-pack taking a lot more blows than he was getting in, Gandil knew he had little more than hope and a prayer. He might land a lucky blow that would do it. But that wouldn't make him better than Chaney. By comparison Jim Henry was an ox, had no style and this was one where his strength alone wouldn't carry him. Gandil averted his eyes from the fight as his man went hurtling into the ward again, and glanced at Speed. The marker man had hustled him well and truly; he stood to sink nine grand; that wasn't his problem, he could afford to lose that many times over. What he couldn't stand, however, was losing, not being number one. He saw Chaney follow his man into the crowd and rose out of his seat to move across for a better view.

Those at the front of the crowd folded back out of the way of the two hitters, and those behind jostled forward trying to get a better view. The fight had left the original marked out ring and rolled on between the stilts of one of the shanty shacks.

Anger was boiling over in Jim Henry now at the stingers that kept hitting him. Anger was all he had and he was wasting it rather than controlling and directing it like Chaney. He swung a heavy boot toward Chaney's groin, Chaney moved to the side but not quite fast enough and studs tore into his thigh, and before Jim Henry established himself Chaney got off a series. They were driving blows and the big man crashed back against one of the shack stilts. Using that for impetus he launched himself at Chaney with a brief flurry of dazzling blows, a number of which Chaney couldn't keep out; figuring he had him up to that point, Chaney was stunned more by the appearance of the counter attack than the damage it did. Chaney went down.

Speed's heart stopped beating as big Jim Henry came at his man with a huge killing kick. At that moment Speed didn't care about the nine G notes, he was only concerned that Chaney didn't get mashed up by this big galoot. He breathed easy when he saw Chaney twist away, catch the foot and topple the man. He found his hands had been tightly gripping Poe's shoulder.

When he got his shoulder returned to him, Poe briefly smiled up at Speed, reassured by his friend's evident concern for their hitter.

Scrabbling along the ground beneath the shanty dwelling the two hitters came to grips again. Half-wrestled, threw punches; Jim Henry pulled the short ends of Chaney's close-shorn hair. Although the big man was plainly the more tired Chaney knew he had to get the fight up off the ground, for there he had the distinct disadvantage. At the first opportunity he scrambled away from the man, but not fast enough. Jim Henry came after him and caught his foot and started to drag him back.

Chaney twisted himself over and kicked Jim Henry in the face with the outside of his left boot, immediately bringing a great wheal up on his already very marked face. The blow had the desired effect. Chaney was free and quickly got to his feet. He waited for Jim Henry to start to his feet and then moved in, hitting him with two good rights, but got too near. Jim Henry took the blows as if by design, his great arms snapped out and around the small of Chaney's back. He knew he had him now. No one ever survived his bearhug. He applied all the tired strength he could muster as he attempted breaking Chaney's back.

The crowd were silent, electric with expectation. Gandil moistened his lips as he stood watching, waiting, hoping.

His back was breaking, Chaney could feel it going and with it his strength. The pressure holds he tried first on the man's neck then head had no effect, he couldn't get any purchase. The image of himself trapped in a hospital bed with the Feds coming down on him flashed through his mind, but didn't help him any. He tried tearing Jim Henry's ears off but the man was prepared for that. What he wasn't prepared for was the only move Chaney had left open to him. Simultaneously he slammed his two hands together over each of Jim Henry's ears, the pressure he created bursting the man's eardrums. Jim Henry cried out in agony and released Chaney, who quickly stepped back. He knew what would happen now. A man in that much pain would try to kill the man that caused it; Chaney understood that. He waited, knowing he had to finish, and how.

Slowly Jim Henry rose from the ground, looked around at the crowd, then at Chaney; then charged him. Chaney hit him with a straight right and wasn't too sure whether it was his fist or Jim Henry's head that broke – neither it transpired. Jim Henry hung like a dinosaur trapped in ice, but he seemed to have no designs about going down. Chaney drove him back with a series of jabs, then landed one that would have knocked a lesser man spark out. It sent Jim Henry crashing back into one of the stilts, which snapped clear in two. The corner of the house it was supporting sagged badly, but held on the lace work of scrap materials it was built from. Jim Henry climbed up again, fetching with him a hunk of wood which he swung at Chaney like a baseball bat. It missed, and Chaney hit the man in the neck and finished him.

At this point the crowd were deathly silent. Only the occasional squeal of pigs kept in pens beneath the dwellings could be heard.

Speed was the first to stir through that half-light. He moved hesitantly forward to Chaney and touched his shoulder, first to make sure it was real, then in appreciation. Then he strutted on to where Jim Henry lay. The significance of it suddenly lifting him over the moon.

'My, my, my, well look at that. Lying there like a dead man. Hard to tell if he needs a doctor or an undertaker, ain't it. Maybe it's just the light. Somebody get a wheelbarrow for Mr Gandil's hitter,' he said mockingly.

Now the crowd started up once again, reverently folding back as Gandil approached. This was the man who didn't allow too many emotions to show, but he was having problems taking his defeat with a gracious calm. Inside he was seething, and already the wheels of his mind were churning. He had never in his life been a loser and he sure as hell wasn't going to start in being one with a punk like Spencer Weed. This was a temporary set-back. Nobody ever put one of his hitters down, simply because the best hitters were always his. If Speed's hitter had suddenly come out the best, then that meant that hitter's next fight was going to be for him.

He stopped and looked down at the bloodied carcase of Jim Henry, then tensely snatched the pot-bet from his shill's hand and thrust it at Speed.

'You've always had an unfortunate way of putting things,' he drawled.

Offering his most winsome smile, which with the nine thousand dollars in his hand, was something of an insult. 'Nothing personal,' he said pleasantly.

It was personal to Gandil and it wasn't stopping here. Speed understood that from his look before he turned away.

The crowd were milling all around now, dissecting the fight blow for blow. Those who betted on Chaney picking up their three to one, others about ready to piss on the floored Jim Henry.

Poe was checking Chaney's cuts when Speed returned, the new pants he had on stuffed full of notes. Just a look passed between Speed and Chaney; there was everything, Speed thought, there was both affinity and infinity; there was something that had bound them together this far, and would hold them together in the future. He knew it. They were at the top now.

'We did it,' Speed said.

Chaney didn't deny him his moment or try and diminish it in any way. He just smiled as Poe threw his coat over and planted his cap on his head.

As they started away off the batture, Chaney paused, catching Gandil's eye. Both men's stares were expressionless, yet paradoxically, each revealed everything to the other. Chaney moved out, thinking about that look, it told him Gandil had seen something Gandil wanted. That prospect didn't inspire him. Gandil was no different from the men who belong to the banking institutions who took all he had for no other real reason than because it was all he had. Gandil was a threat and Chaney didn't want any truck with him, not because he figured he couldn't go after him as effectively as he went after those banking people, but now he couldn't afford that kind of trouble.

They had made it. They were the best there was, there was no one to touch them now. New Orleans wasn't big enough for the celebration Speed had in mind for tonight. First they picked Gayleen up; then waited while Chaney fed his cat and got cleaned up; then they collected Lucy and went to eat in the Quarter. They were the best in town and went to the best in town. That was Antonine's on St Louis Street. The restaurant with its lacy wrought-iron balconies and mellow lighting had an air of quiet distinction which was more than could be said for Speed's party. Chaney was a street fighter and that was what he looked like at that moment. He didn't have a tie on even. Speed slipped the waiter a dollar and a table was found for them. Poe left them briefly, ostensibly to find himself a partner. He returned with one, nobody questioning what else he might have picked up. The woman was tall and had fat tits, fat ankles and a short concentration span. But Poe was a chivalrous escort.

The bill came to twenty-two dollars for the six of them. Speed baulked at it, then paid up and looked big. Everybody was having a good time and Speed wasn't going to spoil it for a lousy twenty-two bucks.

It seemed to Chaney his winning meant more to everyone

else than it did to him. For him it was sixty percent of the pot-bet safely in his possession. Soon he'd have enough money to be moving on, and that was just what he'd be doing. But tonight Chaney was going along with the celebration. He didn't resist the suggestion Speed made about taking a ride out to Jefferson highway to the Cotton Club. Lucy was happy to go along with him. With nearly seven thousand dollars in his canvas belt Chaney figured he could give just a little.

At the Cotton Club they got a very good table on the edge of the mezzanine, overlooking the dance-floor and the jazz band. There were about two dozen couples on the floor; Poe in his high, slightly intoxicated manner asked his date if she'd care to join them. She did. Speed, who like most of the company was only drinking beer, didn't really need anything to make him drunk; success was enough. It was really his night. Chaney sat drinking shots of whiskey alongside Lucy, with the now bemused and cynical Gayleen opposite her.

There was a young, very fat cornet player with the colored band. He smiled a lot and infected people with that smile, and when he stood and blew that horn, people didn't want to do anything but listen. Some just paused in the middle of the floor, then resumed dancing when he'd finished. Poe was out of touch with the latest dance craze, but his partner didn't seem to mind. They moved with a lot of vigor and sometimes even a little grace. It would have been fine except Poe's date stood a head taller than him, and made him appear no more than an erstwhile medical student who'd just sprung a healthy, awakening interest in sex. Chaney wondered how he'd found her at such short notice, besides fulfilling his other needs, but didn't pursue the thought.

When the number finished Poe led the woman up the steps and back to the table, much to Speed's delight.

'Listen kid ... we saw you out there. Smooth, Poe, very smooth.'

'Thank you. Thank you,' Poe said, moving the chair in behind the woman. 'It's all in the partner I have.' He gave a little bow.

Speed flagged his arm at a passing waiter but in vain.

'More drinks,' he shouted, 'all the way around. When I drink everybody drinks. When I pay everybody pays!'

He roared aloud at his own rotten joke, and searched for

another waiter, then seeing the two empty beer pitchers, he rose unsteadily with them and headed for the bar.

'I assume you realize,' Poe was saying to his tall date, his head attentively close to hers, 'that the blood of the fabled Edgar Allan courses through my veins?'

The girl's eyes lifted with unconcealed boredom. 'No, but it sure sounds like I'm going to hear about it.'

'Am I to understand that you and the noble literature are strangers? Then I shall on the occasion of this celebration treat you to a burst of my ancestor's genius,' replied, and immediately began his recitation. 'Hear the sledges with the bells Silver bells. What a world of merriment their melody fortells,' Poe hesitated there as though expecting to be jumped on or shouted down. His date was amazed, and gaped at him. No one else took any notice. And as if that in itself was an invitation, Poe continued. 'How they tinkle, tinkle, tinkle in the icy air of night. While the stars that over-sprinkle...'

Ever since they had picked Chaney's girl up earlier that evening Gayleen had looked for an opportunity of grilling Lucy. Personally she saw nothing special about her and was curious to know what it was that Lucy had going for her which she didn't. There had to be something, she figured, a man always wanted something.

'Tell me,' she said conspiratorially, 'how long have you and laughing boy been together?'

Lucy gave her a pale smile, having been around enough to know a bitch when she met one, and here in poor Gayleen there was one. Chaney sure had a poor choice of friends, then she suspected that they weren't chosen by him for their friendship value.

'I think we ran into each other about a month ago,' she replied, glancing at Chaney who was watching the cornet player.

'I guess it was a case of love at first sight.' Gayleen offered the sweetest smile! It was instinctive, the natural defense mechanism of a bitch and she got a lot of pleasure out of being so smart. Just sometimes she wished she could stop it, but it gave her an awfully good feeling most of the time.

'He ever loosen up around you?' she asked.

'When he feels like it.'

'Wonder how often that happens?'

Recognizing what the other woman was doing, Lucy refused to be drawn, not wanting to bitch the party.

'I'm not complaining,' she said as though she believed it.

'Well, I'm certainly glad to get that news,' Gayleen said, suddenly adding. 'Glad for you, sugar, that is. I'll tell you one thing. If he ever gets rough I wouldn't pick a fight with him.'

'He's all that good?'

Gayleen wondered if she was serious, but could never let such an opportunity get by her. 'Why,' she said, 'I should be asking you that.'

Lucy's troubled expression caused Gayleen to half-regret her remark. She figured Lucy was 'plain folks' so she eased up.

'He's the best Speed's ever had. And I've been with Mr Wheeler Dealer now for about...' She paused as if uncertain. 'Oh, too long. In case you wondered.'

Seeing her chance of getting back at Gayleen, Lucy smiled and said, 'I never wonder about those things.'

Gayleen froze, and considered how she had underestimated this woman. 'That's what's nice about people,' she said, 'it takes all kinds.'

Drunkenly Speed reappeared at the table and slammed two full pitchers down as if trying to draw attention to himself.

Poe's date was either mesmerized or asleep with her eyes open. Either way Poe wasn't too concerned, caught up as he was in his recitation. '... In the jangling. And the wrangling. How the danger sinks and swells,' there wasn't a wrong word or inflection. 'By the sinking or the swelling in the anger of the bells, of the bells, of the bells, bells, bells, bells, bells, bells, bells. In the clamor and the clangor of the bells –'

Speed cut in. 'Jesus! Will you shut up over there with those goddamn bells. I'm going to make a toast.'

Nothing could stop Poe now. 'Hear the tolling of the bells, iron bells!' Poe was there and exhausted as though having done the whole recitation on one breath.

Chaney smiled and gave him a little clap.

Poe appreciated that.

Speed raised one of the pitchers. 'The toast. To the best man I know. To a mastermind. To the Napoleon of southern sports.' He looked at Chaney, then paused and said, 'Me!' And drank hugely from the pitcher.

'Right now friends as we're all feeling so hot. I suggest we all just slip outside the city limits and into Jefferson and shoot a few at the Old Southport.'

Chaney knocked back his drink. It was time to go, but not crap-shooting. 'Count me out of this one, Speed. I'm moving.' He rose, looking at Lucy.

She blinked as though she wasn't sure if it was an invitation to join him, or a good-bye. But she got up anyway.

'Hey. Listen. We're going good. Why end it?' He put a hand on Chaney's arm, but knew he wouldn't get him to change his mind. He turned to Poe.

'I too have headier pursuits in mind,' he said ambiguously. But offered a little prayer for brother Speed, who was riding the crest. He feared it would go the way of all winning streaks.

'Well don't that take it!' he exclaimed. 'What about you, Sugarplum? Want to ride across Jefferson with me?'

'Let's go home, Speedy,' she said invitingly.

'We'll get there. We'll get there. Come on, Gayleen. Let's get there with those galloping dominoes. I'm really running.'

At that moment he was the luckiest son of a bitch in New Orleans, the entire State of Louisiana. Luck shone out of him like the light of God. He figured people just wanted to come up and touch him in order to receive it like holy communion. Nothing could stop him. The Goddess of Fortune was shaping his future, and tonight Speed was going to give her just a little more help.

THIRTEEN

For an hour now Speed had been helping shape his future by shaking those craps. He'd won a little and lost a little, but he wasn't worried about that. Right now he was hot and he was rolling, laying down two and three hundred at a time, and luck was still with him.

While waiting for the dice he'd pushed his roll up past five thousand with bets on other shooters, taking off their luck. Tonight he couldn't go wrong. Only Gayleen, who was at the bar drinking rum like it was water, lacked faith in him, doubted his fortune was going to last.

Skillfully he covered the board. Come-out bets, and place bets. There was no way he could lose. He won on his come-out throw if the dice passed on a seven or eleven; he won if he threw a point-number, and on the place-bet he also had himself covered, should he fail to throw a point.

He started shaking as other bets were laid down. The field was covered, even those big sixes and eights.

'Am I hot!' he yelled. 'Hotter 'an hell.'

With a shriek of delight he rolled. Little joes gave him a point, along with the big eight bets. He canceled the five point-numbers and started throwing again.

'Four's point. Four gets me a point.'

He rolled. Threes came down. He picked up the dice and began shaking them again and let them out.

'Point,' he called as he made it again.

He collected his money, and let it ride. It was a lot of money now, but Speed was unconcerned, was taking his chance. Luck wasn't always this good to him and he was grabbing it while it was. Ten thousand, that was the magic figure. Just ten grand, and he was on his way home, on his way down to Miami with Gayleen. He threw again; there might have been no alternative to winning. He collected his money, and again he let it ride, covering the six point-numbers once more.

He threw wildly, recklessly, delighting in the murmurs and

sighs of admiration and envy around the table. He won another point, collected his money and let it ride. Made some place-bets on his six point and started shaking. He rolled.

'Sixes!'

He collected his money, then put up some more, and fingers burning like they were on fire, took up the dice again and began shaking. He rolled and threw a pass. He'd been waiting for this, it was the beginning of the really big run, he told himself.

He joked with the crowd betting with and against him. 'Ten consecutive naturals coming up now. How about it.'

No one disagreed. He picked up the dice and rolled them around his lucky palm as the bets went down. He let them go as easily as could be.

'Sevens!'

The excitement in him made him jump now, and he could barely keep himself standing up at the table. He began shaking yet again with everything riding. He rolled another pass; let everything ride and rolled again. Another pass. The stake was getting big, so big it made him silent now, and those running the game a little nervous. Shaking them again, Speed let them go and made another pass. Everyone around the game was betting on him to win now. When he clicked those dice a tremor ran through his whole body, its intensity greater than any orgasm, also it continued longer. He let the dice roll making a pass yet again. His breathing was short and fast, like a man who had been screwing too much for his age.

Even Gayleen, who had pushed in right behind him, was shaking now, though not for the same reason. She had seen the light.

'Get out, Speedy,' she advised. 'Now darling. Leave it!'

That was impossible for him now. Even though he was well through that ten grand ceiling he had set himself, he couldn't quit, wouldn't quit. The Lady would never forgive him if he did, would never smile on him again. Every cent he owned was riding on the roll of those two dice, nearer to fifteen grand than ten. His Lady understood the compulsion, he had to go on, understood where Gayleen never would. Speed was going to keep those bones rolling until they begged him to quit or he ended up owning the place.

The dice cracked loudly in his hands. There was a breathless excitement around the game; the croupier's lips moved in silent prayer. With a stylish flick of his narrow wrist Speed let them slide off the side of his hand. They spun down the table and hit the back board, bounced up and tilted over. There was an enormous sigh of dismay around the table before the dice had settled. They had seen what Speed's luck-filled eyes wouldn't allow him to see at first. The boxcar. He had crapped out with two sixes. He couldn't believe it, he wouldn't believe it. Every conscious fiber of his being cried out in protest. The croupier's rake scooped in his huge pile of money; his ticket in style down to Florida. He stood helplessly at the end of the table, a numbness coming over him. He was aware of Gayleen's whining at the back of him.

No one else mourned Speed's loss.

'Put something up, or pass the dice,' a gambler called, impatient to chase the Lady himself.

Finally coming back to earth with a painful bump and a greatly deflated ego, Speed said furiously, 'Sons-of-bitches, mothering dice!'

'Push or shove,' the impatient gambler said.

'Keep this game going. I'm gonna be back.' He turned angrily and shoved Gayleen away from the table as the game started up behind him.

'Get your goddamn purse and coat,' he snapped. 'Let's go. I got business in town.'

Like she had been waiting for this moment all night, Gayleen said, 'Everything, Speed? You asshole, you lost everything!'

'Shut up! Jesus Christ, will you shut up.'

'Well, excuse me, Mr High Roller.'

Outside he slammed into the Buick, wrenched the shift into first gear, and blazed away, thrusting Gayleen back into her seat.

When they called in at the Pan-Am filling station he had to borrow fifty cents off Gayleen for gas.

'Jesus Christ!' she protested.

If he hadn't needed the gas change he'd have canned her there and then.

Driving fast with his stony, embittered thoughts, Speed maintained a steadfast silence all the way to the Quarter. He had a sound plan. He was going to hit on Le Beau for a piece to take him right back into that crap shoot.

The one time he really needed Le Beau he wasn't where he should have been. One of the bartenders in the Absinthe House said he'd left a short while ago to attend to his other business. He suggested where he might find him.

Across North Rampart Street and limited by Claibourne Avenue was the once notorious Storyville, the red-light district. A local ordinance closed the district back in October 1917, and although it never regained its pre-war legal status, business there picked up again. There were no longer any palaces and no cribs to step in off the sidewalks, but twenty years later prostitutes were still getting a living, and their pimps an even better living.

Part of Le Beau's business was pimping. He ran a couple of modest houses on Basin Street. It was at one of those where he was counting receipts that Speed found him.

'Still open for business?' he said, when he was led out back to the man with the concealed throat.

'What kind of business?' Le Beau croaked barely above a whisper.

'Well, I sure ain't looking to get laid. Not at your prices.'

Le Beau studied him. Any gambling man who came to him at this time of night was hitting a losing streak. Those sort of gamblers you had to watch especially closely. Le Beau knew about gamblers, and he knew about Speed. Word had gone round on him on account of the hitter he had got himself hooked up with. He had taken Chick Gandil for big money; that made him a good risk.

'Getting to be a habit,' he said looking hard at Speed.

'I pay my debts. I need two thousand,' Speed was feeling a little desperate.

'That's a real high number.'

'I like to live big.'

'You sure you're not moving too fast?' Le Beau said.

Speed suddenly snapped, 'Maybe I ought to go somewhere else.'

A sinister smile crept across Le Beau's mean expression. 'An hour this time?' he said.

'A week,' Speed replied. 'Don't worry I know the price.'

Le Beau regarded him for a while longer, leaving him on the hook. This guy before him liked himself a lot, he figured, and guessed he'd rob a blind leper to pay his dues before he risked having that face cut. He gave a tiny nod to Doty.

'Let him have it,' he croaked.

Doty stepped forward and produced nineteen bills from the wallet.

'Don't be late,' the little ox-like man said, smiling like he meant him to be, so he'd have a little exercise.

Speed snatched up the cash and turned out.

With nineteen hundred to roll he started living again. He was a gambler back in business, and here to stay this time as they headed back out to Jefferson.

'Didn't have enough goddamn capital,' he said expansively. 'Only reason I went down, you know that. Jesus, that sweet Lady knows you're down to bedrock, she blows.'

'The reason you went down was because you tried cheating on your luck,' Gayleen said, pleased Speed was back in fighting form.

'Horseshit!'

'Speedy, you ain't quick enough for me. I saw you try a slide throw.'

'The hell I did,' he lied.

'I saw it,' she insisted, never understanding why he lied to her on such occasions.

Speed cursed at a bum shuffling down Jefferson Highway where he nearly stepped under the Buick.

'Gambler's skill. I wasn't creating on the Lady. But I ain't relying too heavily on her this time. Where are my own dice?'

'Speed! They see you palming those they'll cut your fingers right off.' There was genuine concern in her voice.

But Speed wasn't heeding her words. He snapped open the glove compartment in the walnut dashboard and scrabbled around for his dice that had been drilled and loaded with mercury.

'Where the hell are they?' He panicked slightly when he couldn't find them. Maybe he intended using them, maybe he didn't.

'They're at the apartment. Forget it Speed.' Gayleen said with an air of finality. 'If you really want to can your ass, try something just as dumb. Stick a short pig's bristle into one corner of the die!'

'Where the hell are . . . Will you shut up? Will you just

shut up. I'm still hot I tell you. I got it figured,' he said snapping the glove box shut. 'I'll play the Martingale, bet against myself all the time.' He suddenly laughed, seeing the sense in it. 'How can I lose? It's so damn smart, I'm a genius. I bet on myself losing all the time, I got to win!'

This time, Gayleen thought, he's really flipped. She shook her head in dismay. For a moment back there she had thought they were going to make it all the way to Miami. But at this rate they weren't even going to get their valuables out of hock.

With a compulsion to lose far stronger than the deathwish of a lemming was how he came back into the game. He batted impatiently at the shooter presently throwing for him to relinquish the craps.

'Pass those dice, friend. Let a real shooter roll those bones.'

Having quit the six-bet system, the win and lose system and the series-system, he now had the certain feeling that he couldn't lose, because he was actually betting on himself to lose.

Taking up the dice, he laid out a single bill on the pass-line. He was feeling hot, and intended to run up several consecutive naturals before starting to bet on himself crapping out. He rolled and sure enough he got himself a natural. He was paid on the bill, and let it ride. He shook those dice again, spun them from hand to hand, jiggled them once more and let them go. The Lady hadn't left him after all, she had merely been playing a game of her own with him. He made another natural; then on the next roll he got sevens again. He was coming in big now, really big, and the chances of seven showing again was a real longshot. This was where he made his switch. He laid all he had riding on himself to lose. To lose on his next throw, which would be one throw in the endless succession of apparent bummers. He knew it was coming for him as he started shaking. He whispered to them, and let it go, but didn't look.

'Win,' someone called.

It was another natural, so he trebled his original bet. Only way to get it back. The Lady loved a bigtime. Three bills down on himself to lose; this time he had to miss. He shook those dice like a Voodoo man's dry bones, stroked them, chanted at them, kissed them. Then he let them go wildly.

'A natural.'

His heart was pounding away again. Three naturals was almost unnatural! He'd never throw the sixth, he told himself, not a second time in one night. He doubled up, laying six bills down on the don't-come area. That was where this roll was going to, he knew it had to. That familiar trembling which began in his calf muscles and worked right through his body started up again as he began shaking. The crowd were with him, most of them betting on him. One blonde with a bob-cut, big tits and a boyfriend with a gun stood alongside him, jumping up and down with him as he shook.

'Shake, shake, shake!' he cried. 'Jesus send me some snake eyes.'

'Shoot it,' someone urged.

Then the blonde with the bob-cut screamed, 'Touch my tits with the dice. I got lucky tits.'

Speed ignored her, staying faithful to the Lady, even though she wasn't too good for him at the moment. He tossed them bones. A great roar went up, an another natural turned up in silent mockery. Speed sweated, it had nothing to do with the heat. Double up he told himself, this time he had to crap out. He had to lose anyway because he was putting the last he had down. He couldn't double up, he only held nine bills. He slapped those down on the don't-pass line. The croupier shoved it back at him.

'Can't fade it.'

'What do you mean?'

'It's over the limit, unless it's riding. Seven-fifty's the best I can do for you, pal,' the croupier said.

Speed stood there stunned for a second. If he couldn't shoot his roll would break the sequence that was turning for him this time.

'Goddamn,' he shouted angry, like he had caught a tin-horn cheating.

'Put something up or pass those dice,' a drunk said.

'Blow it out your ass, friend,' Speed replied.

His mind went blank for a second. It was long enough for the vision he had to fill his inner eye. The Lady had told him what to do, to switch again; there were only naturals in those dice. He split his nine hundred dollars across the table, chosing his odds. Slowly and with a secret smile on his face he began to shake those bones. He was after a win this time. Everyone was with him, waiting on the seven. Speed could feel the energy they were giving him, he was caught by it, seduced by their sighs, their beseeching to the gods on his behalf. He wasn't really in control anymore, and could no longer distinguish Gayleen's whining behind him, telling him to quit, he just knew she was there like a sore spot on his back.

'Goddamn it, somebody get her out of here !' Whether she was pulled clear or not he didn't know then. He went on shaking, pleading for that seven. Then he spun the dice across the table and crapped out. He looked up at the don't-pass line. He hadn't a cent down there, everywhere but there. He stood there in disbelief, mocked by the Lady he'd loved, been faithful to. He'd lost the lot, everything. The weeks of running up, getting to the top, building his roll, and he'd gone right down again to nothing. The woman with the lucky tits and the boyfriend with the gun took the dice out of his hand, shrieked, and rubbed them against her breasts, and started shaking. The game went on, as they always tended, without Speed. He turned away, a sorrier man than he was when he had entered the Old Southport for the first time that night.

Gayleen was waiting for him at the bar and she smiled. The smile was both a little sad and triumphant. 'So now you've really got a problem,' she said quietly.

He just looked at her blankly for a moment. 'I got nothing,' he said.

'You got twenty-six hundred dollars to come up with by next week,' she reminded him. 'And you don't pay the man, he ain't going to like it, Speedy.'

Speedy thought about her words, then nodded to himself, thinking how like Doty she sounded.

FOURTEEN

Sure Speed knew he had a little problem, but he wasn't too worried, for a gambler's life went up and down, and his turn would soon be up again. Anyway with Chaney fighting for him it would be no time at all before he picked up the twenty-six hundred he was shy. When you had the debts Speed had all his life, a week was way, way off in the distant future.

Anyhow he was pretty optimistic, and had a good reason to be. Gandil had sent a message that he wanted to see them, and that could mean only one thing.

When Speed had stopped by for his hitter, Chaney hadn't been interested in seeing Gandil, told Speed to handle it. Panic had enveloped Speed for a moment; he had pleaded and Chaney had come round.

Indicative of his power and wealth was the downtown river frontage Gandil's family owned. It was a very busy and rich piece of real estate situated between the Poydras Street wharf where most of the coffee was handled and the Canal Street ferry. It was approached from where the Streetcar named Desire terminated on Canal Street, taking the right fork down by the ferry on ramp.

Speed swung the Buick down between the huge warehouse sheds loaded with Gandil's goods for shipment, wondering how much he could shake the son-of-a-bitch for up front. He completely disregarded Chaney's mood, figuring he was just grouchy about coming down to see Gandil.

Things were getting too close to Chaney, that was his problem; the fights, winning; Lucy; Speed. And now Gandil. Just a few more fights, he'd told himself in his room earlier that morning, and he'd be moving on. Be cutting off those tendrils of commitment he felt creeping over him, getting stronger the longer he stayed. He wanted a piece more money before moving out, but he didn't know if it was practical with Gandil making his play.

Parking the car on a clear bay, Speed headed for the next block of offices sandwiched between two sheds, Chaney at his side, casting glances about him, measuring, assessing. Speed's walk was all business and false confidence, the suit that was no longer new, totally out of place set against the longshoremen, the black swampers who were about their work unloading the ship that was docked and the trucks that were parked. Cotton and tobacco were the main commodities Gandil dealt in, when it wasn't human muscle.

They climbed the stairs on the outside of the building. The offices started on the second floor. As they paused on the landing, Chaney looked below at them, and seeing the blacks at work there, he felt uneasy. They looked just like so many of Gandil's slaves to him, trapped and held fast by economics rather than letters of bondage, but no less trapped for all that. He already had Gandil figured for what he was and wasn't looking forward to having the opinion confirmed. He knew he had something Gandil wanted; Gandil still had to realize that he had nothing Chaney wanted.

They moved to the back of the large building, started up a rear staircase and toward overhead offices with glass windows looking down on Gandil's lackeys.

Entering the building, they found themselves on a short corridor with a shipment hatch with frosted glass. Before they got to knock the window, the great bulk of Jim Henry, still bruised and cut, appeared at the end of the corridor. He beckoned to them. They went. Jim Henry wasn't a happy man, and Speed rubbed it in.

'How's your jaw, glass man?' he said, as they passed him and entered the bullpen office beyond where there were a dozen people working amid untidy heaps of shipment dockets on desks; file clerks, secretaries, accountants, all beavering away like it meant something to them. To get to Gandil they had to pass into another corridor with smaller offices off it, then through a private secretary's office, their progress meeting more and more luxury.

The inner office was spartan in its furnishings. This place of work wasn't his real life obviously. Here he merely made a lot of his money, which he spent elsewhere. Chaney was surprised by the austerity of the place. Gandil wearing a spotless, uncrumpled white linen suit, was sitting behind the bare desk, he didn't stand as Speed and Chaney entered.

'Speed,' he said, 'glad you could drop by.' They might just

have been passing.

'Always a pleasure,' Speed said, impressed at being invited, like Gandil had invited him to his house for dinner. His was a way of life Speed perpetually tried to imitate, though he never openly admitted it, which was why he bitched it most times.

'You remember Chaney?' he said.

Gandil nodded. 'Sit down. Get comfortable. Let's be a little sociable.'

Speed sat. But Chaney turned away and moved restlessly round the room. He didn't like being here, didn't like it at all. It was as though Gandil had anticipated not getting what he wanted and so had tipped the Feds and was now delaying him.

'Have a drink?' Gandil offered.

'Little early for me, Chick,' Speed said nervously.

Chaney ignored him.

'All business.' Gandil was being winsome.

'That's right. Let's have it.' Speed clapped his hands.

'You've got a direct way of speaking,' Gandil wasn't happy about someone else calling the shots.

Speed was briefly intimidated, and glanced at Chaney, not knowing what way to move. He didn't want Chaney to see this man ride rough shod over him.

'Nothing to get upset about,' he said.

With a curt nod Gandil saw a way of putting himself on top again. 'I like a man that's direct,' he said abruptly. 'Makes everything easy to understand. Like the old days. My grandfather didn't win this business in a raffle you know. He earned it. Started out in life with just a few thousand dollars and the bankrupt remains of the Opelollsas railroad.' It was a joke which neither of them got; then Gandil guessed his sense of humor was far too refined for them.

'I don't think we came here for any history lesson,' Speed said seriously. 'Maybe we ought to get down to cases.'

Gandil's eyes followed Chaney uneasily as he prowled the room. He wanted to tell him to sit down, but he wasn't about to risk it.

'Maybe we should,' he said.

He took a large envelope from his pocket, and casually placed it on the corner of the desk, in Speed's direction.

'Five thousand dollars in that envelope,' he said. 'It's yours.'

Speed baulked at the mention of five thousand, but he was purposely resisting the proposition. No one ever took the first offer. 'I don't think I'm following the drift.'

Gandil showed his white, even teeth. It wasn't a smile. 'I'm buying half of Chaney. We'll do real well as partners.'

As he waited for the shooter's reaction a quiet confidence spread through Gandil. With their money his family had been buying an awful lot of things and an awful lot of people for a long time. He was very used to power. The need people had for money bought him just anyone he chose to own, from the boy uptown to those down on the bowery. Everyone had their price, it was all a question of degrees.

Speed was a little embarrassed. His eyes searched Chaney's back over at the window It wasn't that the idea was objectionable to Speed, especially now as he needed the money so much. But he didn't like to be seen to lick this guy's ass, not here and now. Anyway, he didn't think Chaney would see the proposition as good news.

'This comes a little bit quick,' he eventually said.

'Don't let it bother you,' Gandil said despotically. 'It's done.'

Chaney stood looking down at the river front activity, but he was listening. Gandil's grandfather would have been no different from Gandil, but maybe, and only maybe, he would have appreciated that a man's hire was worth more to him than just money. Gandil didn't understand that and never would. He wanted to own Chaney and thought it was just a question of laying his money down. Chaney would never be owned by anyone, man or woman, and he didn't need money that badly. He would rather be free and riding the freight cars if that's what it meant to have the car fare. He would rather be riding them anyway. And it was time he was.

Apart from the need to own him because he was the best, Chaney felt something else coming from Gandil. It was that negative, destructive quality the rich had, it engendered a kind of determination to pull him down, suck the life, the fight out of him.

'Pick up the money,' he told Speed. 'We got a deal, boy. We're partners. Just like buying a horse. We're partners, fifty-fifty. Now the first thing I want is for us to go up to Lafayette. Got a man big in oil up there ...'

Suddenly wheeling round, Chaney slammed his hands down on the desk, and leant menacingly close to Gandil. 'Talk to me. Not him. You talk to me, Gandil.'

For a long while Gandil held his look, measuring the man, realizing his own mistake. Arrogance had impaired his usually fine judgement. He had seen the kind of guy Chaney was, and knew of course that in any fight with him he would have to play things differently. Chaney was the type who gave nothing of himself until he was backed against a wall, then he had to let go with everything. Unlike regular shooters Gandil was a businessman, he could set up a deal and wait a long time for the dividends. He'd eventually get what he wanted. Certainly when he was dealing with people. Nothing changed his basic tenet, that every man had his price.

Those contemptuous eyes studied Chaney coolly now. Gandil was aware that he'd already scored a point by causing Chaney to explode.

'My, my, my. Why, you got quite a temper, Mr Chaney,' he said chidingly.

'I got no temper at all. I just wanted to get your attention.'

Seeing Chaney's reaction now Speed knew he didn't have a prayer or a hope of ever having any part of that five thousand in his own pocket to pay back Le Beau. But feeling the way the wind was blowing he decided to sail close to Chaney.

'You ought to learn to live with your losses, Chick,' he said carefully. 'You take your chances like everybody else. That's why the man named it gambling.'

Angrily Gandil stood, shoving back his leather buttoned chair. He gave it to them off the shoulder. 'I had the best streetfighter in this here city,' he said. 'Now I don't. And I don't like that at all. That's why I'm telling you we're going to be partners.'

'I like the things the way they are.'

Chaney stared at him. Gandil sighed almost wearily, but apparently unconcerned.

'Hooking up with me means more greens for you,' he informed Chaney matter of factly. 'Bigger bets. In fact, boy, it's the only way there's a living for you in this town. Tell him, Speed.'

'It is something to think about,' he admitted, grudgingly, guessing at the kind of problems they'd run up against now in setting fights.

Slowly and deliberately Chaney said. 'I just said I like things the way they are. We can get along without you.'

Not for a moment did Gandil believe Chaney. No one in his position could turn his back on such money. It was just plain poor-man stubborness, he was letting this become a personal battle between the two of them. He almost smiled. A horse would break its heart trying for its master, just as Jim Henry had; a mule would get its butt broken resisting, but it all came out the same place in the end. And he was going to beat Chaney. When Chick Gandil fought he could hit as hard as any hitter, if in less direct ways. Men sometimes were made so that they could withstand any kind of pain, but they all had emotions too, and that was where they could be hurt.

'I'm sorry to hear that, Mr Chaney,' he said with an air of menace in his tone. 'I like being associated with the best. I hope you'll come around to my way of thinking.'

Chaney turned around and walked out of the office door. Speed offered an apologetic shrug and followed after him.

They walked back quayside to where the car was parked. Chaney seemed to be brooding worse than ever as they waited for a net of bales that were hoisted up off the quay by one of the cranes there and swung out over the hold of the ship. Those hoists had a pretty bad track record and no one happily moved under them.

Speed could hardly believe that the meeting had just taken place. For regardless of what had happened at the crap game he guessed the luck must still be somewhere with him. In Chaney there was a whole future and a fortune tied up.

'I mean to tell you,' he said, watching the dangerous assent of those bales. 'The chickens have really come home to roost when we have Gandil begging for mercy. Every once in a while something happens that's just too good to be true.'

Chaney didn't reply immediately. He'd seen Gandil's look and he knew the man wanted a fight.

'How long an arm's he got?' he asked.

'He's a businessman,' Speed said ambiguously, then shrugged. 'Always worried about his reputation. He won't try any muscle play, least I don't figure he will.'

The look Chaney gave him suggested that he didn't have a lot of faith in that opinion.

'But there's one thing we got to live with. Since you beat Jim Henry you are marked. Not many people are going to be anxious to come up to the line against you. From now on we'll have to give odds.'

'No need worrying about it,' Chaney said, moving on now that the hoisting operation was clear. 'We're getting toward the end of things.'

Alarm swept through Speed. His fortune and his future was suddenly on the wing. What was this talk of the end of things?

'What the hell does that mean?' he asked, trying to keep the concern out of his voice.

Chaney didn't answer. But he could see the end coming up now sure as the sun that rose in the east. People wanted him, wanted to pin him down; next they'd be trying to print programs. He had been reading the danger signals too long. He spat the matchstick he was chewing onto the ground as they reached the car.

'See you, Speedy,' he said, starting past the car.

Speed watched him, feeling very uneasy. 'Hey, don't you want a ride?'

Without glancing back Chaney shook his head. 'I want to walk.'

Feeling that he had been drawn out of himself more than he liked, Chaney wondered if he hadn't already let things run on too long, and had left himself vulnerable as a result. Certainly he was beginning to feel that with Lucy. And now to add to his problems there was Gandil to contend with.

Almost as if without realizing it he had seemed to have slipped into a permanent relationship with the woman. He didn't know what Lucy read into what they had going, but figured it had to be a lot more than he did. He kept telling himself to put it down, that his seeing her so often was weakening him, undermining his independence and consequently his security. The woman was getting to depend on him. But worse, far worse, he was coming to depend on her a little.

Yet despite his awareness and the danger he read there, evening fell and he found he was calling on Lucy, taking her out to eat. He realized she was almost coming to expect his appearance, was putting an obligation on him to show up. That he hated.

A restlessness came over Chaney in the old bar they sat in, having eaten. The bar's smoked stained Victorian mirrors, its dusty gasoliers and marble-topped tables had all become too familiar, even other customers recognized him and greeted him. Abruptly he suggested to Lucy that they quit the joint. He had some thinking to do.

He could see the disappointment behind Lucy's acquiescing smile, but he didn't accept that he'd ever given her anything which told her to expect more. They walked silently along the street, past the crumbling structure of the Ursuline convent. A blind man with a white stick and tin mug lay against the diseased plaster wall, like at the door of a Christian house it was a good place to wait for Christian charity. Tonight Chaney wasn't seeing those around him, wasn't aware of his surroundings or the woman on his arm even. At that moment he was trying to outpace his thoughts.

For her part Lucy resisted what she thought might be happening to Chaney. She wanted to prolong the evening because she didn't want to be alone. She needed people, needed to have a good time. There were moments with Chaney when she thought maybe she really had something going, but then everytime they started rolling, he seemed to pull back sharply.

'Hey,' she suddenly said, seeing a sign, 'let's go in here.'

Over to his left there was a crib set up just off the sidewalk. A sign read: Psychic Readings, Bone Predictions: Tarot.

'It's a goddamn joke,' he said. He wasn't baulking at the quarter it would set him back, but the pointlessness and the trivia with which people cushioned their lives.

'Oh c'mon, Chaney,' she urged, dragging on his arm as he tried to move away.

Regarding her for a moment, he saw the look of expectancy in her face. She was just someone else looking to have her life mapped out for her.

'You really want to.' He gave a shrug and stepped right up to the curtain that separated the future from the sidewalk.

Inside the crib an enormously fat Creole woman sat at a small baize-covered table, the numerous rings and bangles on her fingers and arms almost submerged in rolls of fat. Her tiny brown eyes widened to a recognizable smile at the sight of two customers.

'What do you think?' Lucy said.

A charlatan, Chaney thought, but didn't say so. 'How much?' he asked.

'The casting of bones and the psychic readings twenty-five cents. Twenty-five cents for the Tarot reading, unless you want the full layout. That's fifty cents.'

The price even for the full layout wasn't an objection. Lucy could pay it herself if need be. But she didn't want Chaney's disapproval. There was nothing, she felt, behind that look he gave her as she slid into the chair across from the fat Creole woman.

Chaney pulled the curtain across shutting out the street and waited. He wanted to be alone back at his flophouse, with no greater dependency than that cat had on him, and that was artificial. He would make out in the alleys again. He pushed the thought away, but another immediately rushed him. More and more of late he was finding himself thinking about either the past or the future instead of concentrating on the present in which he preferred to live. The cat was a brief obligation; Speed was becoming a bigger one; then there was Poe; and there was of course Lucy. He knew how it would all come out, and didn't need to have his future told by any quack. He determined the circumstances of his own life, and if they weren't sitting right or put him in any danger then he set about changing them.

Lucy had decided on the full layout, and the Tarot reading seemed to go on forever. Chaney sighed wearily and shifted his weight from one foot to another, tuning in to the reading now.

The woman sat with a series of upturned cards on the table before her, with several from the major and minor Arcane showing. Not only their picture but the way they faced had an important bearing. The Creole seer was revealing it all for Lucy at an easy pace, a world of ambiguous prospects held in her words.

'The six of wands.' She indicated the cards she turned over with her pudgy index finger. 'The seven of pentacles in conjunction with the Empress, shows improving fortune.'

The woman hesitated and glanced up at Lucy, who was held spellbound.

'But the times will not be untroubled. The number three here indicates a fulfillment of physical needs. The union of both the positive and the negative. You are approaching a time of choice.'

'A choice of men?' Lucy asked with uncertainty.

Like so many Lucy became stupidly gullible in the face of the unknown, especially when it came wrapped in fifty cents worth of mystery. Chaney remained sceptical, but there was something about Lucy's question that touched a part of him. He knew what it was, but let it go as the woman closed the reading.

'You have no real dependence on men,' she said. 'Your choices are with yourself.' Then swept the cards together in her fat hands. 'Fifty cents, please.'

Grudgingly Chaney flipped her two quarters. He didn't figure you had to be a fortune teller to work out that your choices were with yourself. But half a dollar's worth seemed to give Lucy something.

'Well,' she said with a smile, 'sounds like things are looking up. Praise the Lord.' She rose and looked dubiously at Chaney. 'Of course you're the kind that doubts all this.'

'I just like things I can see,' he said.

Lucy turned quickly back to the table. 'I'll turn one over and it'll be yours.'

She pulled out a card from the deck and flipped it over. It was the hanged man.

'That's a beauty,' she said. 'What does it mean?'

'One card means nothing,' the woman replied, smiling blandly.

'I don't care about the rules. It's got to mean something.'

Chaney came forward and looked at the card. Despite his scepticism it wasn't a very reassuring sight, whatever it meant. It shook him a bit, causing those Feds to jump right into his mind. They'd take him back to Georgia if they caught him, and that was a hanging state.

'Let's skip it,' he said irritably.

'Please,' Lucy urged the woman.

The Creole seer brought the card in front of herself and looked at it briefly. She was offhand with her delivery, and not because it was free.

'Surrender of self to a higher authority,' she said. 'Duty seen as bondage, but completion of the task can give release. One can free oneself.'

It took the wind out of Chaney though he allowed no sign to get past him. He couldn't figure why but Gandil came into his thoughts briefly, and then there was something about Speed and his involvement there. It was nonsense of course. Even the woman said so.

'A single card means nothing.' She replaced it. 'Perhaps you'd like a full layout?'

Chaney didn't even consider her offer. 'Sounds like you're going to have a few problems,' Lucy said.

'Just so there's a door to go through.' Chaney might have been giving her a warning.

That was how she took it. He always wanted a door to go through, to leave everything behind. Well, maybe she wasn't as dependent on him as he thought. Maybe all her choices were with herself. Wasn't that what Chaney first told her anyway? Wasn't it what he believed?

Nodding reflectively she said, 'You've got all the safe way of doing things figured out.'

He looked at her hard and saw the mistrust re-assert itself. But he wasn't going to put himself further at risk now.

'Not quite, Lucy. But I'm working on it,' he replied coldly.

FIFTEEN

If Chaney did like the safe way of doing things, then he figured one certain way was to hang on to all his options, keeping everything open so that anytime he wanted to do anything he could just do it, without prior consultation or consideration of others. More and more recently he found it was getting difficult to do this. Too many people were wanting too much of him.

He lay full length on the bed in the room and watched the fan describe lazy circles. The rooming house was the kind of place he liked, the kind of place he could shake the dust off at a moment's notice. And where, when he did, he was no more than just another drifter moving on.

He wanted to be off on his own now. Maybe he'd just been around the same town too long and was simply missing the freedom of riding an empty flatcar, watching the night and the stars slide by. Hard times had taught Chaney to ride that way and that was the way he preferred traveling. Maybe he preferred the hard times. He certainly didn't want the ease of domesticity which he could afford now. He preferred washing out his own shirt; waiting around for the laundry meant waiting around to be collared.

The cat mewed around and leapt up on the end of the bed. He watched it. It no longer looked at him the same way it had that night he grabbed it out the alley, like he was a rival for the food, and a threat, but rather like he was touched. It arched its back, stretched its legs then took it upon itself to walk over him and sit on his chest. Somehow it seemed as though they'd come a long way together. Just in passing the time of day they'd shared something. Yet because of that it didn't mean he had to have the cat round his neck fulltime. He pushed the cat off his chest and rose alertly at the rap at his door. Visitors were a rarity in his life that caused that kind of reaction. It was apprehension boarding on alarm.

Reaching for his shirt, he pulled it on and buttoned it. He stopped at the door and listened for a moment before opening it. A young woman with long hennaed hair stood there. She had a pretty face, and pert breasts pushing out from her flimsy dress.

'Hello,' she said, like they were old friends.

Chaney would like to have responded in the same way, but sensed the woman had brought a story with her, and he mistrusted it immediately.

'I'm Chrystal,' she informed him, and let her tongue slide across her pale red lips, moistening them invitingly. 'I came up to make you feel okay.'

A cynical smile flicked across Chaney's face as he waited for the hook.

'Mr Gandil sent me,' Chrystal continued. 'He asked me to be nice. I'm real good.' She smiled warmly wanting to get across the threshold.

She seemed like quite a nice kid, a pity she'd come under the circumstances she had, Chaney thought. So Gandil had made his first move. She was the pawn with which he figured he would capture a bishop – maybe Gandil didn't rate him that high, but had him figured for another pawn. Either way he would learn that Chaney's needs weren't as volatile as those of other men. He prized his complete independence more than the offering within Chrystal's thighs.

'Little early in the day,' he said.

'Breakfast in bed.' She smiled again. Real nice, Chaney decided. Then he felt for her in the same way he felt for bindle stiffs. She was someone trying to get by in these hard times but just wasn't strong.

'You been paid yet?' he asked.

'It's all been taken care of. Don't worry, it's not going to cost you a penny.'

It would cost me a lot more than that, he thought. She seemed puzzled at his silence, and the defensive way in which he held the door.

'What's wrong?' she said.

'Nothing's wrong. I just like to pick and choose.'

'If it's me, I can send up one of my friends.'

'You're fine,' Chaney said, and meant it. 'But go on back. Tell Gandil I had a good time.'

'You sure?'

'I'm sure.'

'Okay.'

Reluctantly she moved back to the top of the stairs, turned and smiled. 'Guess I owe you one,' she said.

Chaney smiled grimly. Another time he might take her up on that.

'I'll think about it,' he said.

'Take care.'

Chaney watched her descending the stairs, her ass bouncing with each step. Goddamn Gandil, he thought. He shut the door, and stood against it for a moment abstractedly watching the cat.

Quite obviously Gandil would get to be a problem. He could go and see him, try straightening him out, but he guessed there was only one way Gandil would be straightened. He was a man used to having other men bowed before him, and that was how he was set on having Chaney too. It started with gifts and soft persuasion, but it would probably get rougher. It was going to mean a fight. When a man like Chaney, who wanted nothing more than to live his own life, ran up against a man like Chick Gandil, who figured on having things a different way, the conflict as a result was inevitable. If ever he yielded to the likes of Gandil, Chaney knew that everything in his life would have been in vain; going after those bankers who had foreclosed on him; his children's death, Alma's death. Conflict with Gandil might bring him unnecessary trouble and he wondered if he shouldn't cut out right now. Yet somehow walking out also meant giving something of himself up to that man. It meant he was letting him dictate his will, if not his terms. Chaney decided to ride it out for a while.

The next move Gandil made in his direction was quite soon after. Chaney was obviously a watched man, and that made Chaney uneasy. Gandil turned up to watch the next fight he picked up. There'd have been little problem had he only watched. But he had his shill bet heavily with odds on Chaney to win, which only forced money away from Speed.

The venue for the fight was over in Algiers in a dry dock at the head of Seguin Street. With the changing economic conditions diminishing the importance of Algiers as a river-shipping center, the drydock had fallen into disuse by ship-owners. Winos and low-lifes used it now and had made it a place fitting for themselves, an air of decay, both human and organic pervaded. The fight was the best Speed could get. The crowd consisted mainly of those dismal figures who were on the skids, betting the last of their money with such odds on their local boy, figuring they'd get themselves a fifth of something when he ko'd the visitor. But as sure as their shaking hands parted with their money they had lost it. It was the story of their lives, and clearly written in their grotesque, unshaven, scabbed-up faces, and cloudy eyes that hadn't seen anything resembling the way out since they first gravitated to the pit, as the drydock was known locally.

They crowded the garbage and debris littered floor of the pit and lined the top of the walls all around. The hitter who was put up against Chaney could probably have acquitted himself adequately in the disorder of a riverside brawl. Against Chaney it was soon revealed that he was no more than a distant echo of a fighter. He took a heavy tumble almost as soon as the fight started. But gamely he got up and swung a few more at Chaney like he was sparring with the smoky air. Chaney came in through those big flailings and it ended.

Chaney walked over to Poe for his cap and coat, feeling a bit disgusted. He looked around at the men who turned unhappily away, taking the defeat harder than the hitter; it probably meant more to them anyway. Chaney didn't want to buy his future this way, he didn't like hitting these guys when they were already down. He couldn't understand why Speed had bothered. The potbet was hardly worth the trouble, and the side bets certainly weren't. Speed was over-anxious to collect the cash from the heavyset man who was holding it. Just lately he seemed agitated and nervous, and it wasn't simply the peaks and troughs of gambling. It caused some kind of gulf between them, and although Chaney welcomed this, he wondered about it also.

Money in his hand always did things for Speed, but even he looked disappointed with the result. Chaney gestured to him to give some of the cash back to the heavyset man. Speed's face dropped, but he saw Chaney meant it. The heavyset looked surprised, and stayed that way when Chaney gave a nod in the direction of his fallen opponent, before turning to move out.

And there was Gandil standing with Jim Henry by the ladder up out of the pit. Chaney resented the man flaunting his rich and secure existence down here like this.

Gandil watched him approach, figuring the hitter owed him something now. Going on Chrystal's report of a good time he had had, he considered he already held a part stake in Chaney, albeit a small one at ten dollars. He was here to remind him of what was owing. He waited until Chaney reached the ladder.

'You didn't bother saying thanks for the piece of cake I sent you,' he said.

Chaney stared at him. He was ahead of Gandil, owing him nothing. It was going to stay that way.

'Bad manners,' he said, and started up, followed by Poe.

Gandil's mouth tightened in anger. No one played games with him and made a fool out of him, least of all someone like Chaney. He wanted him and he was going to get him. He couldn't use violence, as that would defeat his own ends, but there were other means he could use, means that weren't quite so polite or refined as a sweet piece of ass. Gandil was a student of human nature, and knew there would be something about Chaney that would cause him to crack if he did a little digging. Maybe he had a record, or better still was on the run. He'd have some inquiries made. He caught hold of Speed who made his way after Chaney.

'You're turning into a great disappointment to me, Speed,' he said, knowing that in Speed there was a man who wanted to be like him, with all his own needs gratified.

Speed had enough problems without shit from Gandil. Not only was he short the six hundred due to Le Beau in interest against his marker, the two thousand dollars was also now overdue. The pot there was hardly worth a rub, and he was having difficulty setting up the kind of fights for Chaney that would net them more than loose change.

'That's between you and Chaney,' he said shortly. 'He don't listen to me about those things.'

'He ought to listen. So should you. I'd be good for you both.'

That did it for Speed, he snapped wide open. 'Look, friend, I'm suffering a bad case of the shorts. I'd be happy to take your money. Get a real monkey off my back.'

When people lost control of their emotions and gave too much they also gave an advantage. Speed had done just that, and Gandil saw how he might employ this advantage to gain one over Chaney.

'Who are you into?' he asked Speed.

'That's none of your business.'

Speed regarded the man hopefully. He'd known Chick Gandil from around the fights for a long time, and whatever the odds or losses the man had always stayed utterly cool. But here he was running around after Chaney like a fairy after a hoehandle. Speed didn't understand it. Sure, the man's hitter had been wiped out, but so what? That was the name of the game.

'Why are you letting this thing with Chaney turn into such a big deal?' he said.

Gandil spoke coldly. 'I don't like the way he said "no".'

Speed screwed up his face. If all his problems were as small as that he'd be a happy man.

Between putting himself about and trying to rustle up some action for Chaney's talents, Speed tried to work up something for his own. He was trying to scare up some scratch to ease the pressure with Le Beau. But wasn't having much success. And slotted between these activities he had errands to run for Gayleen; such was the price of failure.

The hot long day hustling in the city had left Speed feeling limp and tardy. He felt like getting a steam bath and massage; or a hot-towel and shave with perhaps a little attention on his hair; he saved his money, preferring instead to put it on the nose of something. However, he did need to keep up his image. He got awfully depressed if and when he began to look a little seedy. When your luck was batting you against the sidewalk as his was at that time it was more important than ever that he looked good. He still had his slick roadster, and felt he had always to match that great symbol of masculinity. He couldn't allow himself to drive around looking like a down-and-out. The thought of trying to sell the car to raise a bit had crossed his mind, but 1930 Marquettes were not at a premium. Anyway, he guessed the finance company would object.

If he could pick a horse that didn't come in last it would be something. He invested a nickel in The Item and climbed up into one of the empty seats on the shoeshine stand next to the news stand. Speed folded the back sheet for the racing form and began his search. The only trouble with the scratch sheet was, he found, that they didn't say which horses were going to be first past the post.

The aging black got busy with his rags, glancing up at Speed just once.

'You want one for the fifth, boss?'

'Only if it's first past the post, friend.'

'Crying Shame.'

'Yeah, ain't it just,' Speed said, then realized he was giving him a horse, and checked the form.

'Jesus, it's ten to one. What are you giving me, boy?'

'I gis another customer a shine, and he gis me this, and a whole quarter tip. I figure he's gotta be on da level, boss.'

'So what else you shooting?' Speed wasn't really interested, he figured the guy was simply making up his wages.

'Flying Spirit in the sixth. Das evens.'

'Both those nags'll still be running at Christmas.'

He looked down at the quick black hands that were about to start popping with the buffing brushes.

'Hey, put a little extra on those, boy. I want to see my face in those.' A shine was lucky. You never saw a lucky man with shitted up shoes.

Speed went back to perusing the racing form. He was only vaguely aware of someone who came and sat in the chair next to him.

'Busy?' the man inquired.

'As a one-legged man at an ass kicking,' Speed replied without looking up.

The voice was familiar. He felt a chill, and lowered the paper. Le Beau's flunky, Doty, sat smiling alongside him. It wasn't a smile Speed found very reassuring.

'A man that's got enough money for a shine must be able to pay his debts,' he said. 'S'the way I figure it.'

'I got to keep up appearances.'

'Sure,' Doty allowed, biting off the end of a ten-cent cigar like he had something to celebrate.

Speed was on the spot. He was also speechless.

'You're overdue,' Doty said matter of factly.

Speed wondered about trying to smile, but somehow didn't think it would work with Doty. In any case these days he was even short on smiles.

'Well, look pal, I'm in a little trouble,' he said, hoping for a little love and understanding.

Doty stared at him, then struck a Vesta with his thumbnail. Doty liked trouble, especially when it was other people's and he was going to add to it.

'I can maybe come up with two hundred,' he said nervously.

'Forget it,' Doty replied. 'He wants it all. Time's run out, marker man.'

That shook Speed a little, the expression was familiar.

Doty stared for a second more with cold fish-like eyes. The message had got through, but he showed his needle teeth as if to impress the point. Then he got up and walked away down the street.

Speed shivered a little now he had no time left at all. He liked to keep up an appearance, but if he didn't get something together quickly and pay off Le Beau he was going to look one hell of a mess, and no number of expensive suits or fancy hairdos or shoeshines would improve him.

The boy finished the shine and stared up at him. Speed sat there a moment looking vacantly at the sidewalk, wondering what had happened to all his dreams. He couldn't work it out how he always came back to this; it was fate, always against him and giving him a hard time. It saddened him this afternoon as he got a breath of the cool breeze off the river, bringing with it all the nostalgia of his carefree southern youth. Jesus, he thought, jolting out of his reverie, I wanted to be like that fine strutting Tennessee walking horse, but I'm going to end up flat, and with a fractured skull.

'Dem sure shine now, boss,' the boy said.

Vacantly Speed looked down, the shine now meaningless. He fished in his pocket for a dime, and flipped it to the boy. He climbed wearily off the chair and walked away, his eyes flashing left and right now, looking for Le Beau's toughs. He would have to work fast and fix something for Chaney, it was his only hope.

Scouring the bars looking for takers, he had no more luck than he did over at the Coliseum arena looking at the regular boxers, or hustling the shooters around the cockfight pits and the race tracks. The trouble was that too many of those boys knew the circuit and had heard about Chaney. Some had hitters they thought might be worth a try, but they didn't have any money for a potbet. He even looked up his old opponent Caesare, but he was wiser now and poorer.

With darkness falling Speed got desperate. He became very wary now about walking into bars and even more wary about walking out of them, feeling Le Beau's toughs were going to jump him, and tear him to pieces. Night times were the worst, for he knew Le Beau kept several huge blacks in shackles ready to give the works, and Speed had a fear of tangling with those sort of blacks worse than his fear of any other man. He wondered if maybe Le Beau wanted to put up one of those boys against Chaney. But he guessed not. Le Beau had never made a bet in his life and he only went for certainties.

Finally the goddess offered up what he thought at the time was a little light in a dull fortune. He managed to arrange a fight with a platoon sergeant down from Hammond with some of his boys. One of them was a hard hitter, the sergeant said, and he was prepared to put his money where his mouth was. They weren't high rollers those soldier boys but he figured if enough of them were in town he could collect a nice piece on sidebets.

There were, and they were a hard-looking bunch, all of them looking as good as the corporal they were putting up as their hitter. Chaney waited in the Buick while Speed entered the bar where the soldiers were waiting and started things rolling.

Eventually the whole crowd of soldiers with a lot of liquor on them came out and gathered in the alley at the side of the bar where the fight was going to take place. They made a lot of noise as they waited for Speed's hitter. Speed needn't have kept him out of sight; the soldiers hadn't heard about his reputation and were amused that he was so old. The corporal opposing him was a big guy, well used to dishing it out. Poe took Chaney's coat and cap and the man stepped forward, raising up his palms.

The corporal, having been taught to take whatever advantage, ignored this ritual, and lunged forward at Chaney and scored, his big hard fist cut Chaney across the right cheekbone. The soldiers roared, all wishing it was them in there now. Chaney was angry, not with the boy he was fighting, but with himself for leaving himself wide open and vulnerable like that. That was carelessness which had subsequently cost him;

it wouldn't happen again. He blocked the man's left and came with his own with machine-like rapidity, getting the soldier over his right eye each time until eventually he stumbled backwards, covering his face with his hands. Chaney attacked the voluminous uncovered body with hard, stunning punches. The man was through back against the wall of soldiers who held him a moment while he recovered; then they pushed him forward, and he came back at Chaney really mad. He started throwing punches, left and right, getting a good rhythm going. He knew how to handle himself, but Chaney slid around most of them waiting for his opening. He saw it just after he had opened the split on the corporal's eye further. The soldier bellowed angrily at him and came on like a thresher. He landed one on Chaney's damaged cheek and was so pleased about it when the soldiers cheered that he might as well have turned and taken a bow, he left himself that wide open. The blow hurt Chaney, but didn't destroy him. He got off an overhand right which rocked the man backward, and followed through letting him have another hard one in the face. The soldier was crumpling and Chaney hammered him until his fist hurt. Finally the boy fell like a dead weight toward the wall of uniforms who just folded back, letting him fall.

Holding the flesh of his gaping cheek together, Chaney turned angrily for the Buick. Poe quickly followed after him, while Speed went nervously to collect the winnings.

In the car Poe attended to Chaney's cheek which was badly split. The light available wasn't the best there was for that kind of stitching operation, but Poe worked diligently and with concern; for all his dismissive jokes about his medical student days, he wasn't bad at all. Chaney was grateful, and let him get on with it without a word.

Speed slid in the front of the Buick and began counting the winnings. It wasn't as much as he had hoped it might be, and his piece certainly wouldn't cover his debt to Le Beau. At this rate he was going to have to run round and fix up a lot more fights before he came anywhere near to it. And he was going to have to do it soon unless he wanted to be fished out of the Mississippi like Two-Fingers.

Poe finished tending to Chaney's cheek, and cleaned the blood off that had run down his chin.

'It's a bit on the nasty side,' he said.

'You hurting?' Speed asked, and began counting the winnings a second time, as if hoping they'd increased of their own accord.

'All over,' Chaney said.

'Son-of-a-bitch was good. Better than I figured those meatheads could come up with.'

'I got careless,' Chaney said emphatically.

That was in the fight. He wouldn't be so careless with Speed as to give him any more than he already had by opening up on how he really felt.

'Hazards of the occupation,' Poe said philosophically.

'Could be worse,' Speed said, counting the money yet again, hoping he'd find a bill or two he'd missed. 'You might be him. Did you see that mouth of his?'

'Let's hope he's not a bugler,' Poe observed drily.

'Tell me how bad,' Chaney wanted to know.

'It's going to leave a mark.'

'Big deal,' Speed said as he stacked the bills. 'What do you think he is, some pretty boy?'

'Never hurts much holding the coat,' Poe replied, with genuine concern for his patient.

Speed, more concerned with his own fate, asked irritably, 'Just tell me how long it's going to be, needle arm.'

'Well, that's a pretty bad cut. I'd say it'll need about three weeks.'

The words leapt out at Speed, dealing him a cruel blow. 'Holy Jesus.'

'What's the rush you got on?' Chaney asked him.

Speed sucked some air in his lungs and glanced through the mirror at Chaney. He didn't expect any handouts from him, he'd come to know him better than that, and accepted his terms. There was certainly no point bawling to him about what he owed Le Beau. The hitter would simply give that age old piece of advice that all gambling men got at sometime. Right now Speed wished he had heeded his Ma.

'This is no time in my life for a vacation,' he said, and hit the starter button.

The Buick went away into the night. A cop watched it. He was watching the driving of a worried and distracted man.

SIXTEEN

Later, as Speed drove back to his apartment, his thoughts turned to finding a church where he could do some praying. With Chaney out of action for three weeks or so he had no chance at all of finding Le Beau's money. Crying Shame, the nag that shoeshine had given him was still running. He'd kick that boy's ass the next time he saw him.

Way down town on Royal Street where Speed lived it was very dark, only the occasional spluttering gaslamps lit the sidewalk and those pools of uneven light then darker shadows didn't help. Speed parked the Buick at the curb and shut off the engine. As he got out he ran his fingertips along the hood, as if for luck. The car was about the only thing that had stayed lucky for him and never let him down. Turning away to start up to his apartment, he stopped in his tracks as a Vesta spluttered from the shadows. Doty brought the flame up to the butt of the ten-cent cigar he was persevering with, like it was asserting his manhood. A huge figure stood in the shadows of the stoop right behind Doty, and it was difficult to distinguish him from the shadows, until Doty snapped his fingers.

Then the black stepped from the shadows, carrying a sledgehammer.

Speed, in his frozen state started shaking. The next best thing he had to money he had to offer was his great reservoir of winsome smiles, but even those had deserted him and he just ended up twisting his mouth in a nervous, twitching terror of sheer goddamn fright.

The black approached menacingly slowly, but walked straight on past Speed where he stood on the sidewalk.

'Hey, what's going on?' Speed croaked in an unintentional imitation of Le Beau.

'That fender needs a little attention,' Doty responded, gloating now.

The black lifted the hammer as high as he could and swung it down, slamming it into the Buick.

'Hey, Jesus!' Speed just felt his balls being chopped off.

The hammer swung back and fell again, this time making a mess of the hood. A sound of grating, rending metal tore at Speed's ears.

'What are you doing?' he cried, feeling them going for his pecker now.

The black went on crashing the sledgehammer into the Buick, bouncing it off the hood a couple more times, then slamming it into the spare wheel fixed in the left hand front fender; the door got some treatment, then the protruding headlamps.

Speed saw the whole structure of his life being wrecked here and he was doing nothing to prevent it.

'Jesus Christ. Hey, come on, Doty,' he pleaded.

When the man was unyielding he stepped toward the black, his concern for what was left of the car suddenly over-riding even his personal fears. The big black spun round, stopping Speed cold by laying the business end of the sledgehammer against Speed's shoulder. Doty's voice sounded from behind.

'There's a man that's got some business with you.'

The black jarred the hammer into Speed's shoulder, the blow nearly breaking it.

'Nobody wants any trouble,' Doty continued. 'Just pay your debts. Okay?'

At that the black simply lifted the sledgehammer, and once more sent it smashing into the car. Then he tossed it aside, and rejoining Doty, moved away into the shadows.

Speed stared at his car, feeling wretched and heartbroken. He'd have trouble cutting such a smart figure now. That was a real mean thing to do to a man just for a bad debt. There was only one thing worse that they could do, and he knew they'd do it if he didn't pay up.

'Speed?'

Suddenly on hearing Gayleen's voice he felt worse. She'll love it, he thought, delight in seeing my wheels cut from under me like this.

'What's going on down there?' she wanted to know.

He looked up as she appeared on the terrace above. She was wearing just a robe, her provocative figure outlined against the light from the room behind. If he hadn't felt so beaten, Speed told himself, he might have given her the goods tonight.

'What was all that racket?'

When she saw it her face fell; the car had after all been her ticket out of town too. She watched the man vanish into the house, moving like a man of ninety. She stared down again at the wrecked Buick. Now Speed was really a beaten man, and she figured he had next to nothing to offer her. She turned back inside as he slammed into the apartment.

'So now what are you going to do, hot-shot?'

'I'm saving my life that's what I'm doing.'

He strode through the apartment and into the littered kitchen. He took down the stone cookie jar. It contained Speed's last shot, his very last. He was going to play it tonight, for one way or the other after that it wouldn't much matter.

Gayleen attempted to stop him. 'Speed.'

He looked over at her where she stood in the doorway. She was serious, not even bitching.

'You know what we said.'

'I know what you said, Gayleen.'

'When it gets to the cookie jar we start a different game.'

'Winding up with a broken back is no game I want to stay in, Sugarplum. Jesus, they'll finish me.'

'So we split.'

Ignoring her he reached in for the five twenty-dollar bills. Being a gambler whose luck had frequently been down it was amazing the hundred dollars had stayed intact. But he had never been this low and with such a threat hanging over him.

'That's what we agreed,' Gayleen screamed angrily. 'Do you think I'd a hung round here with a lousy tin-horn gambler without cab-fare out?'

That did it. Speed would knock her teeth down her throat. When he tried to free his hand from the jar he found it had jammed. He shook it and the jar came loose and crashed to the floor.

'That's it you smash up the place now.'

'Jesus. Why don't you shut it and get this place cleared up?' He stuffed the five twenties into his pocket with the other scratch he had and started out.

'Speed it's good-bye then.'

He turned furiously. 'Gayleen, I'm going to a crap game. You can just do what you damn well like, Sugarplum.'

Gayleen sighed wearily as her big gambling man crashed out of the apartment. She knew she ought to quit, but at that time of night and without money, and when she was ready for bed anyway.

The black might have wrecked the Buick's body, but Speed figured the engine was still good. He wrenched open the buckled door, and had to slam it to shut it again. The motor started first time, and with a bit of creaking and clattering the car blazed away down the street.

Crap games in New Orleans sometimes floated for weeks, and in order to keep officially one jump ahead of the police, the same game sometimes switched venues, the cops themselves warning whoever ran the game when it was time to move; the bar fronts were the only things to really change, for one back room of a bar looked much the same as another. The Mississippi Negroes, who quickly picked up the game after Bernard de Marigney brought it to America, played on street corners, and when the police swooped them for real, crouched with money in their hands and on the pavement, the dice were rarely found. They used very small dice which they would swallow.

The way Speed was tonight, spending his last scratch in the world, any kind of hassle from the police was the last consideration he had; he hadn't the time to go beyond the city limits to Jefferson or St Bernard Parishes. There was a game out back of Gordon's pool hall over on North Rampart, that would be the richest game and the nearest.

It was a fast game. Money was bet and won and lost on those rolling almost before you could blink, certainly as fast as the shooter's hand could move. Speed figured the pace was going to get even faster once he got the dice. This low down, you had to start back with a winning streak, that was the way he saw it.

'Hold on, friend,' he shouted. 'Got a wad and a hot hand, so hot it'll brand you.'

'Screw you,' the present shooter said.

Voices came from all around, the man running the game never missing one of them.

'Right.'

'Nine. Nine gets me a point.'

The crowd pressed in around the table, placing bets on the pass line. Speed elbowed his way in amidst protests. The excitement generated by the crowd soon began to affect him, and he could feel himself getting shaky.

'Check these fingers,' he invited. 'Secret to my love life!'

'Somebody throw water on him. Hose him down.'

'Gimme those goddamn dice.'

Speed could feel it now like that brief, precipitous moment before orgasm. This was the way it always happened. Luck taking you like a charge. His heart started thrashing in his ribcage, he couldn't keep his fingers still; he had to throw those dice; Luck was streaking through him seeking some form of release. He grabbed up the cubes and slapped everything he had left in the world down on the passline. He rolled out the dice almost as an anticlimax.

'Read 'em and weep.'

He smashed his hands together as he saw he'd won on a natural. He collected his money, left it to ride, and scooped up the dice again as they came back down the table to him.

'Are they hot.'

He tossed them around so fast they might have actually been burning his hand. Then he let them out.

'I'm really on fire.'

He scored again, and just left his money riding. There wasn't a thought in Speed's head at that moment but those for the game, he was concentrating all his energy on what he wanted those dice to do for him. And they did it time and again.

'Roll that up and smoke it,' he shouted as he threw the dice. He won again.

'Crap out,' a man called.

At that moment as Speed took up the dice he got a flash in his inner eye. As a result he pulled back most of his winnings. This was going to be an off-throw. Sure enough when he rolled he crapped-out. That was how it was with Speed and that was how it was going to stay, his never doing a thing wrong. He had enough now to get Le Beau off his back. But Le Beau wasn't in his thoughts then, and something told him that this was the long run, anyway he put everything down on the line, and started shaking. He threw.

'Shake.'

He won on a nine.

'Nine points, goddamn.'

He took up the dice again.

'Shake, shake! Christ died for our sins.'

Again he won. Now smiles were breaking across his face

like a man reprieved from the chair after his head and leg had been shaved. He wore the shine of a winner and knew it. He collected his money and just let it ride on up.

'Stand back.'

He threw again.

'Pay me, hot-shot.'

'Hey, boy, let a real shooter put his hands on the cubes,' a fat man said, barging in.

'Kiss my ass.'

Speed let all those green backs ride again, and began clicking the dice, oblivious now to everything except the energy he had running into the dice.

'What you thought was a pigeon turned out to be an eagle.' He let the dice out.

'Four's point. Four gets me more.'

Seeing was believing, but even so the run Speed was having wanted some believing. Everyone was concentrating on those white cubes, and no one paid any attention to the would be shooter who now stood in the doorway.

There was rarely any police problems for white gamblers in New Orleans, even though the pursuits weren't strictly legal. Problems only arose if and when the police chief was getting it from the boys uptown, and so gave it to his precinct captains, or when a new detective arrived at the precinct and felt it necessary to establish both his presence and his prices on the gravy train.

Micky Mulligan was one such detective. His voice boomed from the doorway, 'Gentlemen, just hold everything right where it is.'

Five uniformed cops followed the detective quickly into the room. The crowd started up in familiar protest. Speed was rolling, not knowing and not caring what was going on, until the detective stepped right in beside him.

'Everyone stay calm, and we won't have no friction,' Mulligan said.

'What's going on here?' Speed demanded. 'I'm rolling for a point.'

'You were, Pat,' the detective said. 'But we don't like unreported games.'

Suddenly before Speed's eyes one of New Orleans finest began sweeping the money off the table and into a cloth bag.

'Listen. Jesus, listen.' Panic racing through him. 'I got my life on that table.' He pleaded, 'It's mine. Goddamn it, mine.'

'Was yours,' the bluecoat informed him.

'Still is.' Speed grabbed for the cloth bag.

'Get out of my way,' the cop said reasonably. They didn't want to bust anyone, they just wanted themselves a piece of jack.

'Asshole.'

All maxims for safe existence thrown to the wind now, Speed let the cop have one in the guts, then a good one on the jaw. He grabbed the money and ran, but two of the other cops ran faster. One of them got him from behind with his billystick right between the shoulder blades. Speed floundered forward and hit the door. The two cops picked him up, relieving him of their money. The detective walked over to him, irritated by this unnecessary complication.

'You just won yourself a little vacation,' Mulligan said. 'Take him away.'

Had he the money to piece the cops off there would have been no problem, but they had all his money, only didn't appreciate it when he pointed it out to them. Speed was ashamed to admit it even to himself but he cried in the van on the way to the station house. He'd tried his goddamnest, and this was all he got in return. He had no one and nothing, and that was after he'd spent his life trying to help people like Poe, Chaney and the hundred other ham and eggers before him, who without him would have been nothing. All he had now for his trouble was a well of self-pity and a ride in a paddy wagon. There had to be someone whom he could turn to and have them spring bail for him, but he couldn't come up with anyone other than Poe or Chaney. Poe would be doped up and away on his cloud at this time of night, and Chaney wouldn't stand for anyone putting on him. And Gayleen, well she just wouldn't cut it, even if she was still around. So Speed guessed he would have to accept yet another losing streak. There was nothing else he could do except spend a short vacation in the city jail and wait for the winning streak to come through again.

Although Speed didn't know it then, his next winning streak was a long way off. But for him Chaney knew Speed would still be running with small-time hitters who couldn't stay on their feet long enough to see their opponents. Chaney had been his meal ticket, had brought him what he seemed to consider was a small fortune. It had been Chaney who had wanted it, had determined it and had brought about the result. Speed had been useful, that was all, and when he'd served his use, Chaney would let him go. Then he'd find himself back on that familiar losing streak. Chaney hoped that that wouldn't be the way of it, for he had a kind of nice feeling for Speed, but sadly that was a fact of life.

The time was closer than he thought. Chaney was getting restless right now. That corporal splitting his cheekbone had served as a warning, and he was taking note of it. Stop, stand still, accept a pattern and you increased the danger of getting hurt. Having been warned, Chaney was all eyes for the signals which told him things were coming to a close.

He noticed it in Lucy. Maybe he was feeling too sensitive, and shouldn't have visited her of all people so soon after the fight with the corporal. But he did.

He stopped by, and she took him in, she had no option. He didn't want to speak, but just wanted to make love, rest a spell. And afterward he still had nothing to say. The woman had fulfilled his needs, and he hoped in that respect he had fulfilled hers.

Just lying there, watching the junebugs on the night outside the window, and listening to a radio playing out a haunting piano rag on a porch somewhere nearby, his thoughts drifted back to Georgia and his piece of land. His cotton would have been ripening by now, assuming he had got his loan from the bank to buy his seed and guano. He cut the thoughts abruptly.

Seeing his head jerk like that, Lucy knew what it was, but not why it happened, and figured the man wasn't about to impart those thoughts. She considered him now like this. His secret thoughts said all there was to say about their relationship. It was nice to be needed by him sometimes, particularly when he was hurt. But sometimes wasn't all times, and she had to live all of the time. She reached a hand to his unmoving face and touched his healing cut. There was curiosity in her gesture.

Gently, but firmly, Chaney pushed her hand away. He couldn't give himself over to Lucy like that. It wasn't what he needed her for anyway, and he figured if he let her play that part, she in turn would expect more from him. He didn't like being taken care of in that way. He had few reservations about letting Poe handle him, then he knew that Poe accepted what he was doing for ten percent of the take, he wasn't going to make demands on him afterward. It was fine knowing that. So long as there was distance between them some kind of relationship was possible, and perhaps affection too.

'You ever get scared when you fight?' Lucy asked, considering the cut cheek. 'You know, ahead of time?'

'I never think about it.'

Lucy looked askance at him, and thought perhaps he was never scared before a fight, but he was about entering into any kind of relationship. She'd worked hard getting him this far, but she doubted she was going to have any further success.

'The only thing you care about is the money,' she said obligingly. 'Isn't that right? Just so the money's good.'

He didn't answer. Her tone, plus her agitation told him something was eating her, something about herself, and she was throwing her shit on him.

'I'll tell you what I think,' she said. 'I think you like it. Standing out there in the middle and everything coming down on you. I think you love it.'

She paused. She believed what she'd said. Sometime in the past he'd been hurt, any meathead could figure that one; so now he spends all his time setting himself up against getting hurt again, refusing to play the game of living by anyone else's set of rules. His whole life was a set-up, he never risked anything to chance; the last thing he was was a gambler, all chance had long been eliminated from his life. Things came around just as he worked them, and he said, there, that's life. But it wasn't in any one way, and nor did it have to be, Lucy knew that.

'You love it, don't you?' she said. 'Standing up there.'

Chaney held her look for a moment. If she tried getting any closer he would have to cut her right out.

'You got any more questions?' he asked.

She paused. She should have known better than ask something about that what went on beyond here and now. Suddenly she smiled.

'Try this one,' she said. 'Are you going to stay the night?'

'Not tonight.'

She shrugged a little disappointedly, despite herself. She

sensed a stirring, restlessness in the man.

'I don't know why I ask,' Lucy said. 'You never do.'

Chaney sat up, leaned his elbow on the pillow, and his face in his hand. 'Does it matter?'

'Sometimes.' Lucy said.

But it wasn't just stopping over the night. It was everything about this goddamn relationship and the way it held her down. The waiting and wondering when he would show next. She felt like she was nowhere and her face showed it.

Recognizing the look he had seen on the faces of other women in other bedrooms in other cities, Chaney gave a truculent sigh.

'All right, get it out,' he said. 'What's eating you?'

Lucy knew she had forced this moment, knew she had been compelled to, but still she regretted it. She waited a second, then sat upright in the bed.

'All right,' she said. 'Hell, yes. Something is wrong. A lot of things. The rent. Price of groceries. Clothes I can't buy. A few items like that.'

It always came round to this. He knew why, of course, yet still he let it surprise him. 'How much do you need?' he said.

'I don't want any more of your money. I want my money, and not the lousy nine dollars a week I make at the Horse Shoe Pickle Works.'

'You'll catch on somewhere.'

'You ever read a newspaper? Things are tough.'

Chaney slumped back in the pillow. He couldn't buy her off. She wanted that one thing he couldn't give her, that he knew he daren't give her. There had been moments though when he would like to have committed, like to have stopped. But he was going to have to get going soon.

'And maybe I don't feel like bottling pickles any more,' Lucy went on. 'I want something with some life in it.'

Chaney swung out of bed. He began dressing, listening to the woman behind him, but not allowing her words to reach in at him. If he lowered his guard for a moment they would get through with as much effect as that soldier's blow that had cut his cheek.

'The way things are now nothing connects. Like you. You don't connect to any other part of the way I live. Nothing does. Everything's in separate closets.'

Shoving his shirt in his trousers, Chaney said, 'Things are better that way. Keeps them simple. You get less edges showing.'

'That's only good if you're on top of things. As soon as I get on the street with everybody else I get moved around. I don't like that.'

Chaney picked up his coat and reached into his pocket for some money. He proffered it, felt she ought to have it.

'Take some.'

She pushed it away. 'I told you. I want my own. I don't want to depend on you. You're not reliable. God only knows the next time I'll even see you. You come when you want, go when you want, and never mention what comes inbetween.'

'Lucy, there are no inbetweens. There never were, there never will be. That's the way it has to be.'

That was as open as Chaney had been with her, as close as he had come to an emotional outburst, but she didn't yield.

'Suit yourself,' Chaney said and withdrew the money he had offered.

Putting on his jacket, Chaney stood looking down at the woman. He knew what she was asking, recognized the ultimatum she was giving him. It didn't make any difference.

'I'll see you around,' he said.

He turned and walked out, down the stairs, through the apartment house door, across the porch and away along the street.

Lucy listened to his departure, and when she could hear him no more she cried.

SEVENTEEN

Chaney awoke late and alone in his own room, and undisturbed about either aspect. There was nothing so sweet as waking alone and free. A man tethered by a job and relationships and obligations, that wasn't any life. He thought briefly about that and didn't know that he believed it anymore, he wasn't too sure that he had believed it at all over the past six years. But he told himself it just the same.

Rising slowly, Chaney stretched and eased the stiffness out of his shoulders. The times were gone now when he didn't wake up stiff. The cat was sitting on the table watching him. He reached out and touched it with the palm of his hand. The cat purred and nuzzled against his hand, looking for a little affection. Sometimes he still wondered about why he'd picked the thing up. Perhaps it indicated some spark of hope in his unyielding makeup, for having it here gave him a strange pleasure. Maybe it was just a defect in his personality. He pushed away the thought and flicked the cat off the table.

From beneath the pillow he took his canvas money belt and began buckling it on. It held nearly eight thousand, he didn't need to count it again to reassure himself about that. He felt pretty good with all that strapped around him. A fat roll and a future wide open was really something; but having the money and not having anyone to spend it on was something else. Alma popped in his head. He would have liked to spend the money with her.

There was no inherent satisfaction in money alone, he reflected, but he felt a kind of satisfaction as he pulled his shirt on over his belt. He'd been down and had got up again, and he had done it all by himself. That was satisfying. He hadn't asked for help from anyone, nor had he expected it. He had made his roll clean, had remained untouched.

From his window he looked out on the street. It was the same littered, run-down, paint-peeling, shutter-broken place it was each morning he looked out. But today he suddenly felt a bit weary of those same beaten and hollowed out lives before him. Next he'd be taking up a collection for them.

Money was bringing Chaney habits he ordinarily got on fine without. Breakfast was one of them. He had got in the way of walking up Decatur to the French market, buying a paper and sitting reading it in Molly's over a breakfast of freshly baked doughnuts and black coffee.

As Chaney reached the bottom of the stairs Poe crashed through the doorway of the room-house. Chaney wondered if he was doped up. His face was a little sallow and he guessed he had been shooting, but he didn't have that slow, dull-eyed look this morning.

'Join me for some breakfast, Poe?' he invited.

He wondered why he took to Poe as he did. Possibly it was because in his situation he recognized what his wife might have gone through, and Poe made the process appear almost bearable. If it was, then it was something he would never have admitted to Poe.

'Breakfast,' Poe said, like the word reminded him of that normal world which he had long since learned to get by without participating in. 'I'm sorry but I'm due for my medicine quite soon.'

His hands trembled slightly and he pulled his linen jacket straight as if rustling up a little dignity that had gone missing, then got in step down the street with Chaney.

'The reason for my call is our old friend, Speed,' he said. 'He was playing crap and the game was raided. In his defense I suppose it can be said that the fearful uncertainties of the gambler's pursuit, plus the excitement and strain generated during play, do tend to produce high passions. Against him the plain fact must be stated, he socked one of New Orleans finest.'

Chaney sighed, but Poe hadn't finished.

'Rage hits gamblers hard. The gamblers stage is littered with wreckage of such fury, broken men, suicides and murdered men. The New Orleans Police Dept. alas do not take such a wide-ranging view. Speed too could be said to be more than a little short-sighted in his move.'

'Well, Poe,' Chaney said, 'I'm out of the game for a couple of weeks anyway. Might teach him to take a wide-ranging view. How long is he down for?'

'Ten days,' Poe said as they turned into Decatur. 'Then he's back on the boulevard.' Barrels of molasses were being unloaded over on the river and the rich green smell drifted across to them. Chaney was thinking about prison and the lack of options it gave a person, even the lack of smells.

'For once they say he was winning,' Poe added reflectively.

'Game had gone on long enough,' Chaney said, 'he'd have lost it back.'

'Do you plan on visiting our mutual friend during his stay at the big hotel?'

'Jails bother me,' Chaney said. 'Make me nervous.'

'A reasonable attitude.'

Poe himself had taken a few weeks behind the bars. In some ways Chaney and he had a lot in common, each had one big, driving need, though very different for all that.

'Speed does ask a favor.'

Chaney glanced at him.

'Lovely and mellow Gayleen,' Poe said. 'He would like us to take her out for an evening or two. He's afraid she'll get bored.'

They reached the veranda-covered sidewalk, the sudden chill of the morning caused Poe to shiver.

'It would seem that Speed has run afoul of the fates and furies once more.'

'You think that?'

'I take it you have another view.'

Chaney paused to pick up a newspaper, and smiled as they moved on. 'People make their own luck,' he said.

Poe frowned characteristically. 'There is a certain lack of charity in that opinion.'

Chaney stopped and regarded the man as they reached Molly's. He guessed he had a lot of feeling for Speed, and fleetingly he envied him that ability.

'Come and have breakfast.'

'I must keep my appointment. My thanks anyway.'

Chaney nodded, watched him turn and straighten his jacket as he walked away, then turned in for his breakfast.

He sat hunched at the bar, three plain doughnuts and a cup of steaming coffee before him, his newspaper unopened. He was thinking about what Poe had said. He didn't owe Speed anything, and if he did visit him, then if he was ever caught and thrown in the slams, always assuming they didn't hang him, then he too might come to expect a visitor. That would open him up, make him vulnerable; that was just something you couldn't be and go on surviving, least of all in prison. Anyway, jails, like police stations, held an inherent danger for Chaney. So Chaney wouldn't show at the jail. He didn't feel obligated to cheering up Speed and couldn't put himself out on a limb like that. Nor to entertain his girl, and Gayleen had certainly got nothing on him. Speed had chosen her, and if she got bored and went prowling for someone else, then that was between her and him. Despite what he said he figured Poe understood about people making their own luck, and in some ways agreed. The only reason Poe didn't try it as an effective philosophy was that he had nothing to gain by doing so; he could afford to be soft and let go, for he had already lost himself to dope and it almost didn't matter anymore.

Chaney hadn't lost himself, not to dope, and he wasn't going to lose himself to anybody either. He didn't think he'd go along with the favor to Speed and take Gayleen out, not because it was too much to ask, but because he didn't figure he'd be around.

Why he was when Poe stopped by two nights later, Chaney told himself, he didn't know. He knew, it was just that he wasn't ever going to admit it to himself.

Having spent eighty-nine cents on a fifth of the best, Chaney was holed up in his room drinking and watching the cat attempt to catch the flies which hovered over the sugar he'd placed down on newspaper. He heard the Buick's horn sound out in the street, and rose to the window. Poe stood looking up. Gayleen, out to catch a big fish, sat in the driving seat.

'Would you care to join us in the ancient sport of Orleanians?' Poe called up. 'That is to say cockfighting. Not the lady's choice.' Raising the volume of his normally quiet voice had caused him to break into a sudden fit of coughing.

Chaney watched his small, pain-racked frame for a moment, then nodded.

'I'll be down.'

Gayleen with a secret smile on her face, drove them out on State Highway on to the Four Horsemen Pit over in St Bernard just below Menefee airport. She might have been taking them out for an entertainment. Poe sat beside her, and Chaney in the back, where she continually gave him little knowing glances through the driving mirror. Chaney played it dumb. It was the best way to handle a bitch in heat, like Gayleen.

The cockpit was a rusting corrugated metal enclosure, with wooden tiers ranking up around the dirt-packed stage which was about twenty feet in diameter. Like most spectator sports in Louisiana, this one admitted coloreds, and they were there in equal numbers with whites, Creoles, Mustees, all shouting, urging their bird on. The pit was packed and Poe, Gayleen and Chaney had a problem getting a seat; the crowd down in the bullpen area where all the betting was going on was even more crowded, and activity became furious as two of the promoters came out onto the stage and held up the two fighting cocks, each heeled with vicious looking two-inch spurs.

Poe very much to business distributed programs. 'Not a very gentlemanly sport, I confess, but I will pass on the acumen of my knowledge before each fight,' he said. 'I have a brief appointment to keep a little later.'

They identified the match number and Poe struggled through the crush and got a bet down for himself and Gayleen. Chaney demurred.

The cockpit was scratched up and bloodstained from the four fights that had already taken place. The betting done, the two handlers let the birds meet each other still tightly held in their strong black hands. The cocks pecked away angrily at each other, were withdrawn, then set down opposite each other and the handlers quickly got out of the way.

'You must remember,' Poe said, 'these cocks and I have an affinity. I am afraid many of them are wide open to doping.'

Neither Gayleen nor Chaney were listening, but watched as the two fighting birds flew up at each other, clawing, pecking and squawking like they knew only one was going to walk away and walk away badly injured. Each cock made flurries across the other, going for it in the saddle, back and cape with its spurs, came round and went for each other's eyes. One was swiftly blinded, its eyes just round bloody holes where its opponents beak went in. The cock fought gamely on as the other moved in for the kill.

This was a short fight and relatively bloodless. Other fights ranged around the entire pit, the birds refusing to die despite the bloody mess they were in.

The gamecock that was left proudly strutting around the pit was not the one Poe and Gayleen had put their money on.

'Speedy, baby,' Gayleen said, tearing up her ticket, 'you'll be real proud of us boy.'

Poe looked philosophical. 'That fowl seemed to suffer from the distinct impression that he was broiling hen,' Poe said.

'You can say that again, brother,' a tall, lean, reverent-looking man in a black hat, frockcoat and string tie standing near them said.

'I don't know why we came anyway,' Gayleen said, already dispirited not to have won something. 'I don't care too much about those poor little chickens fighting like that.'

Poe frowned at her. He would rather have been somewhere else. Sunday evening offered a whole host of interesting religions. But he had business to attend to and had chosen neither the time nor the place. 'Consider the exhilarating night air, the spectacular forays of competing cocks; a spectacle that both delights and disgusts the finer senses of the beholder. And sometimes his pocket book.' Glancing toward the tunnel that led to the men's-room, Poe saw the party he was expecting to contact. 'I have a small transaction to make. If you will excuse me for a few moments.'

He started up through the tiers toward the tunnel.

'Bring me a beer,' Gayleen called.

'Of course, my darling.'

Chaney watched him disappear, figuring what he was going for and that he wouldn't be back. He turned to Gayleen studying the scratch sheet.

'You going to bet this fight?' she said.

Without looking at her Chaney shook his head. 'I don't bet on anything I can't control.'

Gayleen watched him studying the cocks being held up for inspection down on the stage. That simple, he wasn't a gambler, the essential difference between he and Speed. Jesus, she thought in answer to the soft yearning she had, if Speed had only half as much as this guy going for him.

'You don't like gambling?' she said. 'Then why are you here?'

She smiled, clearly seeing a reason for his being here, and one she liked better.

'Poe asked me,' he said. 'I like the blind courage of those cocks.'

Gayleen slapped the fight program against her palm, annoyed

that having put out an invitation to him, he wasn't even trying for a chance with her.

'You don't gamble and you don't say much. So what do you do?' she demanded to know.

Chaney simply let her remarks slide harmlessly past him like the wild blows thrown by an inexperienced hitter. 'Just take things easy,' he said. 'Smooth and soft.'

What Gayleen couldn't accept after having Speed around needing her for so long was that Chaney, a man like any other man, didn't need her, not one little bit.

'How about women?' she asked.

He shrugged. 'When they're necessary.'

Gayleen saw a chance. 'How often's that?'

Chaney blocked it. 'Now and then.'

The fight went on, Gayleen throwing punches, most of them ill thought out. Everytime she came anything like close he blocked her. If she continued, then quite soon he would weary of the game and have to knock her out.

She moved in again, not exactly a dangerous shot. 'Speed says you live in a dump.'

'He's right.'

'You can afford to move.'

A smile wrinkled in Chaney's brain. When you didn't need anything people always resented it and tried to put some need on you; then subsequently tried using it against you.

'I like it there,' he said, and looked back to the cocks being set against each other.

'You got a way of carrying on conversation that ends conversation. You know that?' Gayleen said, like a hitter accepting defeat.

Chaney didn't reply. Gayleen gave up and turned back to the cockfight. At least she could understand that.

The two gamecocks came at each other, neither giving any quarter. The squawks as blood and feathers flew lost in the roar of the spectators.

It was another short one. The losing cock lying bleeding and twitching for a few moments before the handler came out and threw a sack over it.

'Maybe Poe's right,' Gayleen said. 'That one hadda be doped to come on like that.' She tore up another ticket. There was a ten-minute delay before the next fight.

'I'll get your beer,' Chaney said, getting up.

'Poe's doing it.'

'I don't think he'll be back.'

Down in the wet and reeking men's-room below the stands Poe washed and dried his hands like a surgeon about to operate. Then, looking casually around to check that he wasn't being watched, he removed a crumpled carnation from his pocket and put it in his lapel. He took out what he had left of the ten percent he earned from tending to Chaney and rolled it into a ball, pressing it tightly in the palm of his hand. He walked out of the restroom.

At the top of the concrete stairs to the stand he spotted his man, who also wore a carnation. Poe looked up at him, briefly meeting his nervous, fleeting eyes. The man moved around the tunnel at the back of the stand and casually made for a drinking fountain. Having taken a sip of water, he came back along the tunnel toward the stairs meeting Poe, ascending halfway. They greeted each other openly and with a brisk handshake. In the process Poe parted with his money; then continued along to the drinking fountain. As he bent for a drink, his hand reached under the porcelain bowl and felt the small bag that had been taped there. He pulled it loose, then, as casually as he could with his trembling hand he slipped it in his pocket as he straightened up. With the packet safely in his pocket, Poe was already feeling better than he had all day. The pains in his chest had been troubling him, but now he would see them off with a little white powder, just as the doctor ordered. He didn't go back to the others, but cleared the pit and picked up a cab and headed straight for hope-city.

Back on the rail, Gayleen accepted a beer from Chaney and together they watched the rest of the races. Gayleen having been beaten in a few rounds let up some and didn't do too much bitching the rest of the evening.

But traveling back across town to Chaney's rooming house, Gayleen wasn't about to give up on this guy, and put herself out on a limb again. She put herself out so far that Chaney had to knock her down.

They pulled up outside the crumbling wooden building and Chaney reached for the door handle. Gayleen stared at him and waited for any move he chose to make with her.

There were a lot of noises on the air of the close summer's

night, it was as if the heat was acting like a lid and keeping them down and bouncing around. The spasm band was off somewhere playing their odd, disjointed music. Chaney thought on what someone had said about this southern humidity, that the only sane thing to do in it was to make love. And he thought about the woman sitting next to him. Then he thought about the blue-black sky and the kind of day it promised for tomorrow. And Monday was always a pretty good day to get back on the road.

'So take care of yourself,' he said to Gayleen.

'You know,' she said, pursing her lips, 'I could come up and have a drink. Relax a little.'

Chaney's hand stayed on the door handle. He regarded her passively for a moment. She really wanted to get inside him, and probably for no other reason except that once inside she would have a kind of power over him. She saw a sign saying private, but couldn't accept it. Maybe it was because she had no respect herself, and having laid herself open, wanted the same from everyone else she met.

'I figure I have to ask since you won't.' Her look was defiant, challenging.

But her asking did her no good. Chaney didn't make relationships or friendships for himself, but if he did he would have some idea about how they should be run. And Gayleen with her foot on his balls wasn't it.

'You got Speed down to about three foot tall most of the time,' he said. 'Now you want to take him all the way down.'

She had little defense.

'You think I like it?' she asked, like there was no alternative. 'You think it's easy being a bitch?'

'Seems to come pretty natural.'

'I don't owe him nothing.' She went on, 'Things get tight and he turns me over sideways to get a hundred dollars. I'm just arm decoration for his friends to look at.'

Having set herself up, now she was pitying herself. Maybe she thought she'd moved Chaney sufficiently to put herself right on the line. She leaned over, and put her hand alongside Chaney's face, and wished she had the courage to make it his crutch.

'And rain or shine, with him I only get it once a month.'

For a second Chaney left her suspended on the limb, then a

sardonic smile curled his lip.

'Well,' he said, 'you only got six more days to wait.'

Forcing open the damaged door, he stepped out to the sidewalk.

'Good night, Gayleen.'

'Bastard.'

He slammed the door and she just sat there, furious, exasperated. She told herself she'd hang around New Orleans solely to crack that dumb hitter. But now it was finished, with Speed and the whole stinking scene. She was going to make the break, there was no sense in hanging around. Sure, Speedy needed her but that wasn't reason enough for needs. She'd say good-bye to Mr High-Roller, and maybe find some way of getting even with his big dumb hitter, then blow.

EIGHTEEN

Having packed all there was of hers to pack in the apartment – there was nothing of Speed's of value or she might have taken that – she was all set to go. But standing there by the door with her things in one cardboard valise and one grip and a string bag, she looked around the apartment for the last time as if looking for something to delay her now.

Three years was a long time to be with someone. It was time enough to get attached and used to a person's ways, and time enough to get pissed off and want to move on. Sure they'd had some swell times together, especially in those early days when he'd always called her Sugarplum and screwed her half to death. But where were they going lately? No place and fast, that was where. Speedy was a gambler and forever in the grip of the wheel of fortune, and however often it came to rest with the needle pointing to the good times, just as sure as could be the arrow would zero in as often on the bad times. Gayleen was sick of those highs and lows; the inbetweens didn't make up for the difference, so she was cutting the cords of her bondage and setting out alone. For a while she intended to stay loose, trying to keep her options open. Maybe it wouldn't work, maybe the pattern of life she had been locked into here would simply follow her down to Miami, where she would find another Speed. But for a while anyway she was going to try and change things. She didn't figure she owed Speed much for whatever they'd done between them, they'd done because they both wanted it. Sure he'd taken a lot of her shit, but she knew that he had liked taking it, just as in the beginning she had liked his continually going up and down. But enough was enough.

She looked across the apartment to the kitchen shelf where the cookie jar had been. It was no longer, no more than the hundred dollars they held for the emergency. Had the money been there she liked to think that she would have split it with Speed, but didn't feel that way about the few dollars she had by her now. Without her helping a couple of tears came up and rolled out of her eyes. They were tears for what might have been, also for the times that had been.

She quickly dried her eyes on her handkerchief; hefted her baggage and was on her way.

Before she left the city there was still a couple of things she had to do, and both could be done at the same time. Her mean spirit told her she had to try and sink Chaney. Somehow she was going to bring him down. Why the hell should he be so cool and detached and uncaring when her life and everyone else's was in such goddamn chaos? She was going to get right back at him and knew just how to do it. It involved Speedy, and would doubtless come a bit hard on him, but that was the price. Anyway, he deserved it, she concluded, for the number of nights he'd gone soft on her, or had preferred poker to her.

Leaving the beaten up Buick outside the apartment, she took a cab up to the bus station on Canal Street. She deposited her bags, checked what time the Teche-Greyhound left for Miami then took another cab over to the city jail.

The look Gayleen got from the guard who saw her into the visiting pen made her feel pretty good.

The place was bleak, barred, locked, a steel grille dividing the room with either side separated off into cribs; cigarette butts on the floor, whitewash on the walls; the smell and clangor of an institution. Here Gayleen got a vision of Speed's future. She was right in getting out.

Speed appeared, looking as awful as his surroundings, she thought. His mood wasn't too good either. Probably losing too many matchsticks at poker.

'Maybe I should have brought a file,' she said, as Speed sat in the crib on the opposite side of the wire.

Speed was in no mood for jokes. 'Real funny,' he said. 'You're a little late, I get out of here tomorrow.'

Speed had no smiles, not for Gayleen or anyone else. The smile familiar to the old spirit would have looked ridiculous in a jail outfit, and with his beautiful silver hair shorn like a criminal's. He didn't like himself like this, there was so very little protection from oneself in prison, there all the layers were stripped away. He liked stepping into twenty-five dollar suits, shielding himself from the mundane of the drabness that was life without chance. He liked hoping and gambling and hoping, that was his salvation. Here he was thrown in on himself and made to feel inadequate. Prison was like a mirror he was forced to look into, and he took a poor view of the reflection he saw there. And because he took a poor view, he figured everyone else did also, Gayleen included. He didn't really expect much from her, but goddamn it, he had counted on better than this, her breezing in here like a ten-dollar doxie. But in spite of himself, seeing her here like this he found himself with a yearning for the woman like he hadn't felt in a long while. He wanted to reach out and touch her, hold her; all he could do was put his hands on the grille, and even that wasn't allowed. But she didn't reach out and touch his fingers.

'How you doing, Speedy?' she said.

'Terrific,' he replied. 'Lots of laughs around here. How about you?'

'Pining away.'

'Sure.'

This was the usual pattern of conversation, and it was played like a piece of bad music. But Speed didn't want it this morning, he wanted to add different notes, sweeter notes.

'Isn't that what you want to hear?' she said. 'Sitting around knitting, waiting for my baby.'

Speed tried ignoring the hostility and reverted to the old rhythms. Goddamn it in this place he needed to know his old world was still secure.

'Must make for long nights,' he said, and instantly regretted the words. Then tried in a lighter vein. 'What you been doing for fun?'

Gayleen smiled and let him have it. 'Chaney,' she said simply, and went on smiling.

Sounds of the prison echoed through their silence. Speed was struggling up from the blow, trying to get some air into his lungs in order to speak, but couldn't.

'Oh, I thought you asked,' she said.

Still Speed couldn't speak or move, but just sat there frozen. Gayleen didn't want his hurt on her; so she closed the book on them.

'Look, it's adios baby,' she said, 'I'm going down to Miami. Thanks for all the good times.' She stood up ready to go. 'Oh, I left you the wreck of a Buick.' She shrugged. 'You know I never did get a driving license.'

She turned and walked out, her heels clacking against the stone floor. Seeing her vanishing, Speed's deep freeze thawed and suddenly he was boiling. He shot to his feet and started yelling after her, and punched the grille.

'You bitch! Bitch. You goddamn bitch.'

Gayleen kept on walking, letting him know this time it was for keeps. And Speed kept on yelling until a couple of guards dragged him down and off back to his cell.

Speed was sunk, his very last shot had crapped out on him. Maybe now was the time for suicide, Russian Roulette; that was the way the really high-rollers went, out like a light.

However, he had something else now, a feeling that he'd never known before, a feeling that was holding him in the world of the living and would go on holding him there, at least till he got out. It was anger, blood boiling anger. And it was directed against that no good son-of-a-bitch, piss-ant hitter of his. It wasn't simply that he objected to Chaney screwing his woman, but the way in which he would have done it, and the fact that he didn't need it; the goddamn fact that something which had meant so much to him was taken away and laid just for the kicks. He would have taken her with about the same casual satisfaction with which he took a shot of Wild Turkey, or sent down another hitter.

There were no rules and maxims for living now, not when he had this kind of anger in him. Speed was determined to bust Chaney, as strong as the man was. He'd be out of here tomorrow, and then straight way he was going to cut loose on Chaney.

When he got out and was dressed again in his sharp suit and two-tones, Speed still felt like a con. He would like to have spent the loose change he had in his pocket on a cab back to his place, if only to lift his image slightly, but he resisted and took the streetcar instead. He got his lift when he saw the beaten-up Buick waiting for him outside his apartment.

Up in his apartment he didn't even pause to check whether Gayleen had truly departed, but went straight to the closet. There tucked in the corner and forgotten since those days when he was something of a pool shark was his cue. He wouldn't have had it now if uncle had been prepared to put up anything on it. He unscrewed the two sections and took the thick end only. When he called over at Chaney's place he got no answer, and his immediate thought was that he might have taken off with Gayleen. But the gimp who ran the rooming house informed him that Chaney was still around. So he drove over to where Poe slept. And when he got no joy there started scouring the most likely pin-table saloons where Poe might spend his time. Poe at least had to know where Chaney was.

Maybe it wasn't much of a recommendation for life, Chaney thought, but Poe sure as hell could roll those steel balls. Chaney laid against the bar with a bottle of Jax in his hand and studied Poe's reflection in the glass of the pin-table right alongside him. The little crumpled man was quietly concentrating on crossing the ten thousand line, working like the ace, running up his score.

Chaney was getting to like being with Poe more and more. The man made no demands and yet he was there. He was company, and Chaney just recently had gotten a little bored with himself. The cut on his cheek was nicely healed now and he felt ready to fight again.

Much to his surprise, and a little to his irritation, he had missed having Speed around and looked forward to seeing him later today when he was released. When actually with the man Chaney had been continually on guard against Speed putting some demand on him, yet during his stay in the jail his absence was noticed. Being around him and his high-wire act kind of grew on you, and you come to accept his over-stretched style, and you missed it when it wasn't there.

Catching Poe's glance, like they were sharing some secret, Chaney grinned. Poe was a man who knew how to enjoy himself without people. With a pin-table at his fingertips he never felt better, and right now he was working his punctured arms as though they were as capable as any hitter's. Buzzes were sounding from the machine, and lights were flashing as the score clicked over, points rolling up, and the fins thud-thudding non-stop. He was like a man possessed.

Suddenly he stopped, let the ball roll down, and turned with a big smile. In the scoreboard mirror he'd seen Speed entering the saloon. He held out his arms as Speed came striding down toward them. Chaney looked at him, at his fast, stiff-legged walk, and the hysterical energy he always gave out. Speed was back in shape.

'Old friend.' Poe greeted him.

'Speed.' Chaney said.

He approached the pin-table fast, with a funny smile dancing around his face.

'Always good to see my old friends.'

'An equal pleasure now that you've paid your debt to society,' Poe said.

Speed turned to Chaney. 'How you been?'

'No problems,' he said. Then giving more than he gave to most people. 'Missed seeing you.'

'Just what Gayleen said,' Speed snapped, and thereupon pulled out the top section of the pool cue from under his coat and lunged at Chaney, getting him with a glancing blow across the head with it.

He's gone mad, Poe thought, and jumped him, but proved ineffective. Twisting free Speed took another shot, which Chaney, shaken to hell, received on the shoulder. Speed swung again.

It was the unexpectedness of the attack that damaged Chaney, not the blows themselves. Now he was ready and slid round the third blow, which shattered the glass of the pinball machine.

The bar keeper shouted in protest.

Poe competed with him. 'Put it down. You're crazy.'

Chaney believed what was going on; this was for real, but he didn't know what it was all about. He just stared with blank hostile eyes, feeling slightly betrayed and now regretting waiting around for Speed.

'Some things I don't put up with,' Speed screamed, then took another swing.

Chaney danced it and came up again. 'Put it down,' he warned.

Speed hung on to the cue. 'I don't give a shit how tough you think you are.'

'Put it away,' Chaney said.

He was holding on to his temper, but Speed was trying him. He held back hoping Speed would come round, but if he didn't he would explode. He didn't want to explode because he was feeling hurt and the explosion would wreck his friend.

'We can talk about it, Speed,' Poe said.

'I don't feel like talking. I'm going to get that son-of-a-bitch!'

Speed swung the cue wildly again. Chaney blocked it on the arc of his left arm, and slid his right through. Speed went down at once and Chaney kicked the cue out of his hand; then lifted him up as though he was no weight at all. Chaney was trembling slightly.

'I don't ever want to see your face again,' he said.

'You and that bitch.' Speed spat the words at him as though believing Chaney was trying to get away with being the injured party.

That suddenly gave Chaney the reason for the whole escapade. Gayleen, that bitch had finally worked into him and brought him out. It had cost him Speed, dumb, believing Speed. He shook his head. His anger vanished. He felt disappointed and despondent.

'Stupid,' he said.

He shoved him back against the counter, where the bartender was whining. The great gambler, Speed, Chaney reflected, he had to be the greatest mug of all men; he'd left himself wide open and fallen for everything, every trick Gayleen, and maybe all women everywhere, had ever worked.

'Stupid,' he said again. Then turned and walked away.

Poe with sunken chest and stooped shoulders turned back to Speed, who remained slumped against the counter.

'I have seen human stupidity before,' he said, 'but that was a masterpiece.'

'I don't need any goddamn lectures,' Speed snapped. He straightened up, adjusting his clothing and rubbing his sore face.

Poe was somewhat incredulous that all this could have happened; a wrecked pin-table before him and the end of the current dope supply. And for what?

'Even if she had done it with Chaney, which is doubtful,' he said, 'it would simply be a case of history repeating itself.'

Speed was short with him. 'Let's skip it, shall we.'

He looked at himself in the scoreboard mirror of the pin-table, the full implications of what he had done only then hitting him. He felt like a pigeon who had just had his last five cents taken off him. He had been well and truly suckered, and it had cost him plenty. The best goddamn hitter he'd ever had was all; and Chaney himself of course. He felt badly about that. He became aware of Poe's censuring stare and knew he deserved it now.

'Okay, pal,' he said. 'I'm not the first guy that followed a skirt. Forget it.'

'Hitting someone in the head with a pool cue is the kind of thing that hangs in the mind.'

Contrition hung heavily on Speed's face, pulling at the slack flesh. He was painfully aware of his error and didn't need Poe to rub it in. He needed Chaney, and badly, his whole gambling future was presently dependent upon him, to say nothing of his simply surviving.

'You're right,' he said. 'I totally poisoned my own well.'

'Our well. In case you forget, we are now both unemployed.'

Speed creased his face. He was responsible for Poe too. Someone else he'd let down. Jesus, it suddenly seemed that he owed so much to so many, and he'd failed all round. Chaney; Poe; Le Beau. How come I end up always owing so much? he thought. But he knew. For in some way all these people went to supply his needs. He had to repay them, and he had to go on doing it because he knew damn well he couldn't supply his own needs.

'You think I can go after him and try to make it up?' Speed said.

'A very imperceptive question,' Poe replied.

'You want to go and talk to him then?' Speed said. 'Explain things.'

'I wouldn't even try.'

Speed was on the spot again; owing and feeling guilty about it.

'Besides,' Poe said, 'the word on the street is that you have other problems.'

Speed looked at him pitifully. He knew goddamn Le Beau wouldn't be long in setting his dogs after him when he stepped out of jail.

'What you need is a quick trip out of town,' Poe advised.

Speed stared at his broken, unmanicured fingernails. They were the worst, just like himself, and had little prospect of getting any attention now, thanks to that goddamn cat Gayleen. She had left him without even a hope and a prayer. He needed two thousand now plus two weeks interest, which pushed the debt up to over three grand. And Le Beau wanted interest on the interest.

'I can loan you fifty,' Poe said helpfully. 'It's all I got my friend.'

Fifty on the nose of a favorite was still a long way short of the scratch he had to come up with. I wonder how I'd look, Speed thought, a sharp twenty-five-dollar suit and lying in the morgue with my throat cut out.

'Stand here longer and I'll have to pass up the fifty for this wrecked machine,' Poe informed him, seeing the bartender getting on the phone to someone.

Speed snapped out of his self-pitying day dream.

'Let's get ourselves a couple of beers some place else,' he said.

'Commendable idea,' Poe replied.

They turned out casually and began walking, then a little faster. Finally they broke into a run. The bartender saw them and shouted after them.

'You lousy fags! Take your quarrels elsewhere.'

NINETEEN

Chaney was trying not to think about what had happened. His head still hurt where Speed had caught him but he was trying not to think about that either. He cared nothing, not anymore, not about the pain, nor about the crumbled relationship, nor anything else. He was just here inbetween times and nothing meant anything.

He had been shuffling around most of the day, undecided about his next move. He knew he should be hitting the road, but he wasn't doing it. It was like he had lost his ability to make those decisions then act on them right away. He'd been drinking a little in a bar he'd found which was quiet enough for him to be alone with his thoughts. He got hustled a couple of times to play pool, and finally he gave in and played. By that time he'd reached the point where he needed something to stop himself thinking.

After winning a buck or two at pool, he left the bar and walked along the waterfront. The night was clear with a big bright moon that silhouetted the iron-work of crane on the docks showing them to be huge, stationary birds of prey. The river was cold and had an unmoving appearance, its oily smell came across at him, filling his nostrils and making him restless. He was walking nowhere, he told himself, and he was trying to resist the thoughts he now had.

It was no real surprise to himself when he wound up at Lucy's place, nor any that he found himself jabbing the bell-push on her front porch. It had taken him six years to discover it, but Chaney knew he had a need of that woman unlike any he had known for women since Alma.

On hearing the bell Lucy froze, instinctively knowing who it was. She knew that sometime it would come to this, and that she had to go through with it now. She had learned her real choices were all within her; she'd had a lot of long and lonely nights to do that, and had spent them weighing the balance. Her husband in jail; her work prospects; her sometimes visitor Chaney. She now had made her choice.

She wanted things regular, wanted things even; she wanted to know just where she was and just what the balance of give and take was, and she wanted to keep it equal. For every piece of herself that she gave, she wanted the same back from her partner. That was what she wanted, and what she had gone out and chosen.

When the bell sounded again she reluctantly stirred herself, knowing she had to answer. She left the man lying beside her, and rose nakedly. She pulled on her coat and started out.

Cautiously she opened the door and looked out at him. She couldn't help her irrational feeling of guilt. But there he was, expecting it and wanting it, because it suited him, and not about to understand that that way of things no longer suited her.

'I got a visitor,' she said.

In the past Chaney had always been emotionally ready for such reverses in a situation. Now the casual indifference he managed to display needed a supreme effort, and even then he wasn't too sure how successful he was in his attitude. He shrugged.

'Some other time,' he said, and turned to start down the steps.

'No, wait,' Lucy said, 'I'll walk down with you.'

In spite of herself she couldn't accept the close of their relationship, such as it had been, like this with a simple shrug. She wanted to believe that things had meant a little more to him.

She fastened her coat about herself and stepped out to him, barefoot.

'So how've you been?' he said.

There was a brittleness behind his question. She believed he was hurt in some way and she felt guilty, and avoided his eyes.

'How do I look?'

'No complaints.'

He wasn't giving anything apart from those few uncompromising words. No feeling or impression of self. That marked his pain, and a week ago his double-shuffle emotional blackmail might have caused Lucy to yield. But not now that she had made her choice.

'Look,' she said decisively, 'I don't think you should drop by anymore.'

His face remained as stony as ever.

'Things have changed,' she went on.

Still there was nothing from him. Lucy was getting a little nervous, wishing she had stayed up in her apartment.

'I think I'm moving. Going to get a better place.'

Chaney didn't care, he told himself, he had never let himself care; now he completely denied the hurt. She wasn't canceling him out, he'd never been there in the first place. It upset her more than it did him, he could tell that. It was just inconvenient for him, that was it. But he'd survive without this need fulfilled.

'I got a better offer,' she continued. 'Somebody that spends the night. He's even got a steady job.'

Chaney turned and looked at her now, his eyes were cold. She'd leaned on him all ways about staying nights, about a steady job. And for one moment back there he might have bought it.

His words were hard like granite chips. 'You got all things worked out for yourself.'

'That's all you got to say?' she said.

Chaney held her stare for a second. He wasn't yielding, he simply realized he had made a mistake. And so walked away.

She watched him, wondering where he was going, and some part of her wanted to go with him. But she also felt a part of herself destroyed, even though she realized that he was the most goddamn selfish son-of-a-bitch she had met. Yet still she cried for him, and still she believed he was carrying away his hurt, denying it to himself, and guessed he always would.

Walking on past the dilapidated row of peeling Victorians, Chaney was trying to shut out all the emotions that were careering through him, but he was having no success. The sense of loss he felt at that moment was enormous, the closest he had had to that feeling when the kids and Alma went. He wasn't quite sure how his feelings for Lucy could have established themselves like that.

He turned into a liquor store at the corner of the street. The clerk regarded his angry face, and the mark along the side of his head.

'Wild Turkey,' Chaney said.

'Yes, sir. What size?'

'Fifth. Two of them.'

The clerk reached round for the bottles. He stood them on the counter as Chaney handed him two singles. He considered Chaney's face again.

'You okay, buddy?' he asked.

'I'm fine.'

Chaney swept up the bottles, collected his change and was gone.

He walked back to his rooming house and slammed shut the door to his room. He tossed his coat and cap onto a chair then brushed the cat off the bed; he took the tin mug from the sink, and stretched out on the bed. He poured himself a glass of Wild Turkey and drank it. Then poured himself another and drank that too.

He never got drunk in company, as it would have left him wide open and vulnerable. Instead he got drunk alone, and licked his problems alone. And tonight he was alone and getting drunk, for tonight he had problems, that merely his strength and his will couldn't overcome.

The liquor tasted good where it ran down his chest and through his stomach. Soon his anger and hurt would begin to subside. He thought about it then. It had started with that pool cue coming down on his head. The reason he was so angry about that was because Speed hadn't considered the friendship he had given him, hadn't trusted it at all. Speed had been so stupidly weak and had taken Gayleen's word without question. He felt contempt for the man.

But then Chaney had been more angry with himself, for when he looked at Speed slumped against the counter, he knew instinctively he should have destroyed him, he had wanted to. Any man who attacked or hurt him he always destroyed. Yet looking at Speed he just hadn't been able to do it, and right then he had had to admit to himself: I like this guy too much.

That only added to Chaney's anger, for it gave Speed a hold over him; wanting to give anything to another person meant he had to give up something of himself, some part of freedom, of decision, whatever. Without knowing it he'd been growing attachments here, and narrowing down the big blue horizon.

That was how it was with Lucy too. He reassured himself that he didn't need her. When someone leant on Chaney he didn't bend, he simply became more rigid. But it reached into him, the way she'd thrown him over for a man who stayed all night and had a steady job.

He tried another glass of Wild Turkey, a large one. He swallowed a mouthful like beer, beginning now to feel a softening at the edges, and that was nice. He poured another and gazed across at the cat sulking in the corner, occasionally mewing for something to eat. Chaney felt trapped tonight in this room with the cat; he felt imprisoned and he didn't know why. Why was he here anyway? He had no friends here, no woman, and he had no business here now. He had nothing, which was the way he liked it. Yet here he was half-drunk and in no state to go anywhere. He wanted to get up and move out, right out of the city. But he couldn't. It may have been the booze just now holding him down, but it seemed like something a lot heavier, which he couldn't define, only feel. The whole city was coming on top of him and he wanted release from whatever it was. The next glass of Wild Turkey didn't free him. He lay there in something of a stupor, tired and exhausted and wanting to quit. He was through now. Just lay in a half-sleep, still hurting, and listening to the deadened sounds of the street; on a phonograph somewhere there was the strains of a song sung by a singer he recalled hearing some other sad night, in some other sad city. He just lay there, wound up, wanting to release; he heard a shrill whistle, probably of a train, the one he should be on riding away. He smiled a little, believing he was riding a freight car north. He shut his eyes and fell asleep.

The Northern and Southern Railway Night Special from Memphis, Tennessee rolled slowly along the platform at Terminal Station and juddered to a halt with a screech of brakes. Doors started opening and arms flagged the black porters to have them get baggage.

Along the platform Chick Gandil stood, a camel-hair coat around his shoulders like a boxer's robe, a brown fedora over his eyes at an angle. Jim Henry stood alongside him, his eyes searching up and down the platform for the party they were expecting. That was how he functioned now, he was Gandil's step an' fetch it.

Gandil never gave up, especially not on something such as this. Before Chaney's arrival he had had the best hitter in the whole of Louisiana; then he had offered to purchase a part of Chaney, and had not only been refused, but refused contemptuously.

It was never the money he made out of street fighting which concerned him, he had plenty of money; it wasn't even his reputation, that had taken knocks before, and he was after all a sporting man. It was just Chaney himself, the way he stood up and said No, you'll never get me. Gandil didn't like his authority challenged in that way. It was something he was never going to get used to. He was going to beat Chaney, it simply required a change of tactics. But one way or the other he was determined he was going to beat him.

He had called a friend of his who was a captain of police and asked him what he might have on Chaney. There wasn't anything that was immediately apparent but the captain thought like Gandil, a man who was that little known about had to be hiding something. Certainly he would stand a little closer scrutiny. None of the state wanted bills matched up with Chaney, but a couple of the federal posters might have. His friend the captain was looking into those. In the meanwhile Gandil had made other arrangements for Chaney, so had to have the police lay off again. He was going to call him out, he wanted to see him on the floor, a beaten man. Anyone as proud as Chaney had to get his lumps, and that was just what Gandil was going to see that he got, and very soon. After that the police or the FBI or anyone else could haul his ass off to jail, then it wouldn't matter to Gandil.

Seeing a black standing about eight inches taller than anyone else when he stepped down out of the pullman car, Gandil knew that the moment he'd been waiting for since that night he saw Jim Henry on the ground over at Depression Colony was about drawing near.

The big black moved up the platform toward Gandil and Jim Henry, neither of whom made any move. He reached them and stopped, knowing instinctively who they were.

Gandil regarded the man for a moment with ice-cold eyes as if the reputation that had preceded him could now never have been in doubt.

'Welcome to New Orleans, boy. I'm Chick Gandil.' He made no attempt to shake the man's hand.

'That's what I figured,' the black said in his Tennessee drawl.

The black glanced at Jim Henry, then extended his duffle bag to him to carry.

The move was an affront and Jim Henry stiffened. 'I don't do that . . . Mr Street,' he said.

Street had other ideas and made no attempt to withdraw the bag. After a moment's indecision Jim Henry looked to his boss as if expecting him to tell the black to carry it himself, but Gandil's eyes were smiling now, he was waiting for something to get off between these two hitters.

Nothing did. Jim Henry capitulated and took the valise.

Street smiled. He had the hard, uncompromising smile of a winner.

Gandil's mouth twisted into a sardonic smile; he was able to read the future now. Mr Chaney, he decided, was about to be buried.

TWENTY

Having had Chaney watched by the cops and his movements reported back to him via the police captain, Gandil knew just where to find him now he had something to say to him. Chick Gandil was back in the pick-up fight business, that's what he had to say, and Chaney was going to accommodate him.

He entered the pool room on North Roman with Jim Henry and the black they'd met off the Night Special close on his heels. It was still early but the place had that smell like it hadn't been emptied or aired for weeks. Most of the tables were lit and had some kind of action on them. He spotted Chaney the minute he entered. He was along the floor with his back to the counter, drinking and watching two sleazos on the nearest table as they racked up under the yellow light that was cutting through the cigarette smoke.

From the corner of his vision Chaney noticed the men approach him and knew it was for no purpose other than trouble. He didn't turn around, but went on watching the game that had started. One of the poolplayers was a minor shark, every shot he played he hustled.

'I'll buy you one.'

Chaney ignored Gandil's offer, also when he came and sat on the stool next to him.

'How you been?' he said.

Chaney gave him an indifferent look. The man was still trying. He guessed there was but one way to get him off his back.

'You want to talk about the sporting life?' Gandil asked.

'I'm out of it.'

Gandil let the smile slide off his face. He may have lost his shooter but he still had his reputation, and that was what Gandil wanted, and doubted that a man like Chaney would refuse an open challenge.

'That's too bad,' he said. 'Since I had to give up on you, I went out and bought another hitter.' He jerked his thumb at Street; he'd have shown a horse more respect.

'Must make you a happy man,' Chaney said, 'now you got what you wanted.'

Chaney smiled knowing Gandil didn't have what he wanted, all he had was a compromise and a pretty good one if that was it standing alongside Jim Henry.

'I'll tell you what I got,' Gandil said. 'Five thousand. Him against you.'

Chaney was giving nothing. The man was working for the advantage over him and he wasn't going to get it. He had nothing Chaney needed.

'I don't need the money,' he said, watching the minor shark take the five ball on the pool table.

One note of laughter parted Gandil's lips. 'I think you're being rather presumptuous, boy,' he said, insultingly. 'There's no point in avoiding this thing. It's just going to happen sooner or later.'

'He's right.'

Lifting his eyes to meet the black's, Chaney said, 'You want it that much?'

'Sure,' replied Street. 'I'm getting paid, man. Besides, waiting gets me bored.'

Chaney could see that the man before him was a professional hitter, and figured he got more than just a living. They had an affinity.

'You can always play with yourself,' he said, showing more concern with the pool player making his next shot.

Street leant menacingly. 'What if I reach out and start this thing right now?'

'You won't,' Chaney said, 'unless you're as dumb as your predecessor.'

He was that sure. Street was a hitter who had been hired to fight, and would only fight for a purse. Gandil might have provoked things there and then, he was that emotionally involved; however, Street wasn't. And Chaney was trying not to be.

'You don't think so?' Street said aggressively.

'You're not going to take me on for free.'

The black eased off.

The two would-be antagonists looked at one another in professional, assessing fashion. Chaney saw the hostility in the man's yellowing eyes. It told him he could beat him. But he wasn't concerned one way or the other. He figured he had licked

Chick Gandil; that was enough. Now he could leave on his own terms, and that was what he was planning on doing. He finished his drink and slid off the stool. As he started out he spun the glass for Jim Henry to catch, but before he had time to react and do so, Chaney plucked it out of the air and set it on the counter.

Anger sped through Gandil as he watched Chaney go. He wanted him torn apart and couldn't immediately understand why a man of his importance couldn't achieve that. In fact he could achieve that quite easily, but it was how he achieved it. Unfortunately he had allowed himself to become so emotional about this whole business. That was the trouble. Chaney wasn't at all emotionally involved, and certainly wouldn't be pushed into the fight unless on his own terms, no more than Street would.

An angle other than a straightforward bet was required. He needed to get Chaney emotionally involved, or at least on the hook until he let him off. He considered the cops, they could pick him up if he gave the word, but Chaney couldn't fight in the slams. He thought about that woman he had been seeing; and he thought about the marker man. Speed was the person to influence Chaney still, he felt. And Speed was having big trouble with Le Beau, so he was easily influenced.

To say Speed was having trouble with Le Beau might have made him laugh hysterically. He was having more than trouble. In fact his biggest problem right now was hanging onto his life. He was running everywhere and from everything. Running from shadows, and every tough who so much as looked at him. Le Beau meant business and Speed was taking no chances.

Unfortunately the kind of life style that it resulted in gave him little opportunity of getting the money to stack up to what he owed the man, and as the prospect of his ever doing so grew more distant, so the threat of him getting scalped closer than the job they did on him in prison came nearer. He didn't get up mornings anymore, nor afternoons, paradoxically he felt safer about moving around in the dark. He rose from his lonesome bed in his forlorn apartment, and stumbled shakily to the mirror. He looked at himself and tried to measure himself in a way he hadn't before. He ran his hands through his stubbly hair; with his lucky silver hair all shorn off right back to the gray roots it was no wonder he was luckless these days. He dismissed the wreck he saw, and walked out to the kitchen for some breakfast. From the icebox he took the last bottle of Jax and opened it, his last old friend. He squatted on the edge of the table, pulling on the bottle and thinking. Thought didn't make much difference, there was no way it was going to get him out of his predicament. He could pray, but doubted that anyway, much less anyone of influence up there, even remembered he existed.

Wrecked and beaten, a shell of his former self, yet despite all this he was feeling goddamn sexy this morning. Speed shook his head as if believing there was a circuit loose. Strange, but now he wasn't able to gamble, and now Gayleen wasn't here, he had energy. Perhaps not so strange. He had energy, but nothing he could do with it. He took another pull on the bottle of Jax, suddenly paused midway and sighed despondently. He had the best part of fifty bucks Poe had loaned him, and probably wouldn't have had had he dared going near the tracks or anyone who would have taken a bet from him. As he sat there Speed noticed he was feeling more and more horny. He guessed it would have been about this time of the month. It would really bitch Gayleen if he did his time with a whore he reflected. Goddamn, he decided, that's what he was going to do. Fifty bucks went nowhere toward paying off Le Beau, so he might as well blow five in a brothel. He finished off the beer, then rose to dress.

Cautiously peering out his apartment door, he saw the coast was clear, then scuttled down the stairs; checked at the street door, before jumping into the Buick and blazing away.

He drove across town to the Tenderloin District and slid to a halt outside the only brothel which he knew for certain had no connection with Le Beau. The place looked pretty sordid in the daylight and the windows were shuttered and curtained. Inside the girls tended to lose track of night and day. Twelve noon was much the same as twelve midnight when it was spent in bed. He paused a second and looked at the house, his face screwing up in uncertainty. It wasn't that he had any moral qualms, just that lately he hadn't thought it would come to this, his having to fulfill his sexual needs in the same way he filled the Buick's gas tank.

He got out, and slowly crossed the sidewalk and went up the stoop of the house.

Relief swept over Speed when the black maid showed him through to the Madam in the sitting room. For a moment he thought they were acquainted, and he was sure they were, but she gave no sign of recognition. He guessed it was a long time and that he had changed. She sure had. The place was quietly lit and the predominant colors were varying shades of red and pink. There was a lot of velvet that had seen plusher days, and lace that could have stood a little light needlework. The madam would have had him believe they were in another epoch. Speed knew better; this was no classy joint.

The madam proffered the merchandise for Speed to look over. Eight grinning doxies all looking the goddamn same to him, with professional smiles and tits no longer sensitive to touch. Their faces suggested they weren't sure whether they rose too early or were up too late. In apparent confusion he glanced back to the madam. How could he choose, chosing one in favor of another was invidious.

The madam smiled, just like she'd taught her girls to.

'You're new,' she said. 'That's good. We're going to help you have a real nice time.'

'Gee thanks,' Speed said, like he was a cotton-country boy.

He wished he could just get straight to it, without all this horseassing around.

The madam moved closer to him, taking his arm.

'Would you like me to introduce you to all these girls?' she said. Then leaning in to him, caused him to swoon nearly with the smell of perfume, and added in a stage whisper, 'Confidentially, they've all been specially trained.'

Speed looked at her, just a little worried now. The madam gave him a very knowing look. But Speed didn't know. He was no sexual athlete; matter of fact those specialities worried the hell out of him. It was the most he could do at times to get it together and where it should be.

The madam raised her eyebrows as if about to make him her special confidant. 'Any one of them ...'

'Look, I don't need a sales pitch,' Speed interjected. 'I just came here to get my hat blocked.'

The madam nodded, and extended her mottled hand. 'Take your pick.'

Speed smiled limply at a Jean Harlow-type, who gave a little giggle as if shy and daunted by the prospect of Speed's masculinity. Yeah, he thought, real believable.

'Let's do it,' he said, and started for the stairs.

It was business and as he ascended the stairs he began removing his tie. The floozy followed, still giggling, trained to perfection in making a man feel his was the one.

It was all done in two shakes, the great reservoir of sexual energy he thought he'd found deserting him completely. The floozy had made all the right noises so he didn't have to take it as a reflection on his masculinity. But something was wrong somewhere. He lay quite still for a minute, exhausted, and trying to figure it out.

He wasn't satisfied. He'd got it off, his need apparently fulfilled, but there was something else, some other need. Maybe it was that he needed to be needed. This floozy didn't need him. He doubted that she'd even been aware of him. Gayleen had needed him, and, that even with all the bitching, that had been satisfying. As his thoughts rolled on Speed had to smile. He had started out to bitch Gayleen with the five bucks worth, and ended up realizing his need of her.

Miami, he thought, I wonder. Listening to the girl's breathing, he figured her task was completed.

'What's your name?' he asked.

'Carol,' she said in a bored sort of way, like she knew what came next.

'Well, Carol,' Speed said, 'what did you think of that?'

'Oh, it was terrific. You were great,' she enthused.

He stared up at the ceiling with its browning distemper and pink shaded light, then looked at her.

'You know something?' he said. 'That's exactly what I thought you were going to say.'

He got out of his bed and into his clothes. Then he looked back at her, lying as per house–policy, laid to waste until the gentleman had left.

'Here's to the next time,' he said. 'Bottoms up!'

That was one intelligent floozy; as if it was a five-buck special she immediately raised her ass in the air. Speed shook his head, and left her like that. He had his own ass to worry about now. He was back on the street.

He came quickly out of the brothel but didn't make it to his car. From the adjacent stoop two men appeared and made straight for him. They weren't about to ask the time of day.

Speed turned the other way down the street, but stopped when Doty and the black stepped from a parked maroon Packard. In an instant Speed had it, that madam must have remembered him after all and made a phone call. These were the hunters, he was the quarry. He turned sideways to the curb as the two men behind ran up. Speed spun to his left, kicked a trash can and sent it toward the men. Then he turned and threw another kick at Doty. It connected and Speed felt pretty good. He'd learned something from watching his hitters perform. The black came at him and lunged, but he was just a ham and egger and Speed slid to his right and socked him. That made him mad, so Speed retreated, right into the two men behind him. One was a very big man, solid muscle; and the other wasn't a mouse exactly. A fist that felt like a hammer slammed into the small of Speed's back. There was no appeal. Speed folded to the sidewalk where he saw either stars or sparks as the muscle suddenly landed his foot into the side of his face.

When Speed came around he was lying face down in some sawdust. He groaned and brought some attention to himself and wished he hadn't. The toughs who had coldcocked him were still around and a couple of them handled him to his feet. His head hurt like hell, and his back, also his limbs were leaden. He guessed he had given that hooker better than he figured. His throat ached and it was dry, he needed a drink, anything, even water would have been fine at that moment. He recognized the hell he had arrived at as a bar, one where he probably couldn't get a drink. Strange, he had always imagined his hell would have been a racetrack where he had all the winners but couldn't get a bet down.

The bar was a ramshackle sort of place. It looked deserted, though still had the smell of too much smoke, and stale beer which indicated the patrons had not long left. Speed stood very shakily and tried to brush the gob and sawdust off his suit. His effort caused him pain and he had to stop. Doty smiled thinly at him, and shoved him along the bar toward Le Beau who was standing at the rail. Le Beau looked at him in a way that suggested he had invited Speed for no socially acceptable reason.

'This is your lucky night,' he finally croaked in his whispering voice.

Had he been able to laugh Speed might have done so at

that. But he couldn't do anything until he'd got something wet into his throat. Someone's unfinished beer on the bar did.

'I guess that depends on how you look at it,' he said, like a bad imitation of Le Beau.

'I'll tell you how I look at it,' Le Beau said. 'Normally right now I'd decide whether to break your back or just kill you.'

In the menacing silence that followed Speed wondered how he'd look unkilled and with a broken back. Then Le Beau's face cracked. It was like a fissure across a rock surface, it was the closest he came to smiling.

'But somebody paid your interest,' he informed Speed, and inclined his head toward a booth at the back of the bar. Speed's eyes followed his direction. It wasn't too light down there, and when he focused his eyes he picked out the white suit of Chick Gandil. Sitting alongside him was Jim Henry. Gandil smiled sociably, just like they were at the Athletic Club or somewhere.

'Just for a week, Speed old boy,' he said. 'Your man fights my new hitter and I'm going to handle your debt. Otherwise I'm going to have to give you back to Mr Le Beau. Now Mr Le Beau, he's not a very pleasant man to be into, boy. So your man had better have some concern for you.'

Speed's face screwed up in a painful contortion; that was how he viewed his prospects. Chaney was no longer his man, never had been, and Speed knew the one certain way to ensure that Chaney would cut out was to try and put pressure on him like this. Chaney didn't bend, especially not to any kind of emotional blackmail.

'You're plumb crazy,' Speed said. 'Chaney don't owe me nothing. He won't do what I ask.'

Le Beau's face cracked once more. He looked at Doty, who was happy to do this. He was smiling for him. 'Tell him,' he whispered.

'Then you're dead.'

Speed shook and hurt and wondered fleetingly if being dead could be any more painful than the way he was right now.

TWENTY-ONE

Poe was now one of the masses of unemployed, and he had believed things were on the up and up for him. Because he could no longer afford happy dust, life had to comprise of the small efforts, so he was lying across his rather worn sofa reading a Diamond Dick novel. He was neither happy nor unhappy. He was coughing again, his eyes were watery and he kept sniffing; these were the withdrawal symptoms of the drug addict, and Diamond Dick was a thin substitute.

His future in the world was without prospects, but that was of no particular worry to Poe. Within his head he roamed the higher stratospheres of life and not much that was terrestrial could touch him there. Yet time and again he was brought back to earth, with his sneezing and body convulsions continually reminding him that he was only mortal.

He was of men, and often may have wished he wasn't, but when reminders were put upon him, he accepted the fact. He was of men and needed the same comforts as other mortals, who sometimes even needed him; that wasn't often, but when they did he gave himself up. Life, he found, was like an energy charge with a continual positive-negative shift, and one simply learnt to adapt. Having studied medicine for two years, he had something which he could occasionally give which was useful to men. The pity of it was that he could rarely give to himself. There wasn't a thing he could do about his drug problem, save feed it, nor about the world situation, except ignore it, nor about his position in it, apart from bending. Some men did everything for themselves, while others were unable to do much at all. Poe fell into the latter category. The most he could do to justify his existence in this world was to help others with their hurts and pains, and he was not frequently called upon to do so.

That morning Chick Gandil made a similar call on him. But it wasn't exactly a mission of mercy that he had in mind, though that was how he dressed it up. Rather than knock he had Jim Henry kick in the apartment door, causing Poe to leap from the sofa in both a state of agitation and alarm. And the reason wasn't that he had yet to finish his novel.

Gandil walked in smiling confidently and charmingly.

'Hello, Mr Poe,' he said.

'Jesus, Gandil. That ain't a polite way to come calling. There are some social conventions left you know. Such as presenting one's calling card.'

Poe didn't move, but watched and waited for the next move. He wasn't scared, in fact, he was greatly relieved it wasn't the narcotics squad, not that he had anything to interest them. There was something about Gandil which Poe had never liked, not just his wealthy social and economic connections, it was a sly and cunning quality that the man had and indulged when he had no need to in order to survive.

The reason for Gandil's call was that he was putting the arm on Chaney, and believed he was going about it in a way which Chaney couldn't refuse. For a start he had Speed with his head on a block. Chaney may not care too much about his ex-shooter, but Gandil knew he had been seen frequently with Poe. So he intended to hold Speed over Poe, and have Poe put the arm on Chaney. Either way Gandil figured he would win.

That was something about which Poe harbored very serious doubts as he listened to Gandil's proposal. Setting Chaney up to fight the Memphis hitter under threat of Speed winding up dead in the Mississippi seemed a reasonable lever on the face of it. Only Poe saw its shortcoming which was Chaney himself. He didn't care, and Poe acquainted Gandil with the fact.

'You'd better make him care, Mr Poe,' Gandil said testily. 'That is, if Speed ever meant a damn to you.'

He glared at this crumpled little man before him, as if to question his right to put problems in his path. Why so many problems continually beset him he couldn't make out. But one thing was for damn sure, he wasn't going to be the loser in the end. He turned out. Jim Henry followed.

Poe shut the torn apartment door they left open, and leant against it and thought about the situation. He had to go see Chaney. For Speed's sake he had to at least try and persuade him to fight, as much as he disliked doing it. He didn't like blackmail, and felt uncomfortable about having to approach Chaney. Although he'd not seen him since Speed slugged him, he thought something in their relationship which worked right now, and he knew it wouldn't go on working if they started asking things of each other. Chaney had never asked for nothing, so why should he concede to anything which he asked for? Perhaps because Chaney is a man, Poe thought, is mortal, and at rock bottom we have these things in common.

Chaney heard Poe's approach while he was still well down the stairs, his cough sounded like a loose bannister rail rattling. He was shaving when the knock came on the door. He didn't open it, but went right on with what he was doing.

He wasn't giving to Poe. He liked him still but he was all a part of Speed's set-up, and since that crazy scene in the pin-table saloon he was through with it.

In a moment Poe entered the room in an unsure, hesitant manner. Chaney acknowledged him with a brief look and went back to the cracked piece of mirror.

'I don't want to interrupt anything,' Poe said reticently.

He waited, uncertain how to put the proposition. He recognized how Chaney had sealed himself off from all contact.

'We've got a problem.'

Chaney went on shaving, he thought perhaps Poe was upset he hadn't stopped by, and he didn't like to see the man suffering.

'You and me don't have any trouble,' he said to try and put him at his ease.

Poe watched him continue shaving a second, then turned and stared, a little surprised at the cat sleeping on the bed.

'I'm afraid we do,' he said. 'Old friend, Speed.'

Chaney thoughtfully dragged the razor down his cheek on a final stroke. Speed putting on him was one thing; Poe was another.

'He sent you?' he asked.

'He doesn't even know I'm here.'

Poe shifted uncomfortably and shuffled to the window and back to the bed. It was more difficult asking for himself than for Speed.

'Speed and I aren't related anymore,' Chaney said.

He rinsed the razor and put it aside. He was brusque, not wanting any favors asked of him because he didn't want to have to refuse Poe.

Poe watched him, now witnessing the difference between

them. Chaney never needed anyone; Poe did, and in the past had needed Speed.

'Things don't work that easy,' he said. 'He's in a lot of trouble.'

'I'm not interested.'

Chaney leaned the bowl of water and began rinsing his face. He owed nothing to a guy who'd hit him over the head and broken a relationship of his own doing. Speed had burnt his bridges.

'My bag's packed and I'm on my way,' he said. 'Heading north.'

The words distressed Poe, for his own sake as well as Speed's. He guessed Chaney didn't know the full facts and was assuming Speed simply wanted him back in the life.

'This is different,' he said. 'He ran a marker to one of our local riff-raff. They're putting the arm on him. Gandil's going to pay it off if we come up with the money to fight his man.'

Chaney slowly turned to him. It was another play by Gandil. Gandil gets Speed out of hock, if Chaney puts up his money to fight. Chaney knew that if he accepted and lost, it would be the equivalent of him bailing Speed out. If he accepted and won, Gandil was going to be out of pocket, and heavily. However, that wasn't the point.

'You mean it's my money we'll be coming up with?' he said.

'Where else is it going to come from?'

Poe shrugged, feeling both embarrassed and inadequate. If a man didn't have any emotions at all how did you reach them? How did you connect?

'I don't owe him anything,' Chaney said.

He reached for the towel and buried his face. It wasn't so much Speed who irked him in this situation, but Gandil. Again that man was trying to force him to bow to him.

Shifting his weight from foot to foot, Poe was really on the spot, and he felt he just had to make Chaney understand. Pride counted for nothing when a man's life was at stake.

'That's not a matter for conjecture,' he said. 'It's real simple. He's in the ringer. You're the only one who can get him out.'

There was little more to say that meant anything. He'd put it all on Chaney's shoulders, and he didn't believe he could easily throw it off. Chaney set himself alone, set himself apart. In doing so, he was kind of asking for everything to come up to him. If a man stood up saying he needed nothing, that he was strong enough to survive, then naturally he was asking weaker people to look to him for strength. Now Poe was asking.

Chaney understood why Poe was asking for help, and knew that he had it to give if he so chose. He'd missed out helping Alma when she needed it. Maybe he shouldn't miss out on Poe. However, it wasn't as simple as that. Because there was still Gandil, up on his back, trying to break him; these were his terms and had nothing to do with anyone else.

'That's it,' Poe said resignedly. 'Plain and simple.'

Chaney threw his towel onto the bed alongside the cat, and walked to the window. He leant his hands on the top of the frame and looked down into the street. It was getting to be a very familiar sight, too familiar, even the spasm band up to their antics along the sidewalk failed to move him anymore.

Poe stood uncomfortably a second or two just watching this powerful man who had so much to give yet raised so many objections. He thought fleetingly how he would like to have known him, then turned away and shuffled out as only the old or the very weary could.

Hearing Poe shut the door behind him, Chaney didn't turn. He waited at the window for his appearance down on the street, his back heaving as the cough came on him again. He looked a pathetic sight, Chaney thought, but resisted his feeling of pity for him.

Chaney turned away from the window as Poe disappeared along the street. He wasn't feeling anything now, not angry or hurt or accountable. He had effectively dropped that shutter down through himself, closing out all those feelings just as he had after the death of his wife. But they were there waiting for him now, just as they had been all those years ago. That disturbed him.

He looked at the cat on the bed and didn't feel anything for that either. He was watching him, waiting for him, wanting his attention. But he had nothing more to give it. If he did then he knew he would have to take it with him.

Collecting up his shaving tackle, he wrapped it in the towel and fitted it into the duffle bag. He pulled into his lumber jacket and planted his cap on his head.

It was time to go. The cat was still looking at him, and he hesitated, wondering what to do about it. That hesitation almost lost him. He opened the window for the cat; it could go or stay, the room was paid up till the end of the week. He guessed it would go soon enough when it realized there was no more food around. Chaney took out the last of the fish there was in the icebox and laid it on the floor for the cat. Then left.

Heading on out to the freight yards over by the Navigation Canal, he figured to pick up a ride across Mississippi, maybe as far as Alabama or Tennessee. Why either of those he didn't know, only why not. His route across town took him along Almonaster Avenue, and from there realized he was only a short distance from Lucy's place.

Remembering what the woman had said, he hesitated about going down to her place. Maybe she had already moved away. But Chaney realized he wanted to see her again, if only to say good-bye.

He saw the woman as he turned into the street. She was emerging from her apartment house with another woman and two guys. He stopped as they turned along the sidewalk in his direction. One of the guys, who had on the loudest plaid suit, cracked a funny and all four of them laughed. They seemed really happy together, close, loving even, not needing anything outside of themselves and their circle. Chaney watched them draw nearer and he thought how good Lucy was looking, better than he'd seen her looking since that night he first saw her in that cafeteria. He felt suddenly low just then watching her bounce along on that guy's arm. Seeing her separate and apart from him now he wanted her, and regretted her loss, regretted not at least having taken a shot at fulfilling the conditions she had given him. Without warning that shutter inside him had opened and he was hurting. He wanted her back, but realized to his regret that it was too late now.

At that point he knew he had to either turn away without speaking to her again and live with the regret, shutting it out, denying it, or go forward and take a shot at what he had had and had let pass him by.

In fact he did neither, but just stood there a moment longer, letting the shutter close back on his emotions. Then he started forward.

Lucy's expression opened in a surprised smile, but didn't really suggest she was pleased to see him.

'Well, look who's here,' she said.

Chaney went on looking at Lucy. No one bothered with introductions, and the two guys obviously wanted none. The guy in the plaid jacket seemed a little put out.

'Hey, buddy we're in a hurry,' he said. 'So unless you're a cab driver, you're not needed.'

Chaney looked at the man, then his friend, he didn't like being told he wasn't needed, especially not now, and his look was mean. The man backed off and looked for a way out. Lucy's girlfriend gave it to him.

'Why don't we let Lucy catch us up?' she suggested.

Lucy encouraged them. 'You go on, Bert. I'll just be a minute.'

Bert realized it was a good idea, and started away slowly, trying to save a little face. The others followed. Lucy looked back to Chaney and smiled. He was the same as ever, and she experienced the same ambivalence toward him, both attraction and mistrust.

'You sure are to the point,' she said.

'Save time that way,' Chaney said.

Lucy gave him a look. 'You come here to be hard on me?'

'Just wanted to say good-bye.'

Standing off from him as she thought he was from her, Lucy regretted her posture when she heard those words, wanted instead to throw her arms around him.

'For old time's sake?' she said.

'Something like that.'

'You know,' Lucy said, 'sometimes I think you should have come around more often.'

To her surprise the man nodded vaguely. But then he canceled it out. 'It wouldn't have made any difference,' he said. 'Things end up about the same.'

Chaney told himself if he stayed he would feel restless and edgy, jump at shadows and would grow to hate the woman for tying him up.

Lucy shrugged. She looked along the street and saw Bert waiting impatiently by the cab he had hailed. Chaney she had loved, but being with Bert made sense. She had to go.

'Well,' she said, 'you have to have a few wishes now and then. Keeps you going.'

'What's your wish for now?'

Closing her eyes briefly she found some strength. She shook

her head vaguely. 'Bye, Chaney,' she said, her words lost in her throat.

Cautiously she started on past the man, her pace getting faster as though believing he might pursue her. Finally she broke into a run and joined her friends.

Chaney watched them disappear into the cab. Lucy didn't look back through the rear window. He didn't expect her to nor want her to.

Hitching up his duffle bag that was slung across his shoulder, Chaney started back up for Almonaster to head out to the yards.

He was moving on now. Things were coming around. Chaney could feel it.

A nickel had got him all the information he needed on the trains rolling out, their times and destinations, as near as made any difference to him. And those his black informant didn't know about he invented just to oblige, Chaney was sure of it.

Squatting out of sight by the side of the track Chaney waited on the Nashville freighter due up in about an hour's time. All he had to keep company with was his thoughts. He almost wished he'd fetched his cat, but dismissed the thought. Next he'd want to bring Poe along and Speed, the whole shooting works. That wasn't what he was doing here, he was leaving.

Since being here Chaney had grown attachments. The dull ache he felt over losing Lucy brought it all home to him. He'd let himself get attached to Lucy; to Poe, even to Speed. Here he recognized for the first time in his life Speed had been striking out for what he wanted when he had jumped him with that pool cue. Chaney always felt an affinity with a man who tried things for himself; that was why he had taken to that goddamn garbage cat. Unconsciously he'd begun growing roots, and now he could feel them trying to hold him, to drag him back to meet the obligations and commitments that they would like to have forced on him. He wasn't going back he told himself.

An hour slipped past with the ease of a minute while Chaney remained in his squatting position. Thoughts about the demands that Poe and Speed and that damn cat were hitting him with careered around in his head. They needed him but the shutter was down and there was no way he was going to let it up, so no way he was going to respond to their needs.

There was a long blast on a steam whistle as that Nashville-bound freighter headed up on the track. Chaney rose off his haunches and flexed his legs, taking the slight stiffness out of them. He saw the train coming on, picking up as it did. He waited. It ran toward him almost silently.

Without warning Lucy jumped into his head. She managed to prise the shutter open and he hurt. He saw her with the guy in the plaid jacket and it really stung. He knew what he had passed up, knew he should have hung on there; knew a part of himself was dying because he was here and not there, the part he had been killing for the past six years. He doubted there would be another chance for him, and bitter regret rose through him.

The locomotive came on past him, and automatically Chaney's eyes were searching the back of the train, checking that the bull wasn't hanging out of the caboose, picking out the boxcar he was going after.

With great strength Chaney sent himself hurtling toward the train. He reached it and ran alongside, slackening his speed slightly to let his car come on level with him. He had no problems with the hasp and getting the door open. He tossed his duffle bag up in, then jumped himself, he hung in the doorway for a second, his feet clear of the track.

Poe and Speed, he realized, they were providing him with the chance that he'd let go with Lucy. They were two human beings who needed him. All he had to do was give. But he was aboard the Nashville-bound freighter. His feet were clear.

He hung there indecisively.

TWENTY-TWO

Speed was in the custody of Jim Henry and two of Le Beau's toughs. Jim Henry wasn't being friendly. He hadn't forgotten the insults Speed had so often laid on him, and was waiting his opportunity to crush the man.

They were meantime playing a very ungentlemanly game of poker in one of the empty offices down on Gandil's wharf. Speed, needless to say, wasn't having any luck; he could scarcely draw two cards the same color, much less the same value. He thought about trying a couple of double-shuffles to cheat these meatheads but his hands were shaking too much to risk it.

'How many?'

Speed was disinterestedly trying to fill an inside straight. He glanced up at the bruiser opposite.

'Give me three.'

Three cards came clumsily out of the top of the deck. When he lifted them, Speed's hands suddenly stopped shaking. He couldn't believe it. He had a straight flush. He felt a little of the old excitement, his heart began beating faster. Luck was picking him up, lifting him from the jaws of Jim Henry.

'Goddamn,' the bruiser who wasn't dealing said. 'We ain't got no cigarettes left.' He looked across at Speed. 'You smoked them all. I seen you.'

Speed tried a smile, tried his luck – and their patience. But perhaps Lady Luck had paved the way for him just as she had laid the straight flush on him. 'I'll be happy to walk down the block and get some,' Speed offered, and casually got out of his chair.

Jim Henry stood threateningly. 'You're not walking nowhere tonight.'

Speed sat down again and the three guards stared at him. They had the kind of faces that scared people to death.

'Things don't work out,' Speed said, 'which one of you gets to do the job?'

A cruel smile twisted Jim Henry's mouth as he reached into

his coat pocket and pulled out some metal palmers.

'Guess,' he invited.

If only he had taken the advice of his Ma, Speed thought, and not become a gambling man. If only he had lost that first bet he made way back in school, he had won two dollars and eighty cents on the result of that ballgame. That had led to this.

Figuring he could only get killed once, so with nothing to lose, Speed said, 'Yeah, that's right. It's been a while since you won one.'

The point drove into Jim Henry, who bristled, 'Don't lean on it,' he said.

'Chaney really cleaned you low didn't he?'

Remembering and not liking the memory, Jim Henry curled his hands tensely around the pieces of metal.

'How'd it feel?' Speed went on.

Jim Henry stood threateningly. 'You wanna play cards?' he said, 'or play some of this?' He clicked the palmers in front of Speed's face.

The threat set Speed a-shaking again and even with a straight flush he was in no state to go on now. What was the point anyway? If he won he simply lost. Chaney wasn't going to show up to accommodate these assholes, he had more sense. Speed only wished he had had half as much, as he wondered how long Chick Gandil would wait, thus keeping Le Beau at bay.

'I don't think so,' he said, and threw his cards in the air.

Carelessly, like gambling had gone out of his blood forever, he watched the straight flush shower to the floor. It was like tossing his life away. He sunk his head on his arms and awaited it.

'You think he's going to show up?' he heard one of the toughs say.

'Don't matter none. Either way he loses. That dude's wanted on a murder rap up in Georgia,' Jim Henry replied. 'The cops are waiting to pick him up just as soon as Mr Gandil gives the okay.' He smiled sardonically at Speed.

The news startled Speed, yet somehow didn't surprise him. Suddenly it explained so much about the man; the closeness of his cards to his chest; that impenetrable shield he had erected, why he refused to commit. He sat back and stared at Jim

Henry, like he personally was responsible for what was going to happen if Chaney showed up. At first he couldn't believe that Chick Gandil could be so desperate to win that he would be the all-time scumbag asshole if he lost. Then he believed it. Up until that moment Speed had wanted more than anything for Chaney to show up and fight Street and get him off the hook; now all he wanted was for that hitter to stay clear away.

Nothing ever seemed to go consistently right for Speed. With the straight flush he had managed to fill, it seemed that his luck had been on the turn. But then with his diametric shift in attitude with regard to Chaney, he managed to completely muddle luck.

Heat was building up like a Turkish bath, and steam was rising off anyone who so much as moved. The heat was building toward rain, everyone knew it, everyone expected it, and everyone got as nervy and as irritable as hell while they waited for it.

Just like everybody else Poe sweated as he steered Speed's wreck down alongside the Canal Street ferry, heading for Gandil's wharf. Unlike everyone else though, his was a cold, fevered sweat.

The riverfront looked pretty deserted when Poe drew up outside Gandil's offices, where lights were showing. He glanced across at the silent figure next to him, and gave him a long, measured look.

'You sure you want to go through with this?' Poe asked, his voice slightly hoarse.

For a moment Chaney sat unmoving, as if uncertain. Then he said 'Let's get started,' and climbed decisively from the car.

Watching Chaney move away to the open, dimly lit warehouse, Poe sighed and climbed wearily from the car. He had neither the strength nor the inclination to climb the stairs to the office. He found a claw iron lying on a crate, and mustering the strength he hurled it through the second floor window where a light was showing. When there was no immediate response he searched around for something else to throw.

Suddenly the door was wrenched open and Jim Henry appeared at the top of the stairs.

Poe stood and gave him a contemptuous, dismissive look.

'Hey, meathead,' he said. 'Tell that riff-raff we're not going to wait all night.'

Jim Henry stared down at him in disbelief then looked toward the open doorway of the warehouse where Chaney stood waiting. Then turned and quickly went back in.

Wearily Poe shuffled across the crate-littered wharf and joined Chaney. Together they moved down into the warehouse.

Gandil made an entrance with his entourage, which comprised Le Beau, Doty, Street, Jim Henry and assorted bruisers. They moved through the warehouse and into what was effectively a ring formed by balls of cotton that were stacked up. They formed up on the opposite side of the ring to where Chaney and Poe stood. Gandil smiled across the open no-man's-land, much as a rattlesnake smiled at its prey. He then reached into his pocket and produced an envelope which he handed to Le Beau pointedly.

When he opened the envelope and checked the contents Le Beau came as near to smiling as he ever did. He nodded his approval. It was business, nothing more.

'Where's Speed?' Poe croaked like a man asking for the last rites.

Gandil flicked his hand towards the door and Speed appeared right on cue between two heavies.

Speed's obligations having been met, he came through the warehouse and looked all around him, unsure if he was really going to be allowed this newly found freedom. No one stopped him as he walked stiff-legged over to Chaney. He had almost expected to see the place crawling with cops.

Speed looked at the man not knowing quite what to say. He knew Chaney owed him nothing, yet here he was giving to him and putting himself in a lot of danger by doing so.

'You gotta get outta here,' Speed said in a furtive, urgent whisper. 'The cops are expected. They know about the trouble up in Georgia.'

For a moment Chaney didn't speak or move, but just looked at the man who had warned him.

'Didn't you hear what I said for Christsake?' He was getting very agitated.

Finally Chaney nodded slowly, almost with an air of resignation, like there was no place to run anymore. Speed hadn't forced him into this, nor Poe, not even Gandil. It had just been waiting for him for the past six years. Things had a way of coming round.

'You ever seen him work?' Chaney asked calmly.

'Shit,' Speed said with a weary, defeated sigh as if realizing that this was the way it had to be. Then he shook his head.

Street was unknown quantity, and he didn't even know if Chaney could lick him, especially not with what Chaney was up against now. The way he felt right then he knew that this one they were going to have to fight together, all three of them. Chaney, Poe and himself. Chaney was going to need all their help. Measuring Street with a look he knew that the black was only the preliminary to the really big fight where the stake for Chaney was everything.

'I never had the pleasure,' he said tersely. 'But I figure he didn't bring him all the way from Memphis to lose.'

Chaney regarded the black, knowing his weakness, he was trying to assess his strength. Speed caught his eye and they gave each other a look, reaffirming where they were at that moment. Chaney nodded.

'Let's do it,' he said.

Then Speed accepted Chaney's resignation and went into action. All the old energy ran through him, that old sparkle and panache was back in his eye. He strutted out to the opposite group.

'All right, you piss-ant big shots. We're ready over here,' he challenged.

The two groups moved warily together, getting ready for business.

'Anybody else have anything to say?' Gandil asked, annoyed by the sudden bounce in the marker man.

Street nodded to Chaney, 'Glad you could make it.'

Chaney held his stare but gave him nothing. 'Things have a way of happening,' he said.

Stepping right up, Gandil produced his five thousand dollars.

'You know, I envy you, Mr Chaney. It must be very exciting to gamble with far more than you can afford to lose.' There was a treacherous smile dancing through Gandil's eyes.

'Who's going to hold the money?' Chaney asked.

Speed looked over at Poe and said, 'He is.'

Chaney handed him the cash. There were no objections raised by Gandil, who simply passed his five large bills to the crumpled, fever-racked man before him.

Five thousand, win or lose, it was all meaningless to Chaney at that moment. This fight might cost him his freedom, but for a fleeting moment he figured it was going to be worth it.

Whatever the outcome here, only one thing was certain to Speed, that was that Gandil and himself wouldn't be doing any kind of business for a long while to come. Even if that was a prospect he still wouldn't have resisted that last insult.

'I'll tell you something, Chick,' he said. 'No matter how far you go, how big you get in this state, you'll always be a scum-bag.'

Although irritated Gandil had no need to retaliate, not here and now. He turned and called down the warehouse to the two toughs by the open door.

'Close it up.'

The warehouse roller shutter roared downward and slammed shut. The building was sealed off, and suddenly filled with a strange, expectant silence.

Speed glanced to Poe, then to Chaney and gave him a grim smile.

Gandil looked nervously from Jim Henry to Street. There was no more to say.

Everyone was ready. Everyone waited.

Slowly Chaney's eyes traversed the scene before him. Gandil and his cronies; Speed and Poe alongside him. Still he didn't know how the hell he had got involved like this. He had been hanging on that Nashville freighter. He should have stayed aboard along with his duffle bag. Now he was here, heavily committed, the cops coming for him like he always knew they would if he stayed in one place too long or allowed anything to go deeper than the surface.

With a lot of effort he managed to push the thoughts aside. He was ready. He took off his cap and coat and handed them to Speed. Speed gave him a smile. Chaney turned back to the center, and came face to face with Street. Both of them were sweating and hadn't swung a fist yet. Everyone moved back a little. Ringed by the strapped cotton bales, Chaney loose and easy; Street, big as ever, his massive hands poised, ready.

The fighters took a step toward each other, and went through the ritual of raising their palms, paused; neither would jump the gun here, both were professionals. They stood motionless, both perfectly calm. There was no emotion yet. It was the way

Chaney liked it. He looked at Street, who held his stare; they were well matched, Chaney felt, and found looking at the man was almost like looking into the mirror and measuring himself. Street would be that good; so this was the test for Chaney. Never having before cared how he measured up to other men, here Chaney cared, because here he would be measuring himself, and if he lost this he'd be down a long time.

Without warning, rain tattooed on the vast tin roof of the warehouse, startling all those present except Chaney and Street. It continued incessantly as Street came on the offensive. Chaney let him come, then moved almost casually to the left, swung back immediately and hooked Street with a stinging blow right over his heart. But Street was quick, and didn't allow Chaney to dance away. The two men were quickly joined and raining jabbing blows into each other's body, competing with the rhythm of the rain. The noise up on the roof drowned that of fists landing squarely and painfully on bodies.

As suddenly as they came into the clinch they were out of it, and dancing away from each other's blows. Chaney had so far resisted using feint to try and lure the black hitter in, figuring he was too smart for it, just as he himself had read Street's feints and passed those up. So when Chaney did finally feint to the left like he was going to try a right cross, Street bought it, went for the opening and met a left hook that did him quite a bit of physical damage, but more psychological damage. He went down and drew two swift rights to help him on his way.

Expecting Chaney to kick him as he went down the black scrabbled away, got to his feet and swung back, figuring Chaney would be right there on top of him. The fact that he wasn't only added to his anger that had started with his going for that feint. He came back like a tiger.

Speed was rigid and muttered, 'Jesus.'

A grin started through Chaney's face. Up to that point he wasn't sure that he could beat the black, whose blows were hard and damaging and whose skill was as sound as his own; here it would have been a question of sheer strength and endurance, and he thought the black had more of both. But now he thought differently about the outcome.

The fighters moved into each other again, locked and rained blows on each other. The punches were hard and furious, each one reaching home with a trip hammer concussion.

As if believing he had a lot of ground to win back Street changed tactics. Chaney had been reaching him too hard. He grabbed hold of the left Chaney threw, pulled him close, then smashed his forehead into Chaney's face. The impact of that sent Chaney reeling back onto the concrete floor. Following through Street missed with the kick he tried, for Chaney rolled, raised himself and sunk the toe of his boot into the black's kidneys. It was a lucky shot and did a lot of damage. Chaney swung to his feet and followed through as the man came to stop at the bales of cotton. Chaney slammed blow after blow into the man's kidneys and watched him struggle for breath as he went down.

Chaney walked away, breath crashing through his chest, his face stinging and wet with both blood and sweat. He was almost grateful for that forehead he had taken in the face, for if Street hadn't moved like that he would have tried boxing him and probably lost.

Not for a moment did Chaney figure the man would get up, but the fact that he did and came at him again was an indication of his strength. Chaney swung back as Street threw a right. He blocked it, took a left; got a right in himself.

They danced around, throwing blows, holding, throwing more blows. The black was sticking to boxing now, it seemed, but that was a mistake, because he had taken a lot of stick to the kidneys and was getting damaged as a result. He had been slowed up to about Jim Henry's speed and his punches began to get woolly and disconnected.

Street moved in with his right, sending a fable first, Chaney stepped around it, and shot forward with a left to the head, then right cross to the heart, a left cross to the chin. Street rocked back; Chaney danced in again, hitting, sliding back, hitting again, twisting around Street's grinding reactions. His blows fell fast, hard and accurately, yet Street took the punishment. Chaney couldn't make out what worm had gotten into the black's brain that made him fight like this, instead of trying to win no holds barred, which was what street fighting was about. He doubted Gandil was paying him for an exhibition in boxing; somehow he doubted Gandil would pay him at all now.

Flying at Street first one way then another, Chaney put everything into it, every ounce of concentration, energy, strength and belief in himself; his sinews screamed and the fibres of his muscles tore with the continual impact. One blow across the black's heart put him down, and this time he really looked like staying there. But this time Chaney waited to see.

The breathing of the two fighters heaving like steam traction was the only noise aside from the rain. Then a third was introduced, it was metal bouncing against cement as Jim Henry threw the palmers on the floor in front of Street.

Gandil suddenly shouted, 'Use them.'

Street was stirring, game for more. He looked at the metal palmers and began to rise without them.

Gandil stepped forward. 'Use them, black son-of-a-bitch. Pick them up. I didn't bring you here to get your black ass whipped.'

Speed suddenly furious, jumped forward.

'Foul! Goddamn it, get those palmers out. Money's forfeited. What the hell do you think this is?'

Street looked dazedly at Gandil, then to Chaney. Chaney held his look, knowing the palmers would do him little good now, but guessed he'd pass on them anyway.

He did. He rose, kicking the palmers. Still somewhat stunned, he tried to crowd Chaney, but he wasn't fast enough. All he moved onto was a machine-like series of rights, which all but put Street back on the train for Memphis.

Chaney was numb, and every part of him screamed from the effort here and ached from the punishment he had taken. He stood over Street sprawled out before him, and saw a bit of himself there, too, a while ago. He stooped over him and placed a hand on his head. He was alive. He would have had Poe check him out, but Poe was in no condition.

Slowly rising he walked back to Speed and took his cap and coat and put them on. Nobody else moved for a moment. And Chaney wasn't giving out anything more, he couldn't. The way he felt he had to keep it all in, contained his ache, his demand for release, or he'd crash out over the floor. Later when the moment was right, later that night if he managed to beat the cops and make a freight train, then he'd find his release.

His coat done up, he glanced once at Speed. Speed was really moved. He couldn't even say anything. Chaney collected the roll off Poe, then turned and looked across to Gandil, challenging him to say anything about that move.

'It's over,' he said.

'I guess,' Gandil replied. 'You cost me a great deal, Mr Chaney.'

'You'll live with it.'

Gandil nodded. 'Somehow I don't think you will, boy. I've never lost anything in my life.'

He watched Chaney turn away, and together with Speed and Poe started across for the big doors, Speed moved impatiently ahead. Chaney stopped alongside Street and stared down at him. Blood was masking his black face almost. From his roll Chaney took a bill, and dropped it on the man. He was going to need his fare back to Memphis. Then he moved on to the warehouse exit where Speed and Poe were peering out of the wicket gate and through the pouring rain.

'I can't see no one,' Speed said. 'But I sure as hell got a bad feeling.'

'It ain't your problem,' Chaney said curtly. 'I'll make out I guess.'

'We got you into this,' Poe said expansively. 'Honor dictates that we make some effort to get you out.'

'Let's try the car.'

Speed stepped through the wicket, followed by Chaney, then Poe.

They didn't reach the parked Buick before a voice through a bullhorn barked, 'Hold it right there. Police.'

As one they turned and sprinted away through the rain. As they did shots rang out with a muffled, deadened effect. They kept on running. Straight up river onto Poydras Street wharf. A searchlight poked through the rain, but it was as pointless as the shots that were fired. There were the sounds of motors starting behind and of running feet.

The three fugitives cut up between the huge sheds. Poe's pace began to slow and he waved the other two on without him. Chaney caught hold of him and half dragged him.

Twenty-five dollars was being ruined on his back in this rain, but even so Speed knew that Lady was smiling right down on him. They would never have got clear of those cops on the wharf but for the zero visibility caused by the rain. They were clear, and safe, and they had really hit Chick Gandil. He wanted to laugh, he wanted to dance and whoop with delight. But what he did was flag the cab that almost knocked them down. Even that was the Lady's doing.

'It sure is coming down this time, boss,' the cab driver said. 'Ain't it just beautiful?'

They climbed in. The last door slammed. A moment went by.

'Where to gentlemen?'

Both Poe and Speed looked at Chaney, waiting for his direction.

'The freight yards up on the canal,' he said.

Speed looked round at him for a second. He didn't say anything, he didn't have to, not now. Chaney's face was a little puffed after the fight, but looking cool with the rain on it.

'Railyards,' the cab driver said, like his fare was in doubt.

They drove in silence each with his separate yet harmonious thoughts.

Chaney listened to the squelch of the tires as they plowed through the rain; the swish of the windshield wipers against the car. He ached and felt tired, but at the same time he felt good. He hadn't felt this good in a long while. He had wanted release, now he had found it, and for the first time he regretted that he had to move on. Chaney closed his eyes as if his thoughts neded to be seen to be acknowledged.

He didn't open his eyes again until the yellow painted Packard drew up along Alvar Street on the ramp to the freight yards. Pools of floodlighting slanted down through the rain, causing small areas of the track to glisten where they ran empty to the next bend. There was a silence which none of the three in the back of the cab wanted to break. No one attempted to move.

Speed had so many words and thoughts tripping around inside his head, but couldn't get out any of what he wanted to say.

'It was beautiful,' he said. 'It was a real peak, everything coming together.' They were the only words he could make.

Chaney nodded as if understanding. He reached into his lumberjacket pocket and pulled out the roll of money.

'Poe,' he said, 'do me a favor. Go back to my place. There's a cat there. I want you to take care of it.'

He handed Poe one of the big bills. Poe was quite unsure about accepting it, knowing what it really meant.

'A thousand dollars buys a lot of cat food, my friend.'

'Speed,' Chaney said. 'Take this. You take care of Poe.'

He gave Speed more money, a whole lot more. Speed too sensed what was going on and for the first time in his life he felt guilty about accepting money.

'For a man who came to town to make money, you're giving a lot of it away,' he said.

'You're forgetting about the inbetweens.'

'You filled those up pretty good.'

Stuffing the rest of the cash back into his pocket Chaney reached for the car door. He hesitated and tried to stare through the rain at the tracks that lay beyond.

Muffled through the rain, yet quite distinct, came the sound of a train whistle.

'Where are you off to?' Speed said, a sense of urgency creeping into his voice.

'Oh, wherever that train lets out for.'

Speed stared at him, knowing it was the end, that it had to be, but not wanting it.

'I guess we should say something,' Poe said. 'But what are words ...?

Chaney smiled grimly, then pushed out of the cab, into the rain. He didn't look back, but just kept on walking in the direction of the train that was now heading on up.

Speed slid over to the door and rolled down the window and stared off into the night. There was no sign of Chaney now. He continued staring into the rain. He didn't look at Poe alongside, but knew he was feeling the same way. There was a long silence.

'You want to go someplace else now, boss?' the cab driver asked.

'Maybe we should go on down to Miami,' Speed finally said. 'Get something going down there ...'

Poe didn't respond.

'That's one hell of a town I hear tell. Right on the ocean. That sea air'll be just dandy on your health.'

'Uh huh,' Poe intoned unenthusiastically.

Speed stared away into the night, wondering about Chaney disappearing like that. His own sense of loss receding a little. He looked at the three G-notes he had in his hand. Then gave a perplexed shake of his head.

'He sure was something,' he said.

Poe nodded. 'Let's go get the cat,' he said. He waved the puzzled cab driver on.

The Packard swung off the ramp and wheeled away, leaving behind the pools of light reflecting in the rain and the sound of the freight train coming up out of the switching yard.

More true crime from STAR

DUMMY
Ernest Tidyman

The bestselling author of SHAFT explodes the myth of fiction and reveals the true horror of the real world of crime and the machinations of the Supreme Court stretched to its limits. Now a major film. *45p*

KILLER:
Autobiography of a Professional Murderer
Joey

This is the horrifying story of a man without a conscience. In his own words: "I have never killed an honest man. And I have never been convicted. All I need is a clientele – a demand for my services." *50p*

THE LONG TATTOO
Eric Corder

Power, lust, vengeance and savagery, here is the American Civil War at its most brutal and violent. A shattering novel of raging passions that could only have been written by the author of SLAVE. *40p*

THE LAST ENCOUNTER
Robin Maugham

Bestselling author and traveller, Robin Maugham, has written a major novel around General Gordon of Khartoum's famous last journal. Here are heroism, soldiery, the torture of siege and the glorious madness of man's destiny in the desert. Our image of General Gordon and the Mahdi will never be the same again. *40p*

THE TAKEOVER
Niven Busch

The fierce battlefield of politics versus law. Four men, all well on their way to becoming billionaires, pass a death sentence on a fifth – Jed, the President of their Corporation. Soon enough its the White House itself that needs paying off . . . "As up to date as this morning's headline news. A fast-paced, spellbinding story, Niven Busch's finest book so far." ARTHUR HAILEY *50p*

STAR BOOKS

are available through all good booksellers but, where difficulty is encountered, titles can usually be obtained *by post* from:

Star Book Service,
G.P.O. Box 29,
Douglas,
Isle of Man,
British Isles.

Please send retail price plus 8p per copy.

Customers outside the British Isles should include 10p post/packing per copy.

Book prices are subject to alteration without notice.